CW00860021

# THE SPACE TRAVELLER'S LOVER

OMARA WILLIAMS

authorHOUSE®

*AuthorHouse™ UK*
*1663 Liberty Drive*
*Bloomington, IN 47403 USA*
*www.authorhouse.co.uk*
*Phone: UK TFN: 0800 0148641 (Toll Free inside the UK)*
*UK Local: (02) 0369 56322 (+44 20 3695 6322 from outside the UK)*

*© 2022 Omara Williams. All rights reserved.*

*No part of this book may be reproduced, stored in a retrieval system, or transmitted by any means without the written permission of the author.*

*Published by AuthorHouse 02/09/2022*

*ISBN: 978-1-6655-9247-5 (sc)*
*ISBN: 978-1-6655-9248-2 (hc)*
*ISBN: 978-1-6655-9246-8 (e)*

*Print information available on the last page.*

*Any people depicted in stock imagery provided by Getty Images are models, and such images are being used for illustrative purposes only.*
*Certain stock imagery © Getty Images.*

*This book is printed on acid-free paper.*

*Because of the dynamic nature of the Internet, any web addresses or links contained in this book may have changed since publication and may no longer be valid. The views expressed in this work are solely those of the author and do not necessarily reflect the views of the publisher, and the publisher hereby disclaims any responsibility for them.*

*To my husband, Ithel, and daughter, Amalia, with all my love.*

I bow to you
My soul honours your soul
I honour the light, love, truth, beauty
within you, because
It is also within me.
In sharing these things, we are united
We are the same
We are one.
*Namaste*

# CONTENTS

## PART I



## PART II



## PART III

## PART IV



## PART V

# PART I

# CHAPTER 1

# DREAMS

*Who is this man I'm about to reach and then vanishes?*

*Sometimes, the one thing you desperately want is the one thing that keeps slipping away. Then you try harder,* Erin thinks to herself as she closes her eyes.

All she can hear is her fast breathing, but she won't stop running through the endless corridors, her bare feet stamping hard on the marbled floor. A bright, beckoning light flashes in the distance, and she accelerates even more. Soon she finds herself at the shore of a multicoloured ocean, separating her from a sky-piercing tower. Flickering sunbeams break through the far horizon, reflecting on the thin edges of the glassy structure.

A sudden gust of wind lifts her body and spins it over the ocean, her long waving hair wrapping tightly around her neck. She cries out loud until her hurting throat makes her cough. She kicks and flutters, trying to find her balance, but ends up spinning even faster.

Through her blurred vision, she discerns the dashing silhouette of a golden-uniformed soldier standing in front of the tower. She anxiously extends her arms in a vain attempt to reach him while he speaks to her softly, as if oblivious to her torment.

A rising fog obscures his face, but his enigmatic presence and low soothing voice lure her. She soon forgets about her fears. Just when she thinks he's within reach, he disappears behind a dark cloud, his voice fading into a whimper. Suddenly, a blunt blow to her back pushes her harshly into the water. She's sinking fast into the deep black ocean, her body still spinning out of control, faster and faster.

She tries hard to open her eyes, the pressure on her shut eyelids working against her willpower. Still, she keeps trying. At last, the light breaks through her contracting pupils. The impatient figure standing in front of her makes her jump and sit up straight. She buries her head in her hands, as she realises she was only in her bedroom. It was a dream, the same kind of dream that keeps haunting her. *Who is this man I'm about to reach and then vanishes?*

"It's time to get up, you lazy girl," shouts the plump woman, her unkempt curly hair bouncing as she pulls the sheets away and noisily opens the curtains.

"Sure," Erin mumbles. She nearly falls over as she rushes to the bathroom door across the aisle.

Mornings are the least favourite part of Erin's day, especially when she oversleeps and her adoptive mother, Pat Lobart, has to wake her up.

The woman shakes her head, frowning in disapproval. "Hurry up, or you'll be late," Mrs Lobart shouts, continuing to shake her head as she leaves the room.

Erin washes her face and combs her long, sun-streaked hair while thinking about her dream. A swirl of emotions makes her body shiver. She relives the hopelessness and fear. But it's the alluring image of the unreachable soldier that makes her heart flip. "It's all in my imagination," she whispers as she ties her long hair in a ponytail.

She pulls down the blue overalls hanging from the wall and slides them up her body, giving a final glance in the mirror. "That will do for today," she says to herself.

As she enters the kitchen, Mrs Lobart still has a bad temper. "Erin, you'll be such a bad example to the others in the tuna farm … arriving late."

"But I'm on time," she protests.

"As always, at the last minute," Mrs Lobart snaps as if she doesn't want to hear any more excuses.

Erin grabs a piece of bread and takes a sip from her black coffee mug before running out the back door. Blazer, her smooth fox terrier, runs joyfully towards her, jumping on her chest with his two front paws. She strokes his soft, white and tan coat while sharing the rest of her bread with the overexcited dog. She takes a deep breath, looking towards the winding country road that will take her to the tuna farm. The weather is good today, with no bulging clouds or dense mist covering the otherwise perfectly blue sky. She can even see the flocks of seagulls circling over the steel suspension bridge joining the island to the tuna farm's control tower.

The wind brings the smell of the salty sea and the shrieking calls of the agitated birds. Erin looks at her watch. She still has a few minutes to spare before her shifts start. *Shall I go running or get my horse?* She ponders while looking towards the stables.

"Erin." Mrs Lobart's stern call makes her jolt. She jumps over the fence and onto the footpath. "Ah, Erin … Happy birthday! Come back early today … will you?" She hears Mrs Lobart's fading voice as she runs towards the coast.

All the while, she cannot stop thinking about the mysterious man in her dreams, wondering why he keeps turning up ever more frequently, night after night.

# CHAPTER 2

# THE ISLAND

*Everyone knows she's smart, out-of-the-ordinary smart.*

The Lobart family live on the remote island of Tinian, part of Mariana's archipelago in the Pacific Ocean. Erin's adoptive parents, Albert and Patricia Lobart, brought her to live on the island when she was eleven years old. The family moved from LA (Los Angeles, California), when Albert took over the running of the tuna farm.

Anyone on the island can tell you that Erin is a one-of-a-kind girl. Her dreamy gaze and her aloof demeanour are as irritating as self-evident. She prefers to stay out swimming alone in the open ocean or horse riding by its shores, watching the night sky, or playing with her pet dog. Still, despite spending most of her time in outdoor activities, occasionally looking at her school notes, she always comes top of her class. Everyone knows she's smart, out-of-the-ordinary smart. But most of those who admire her are also dismayed at her unruly nature. Behind her delicate, girlish appearance, there's a strong will and a zest for independence. Erin always finds a way to do the opposite of what others ask. This infuriates Mr Lobart, who is accustomed to being obeyed to the letter by everyone else.

Mr Lobart runs the tuna farm like clockwork. Mrs Lobart proudly claims her family saved the tuna from extinction after the most significant decline of the species in recorded history. Although very small, the island is of great importance to the world's food supply, as it's the site of the biggest and most successful tuna breeding farm ever built. The fortified steel control tower, located two kilometres from the island's rugged west coast, rises as far as it sinks. From its sturdy underwater spine, stacks of tubular channels extend and wrap around the island, forming a long spiral right down to the seabed. It's here where the islanders breed large quantities of giant bluefin tuna for the world's food supply. And it's here where most of the world's tuna population can be found.

By the end of the twenty-first century, the unpredictable weather had caused a devastating impact on food production. Nowadays, the very survival of humankind depended on carefully managing resources and selflessly helping each other. For some time now, the sun's periodic cycles had become impossible to predict, a long period of high activity is lasting indefinitely, surpassing the expected eleven-year cycle. An unusually high number of sunspots had appeared and doggedly stayed put, causing frequent eruptions of solar flares and coronal mass ejections. Freak snowstorms, seemingly endless deluges, massive sea surges, raging wildfires, swallowing sandstorms—all could be brewed and unleashed unexpectedly from the rapidly fluctuating supercharged atmosphere.

The changing global temperature and ubiquitous low-pressure systems provoked long spells of disruptive weather, making reliable forecasts almost impossible. With recurrent episodes of widespread floods and droughts, this worldwide unstable climate caused the whole of humankind to reorganise themselves to survive against all the odds—even if it meant the total upheaval of long-held customs and values.

Managing food and water supplies and efficiently distributing them to the areas where they were most needed demanded a rigorous, centralised effort for a faster, worldwide, effective response.

Survival had become the number one priority. "First and foremost, survival"—that was the slogan of the time.

The existing world order was not good enough, fast enough, or fair enough. There had been no other option but to change it. Countries had merged into regions, and regions had merged into alliances. Alliances had merged into one administrative coalition—the ARA (Aid and Recovery Alliance).

The ARA's INST (Instant) Network regularly updated the food storage levels and distribution status, weather conditions, and areas in most need of help. Self-organising rapid assistance brigades were always ready to act, as they were dispatched to assist the ongoing emergencies. The whole interconnected world was now in a constant state of alert, response, and action.

During her first year at high school, Erin often volunteered to help distribute food and drinking water to evacuees of powerful storms on both her island and others nearby. She took it close to her heart, not only the plight of the islanders but also that of Mother Nature. Through her tireless work, she became widely known and admired, and she felt revived and accomplished. At her teacher's insistence, Erin applied and was admitted to the prestigious university's early entrance program in Los Angeles when she was fifteen. But after finishing the first year of her math degree, and to everyone's surprise, she decided to go back home, much to the Lobarts' chagrin. She explained she missed her island dearly—the immense blue sky, the boundless sea, and her beloved farm animals.

But her adoptive parents could not fully understand why Erin chose to go back to finish high school instead of staying at the university. "The university can wait," she had said. Of course, they were then quick to conclude that it was all about a boy, the charmingly attractive Sam Sheppard.

Sam had welcomed her decision with unreserved pleasure. After all, Erin had been his best friend since she arrived on the island. Even better, she was working at the farm for the summer season as well. *This time is the perfect opportunity to tell her about my true feelings*, he thought.

Erin's main job at the tuna farm is checking on the timely execution of the daily upkeep activities and it's demanding work. But for her, being at the tuna farm's control room is her favourite part of the working day; she hates it when it's time to go home for dinner. In most cases, the conversation with her parents will end up in disagreements and reproach.

At dinner, Erin always sits as far from Mr Lobart as possible. She doesn't like his serious face, although he's usually looking down at his plate, tucking into his big servings. But when he gets angry, he even throws the dishes against the wall; once, he missed her by an inch. That's why she's learned not to contradict him while he speaks.

Albert Lobart is a short, stocky man with small eyes and a big curved nose. The islanders know him as "the Mad Bulldog" because of his short temper.

He is a man of brief words and little patience. When he opens his mouth, it is most certainly to give orders. Patricia accepts his irritable mood as part of his strong character. To her, he is the best man in the world, and no one else could run the tuna farm as he does. But their marriage has always been pure business for Albert. Marrying Patricia Lobart, the farm owner's daughter, was his way to take over one of the world's essential feeding industries and become a highly respected man.

As for Erin, she tries to avoid being near the Lobarts as much as possible. The outdoors is her refuge, her private paradise. She belongs to its blue ocean and carved-up cliffs, its green meadows and soft rolling hills. She cannot imagine living anywhere else. *It's the place where I can truly be myself.*

At home, she tries to spend most of her time in the back garden with her beloved dog, Blazer. After taking him for long walks, she stays inside the dog's outhouse, reading her favourite science books while Blazer rests by her feet. She feels safe and tranquil there, even after nightfall.

*I should be grateful I'm living on this beautiful island. The alternative could have been much, much worse. It's certainly better than if I'd stayed at the orphanage. That's what Mrs Lobart says.*

## CHAPTER 3

# BEST FRIENDS' SECRETS

*No one will believe us, you know … it's better if we don't say anything.*

Erin walks into the spacious control room and sits in front of the tracking monitors. Today is her sixteenth birthday, and she's looking forward to the evening. Sam promised he had a surprise for her.

She touches the flashing green button from the computer menu. The whole map of the tuna farm's maintenance plant fills the screen with its crisscrossing, distinctly coloured lines.

A flashing green dot over a five-digit number marks each worker's position. The markers move along the lines, updating each point's time and coordinates.

At a glance, Erin checks the position of each marker and its ID number. She knows by heart the expected time and location of everyone.

She notices that one marker starts flashing in red, but she hears Sam's voice through the intercom before she has time to worry.

"Sam Sheppard … signing in. Checking Level D."

"Sam! Just in time," she gently reprimands him.

"Erin, you shouldn't worry about that. We all know we have to keep to the schedule or else," Sam replies calmly. "I'm on level D, section A4 now."

"That's better!" Erin says while verifying the red flashing dot changing into green.

Sam and Erin have been close friends since they met on her first day at school on the island. She was sitting by herself in the canteen when a cheerful boy with curly brown hair and a cheeky smile sat beside her and asked her name. As she turned around to look at him, he jumped up on his seat.

"Yours are the biggest, bluest eyes I have ever seen." He exclaimed.

"They're not blue … they're purple, horrible." She lowered her eyelids, unable to hide her blushing.

"They're beautiful," he countered.

"Well, everyone makes fun of me because of my eyes. They even call me 'Big Eyes'," she sighed, clutching her hands nervously but daring to stare back at him regardless.

His broad friendly smile made her feel more confident almost instantly.

He regularly invited her to go for horse rides by the sandy beaches not far from the Lobarts' ranch. Erin would accept sometimes. As their friendship blossomed, she even offered to help him study for the exams, something that turned Sam into a very keen student.

When she announced she was leaving for Los Angeles to start university, his heart was broken. He thought about telling her before she left, but his mind froze, and his mouth dried at the thought that she would reject him. She would never give him any clues; she never flirted with him.

But when she came back, Sam started to think that he may have got it all wrong. *Of course, she's coming back because she misses me*, he thought. *I must tell her how I feel, but I'll find the right place, the right time.*

That same summer, they had gone horse riding to the northernmost part of the island, into the narrowing curved peninsula known as El Cuchillo, stretching out into the rough ocean for two and a half kilometres.

They were enjoying the magnificent views of the radiant sunset before they were due to start their summer jobs at the tuna farm.

Erin loved to ride her horse to the end of El Cuchillo to enjoy the view of the impressive black cliffs, especially around the area known as Diablo's Point, where the power of the waves had carved jagged stone arches and pillars around the sprawling coastal caves. The cliffs' rocky crevices led into a maze of underground tunnels and high chambers, forming a unique, intricate cave system that attracted the most daring explorers. But everyone knew there were some routes they must avoid—the deep waterlogged passages leading towards Diablo's cave's gorge, where an underground waterfall kept plunging through a vast chasm and into an underground river.

They trotted carefully on the stony path as the waves kept crashing on each side of the narrow peninsula, squirting random water jets through the blowholes. They enjoyed the refreshing splashes on their bodies, laughing at each other whenever they were showered by the sudden sprays.

The cries of the nesting seabirds and the hissing of the water jets combined into a unique rhythmic sound.

Although it was very cloudy, the Sun had managed to come through a small opening, unveiling its reddened edge and bathing the ocean surface with its fiery shafts of light.

The wind was playing on Erin's long blonde hair, weaving it in thick strands in front of her face that she kept pulling apart as she admired the breathtaking view. Sam couldn't keep his eyes off Erin. Deep in thought, he struggled to arrange his words into a sentence.

"One day, I'd like to have a peek inside Diablo's cave," Erin said as if talking to herself.

"That's something I've been practising … I tried it once with my father and we made it into the second lake … But after that—"

"What did you do?"

"Well, we immediately turned back," he replied in a self-deprecating tone, bursting into laughter that she promptly joined.

Erin kept looking towards the cave's entrance as a fluttery feeling of anticipation revolved in her stomach. Her heart missed a beat when she noticed the shimmering object once again—that same object that sometimes appeared out of nowhere while she had been swimming in the ocean.

"Sam, look!" She eagerly pointed in the direction of Diablo's cave.

Sam stared, completely bewildered, as a shiny metallic sphere emerged right at the entrance of the cave, getting wider and brighter as it rose gradually out of the water.

"What is it?" Sam yelled while trying to keep his horse still.

"I've no idea ..." Erin kept gazing at the luminous sphere, her heart pounding ever faster, but she didn't feel in the least frightened. Instead, she was utterly spellbound.

By now, the object had started to shine so brightly that they had to look away. A warm air current surrounded them while a low booming sound pounded in their ears. They tried hard to contain their nervous horses, tightly clutching their reins for a long tense minute.

As the humming sound and the bright light dwindled, a cool breeze coming from the sea refreshed their sweaty skin. Relieved, they opened their eyes and looked back towards the cave. By then, the shiny object had disappeared.

Only the agitated waves crashing against the dark entrance gave a hint that something had been there and suddenly had plunged into the water.

A wide-eyed Sam looked back at Erin, trying hard to open his stiffened mouth. "Wh-wh-what was th-th-at?" he stuttered.

"I wish I knew," she mumbled. "It seems like it's following me—"

"Jeez! You mean you've seen it before? Why haven't you told me?"

"You would've never believed me … Anyway, I'm glad you've seen it," she said with a smug grin while patting her horse's mane.

"You don't seem very scared—at all," Sam noticed while looking at Erin, intrigued.

"It always keeps its distance … and it looks beautiful."

"When was the first time you saw it?"

"This summer. Only happens at sea. Seen it twice before …"

"What can it be? What can it be?" Sam pondered as he scoured the rocky shore.

They kept looking around the cave's entrance, closely following the erratic movements of the choppy waters. But as the swell started to dissipate slowly, it appeared as if the bright metallic sphere had been a mirage.

"No one will believe us, you know … it's better if we don't say anything," Sam concluded as they cautiously led their horses away from El Cuchillo peninsula.

"Agreed," Erin said while looking back, wondering why she felt so attracted to the mysterious sphere and why she could sense its appearance, even if she didn't know where it came from.

That was the only time Sam ever saw it. But for Erin, it would appear numerous times, especially before one of her recurrent dreams. She was convinced that both events were connected, and she never mentioned it to anyone, not even Sam.

Today, while wondering what surprise Sam is preparing, she goes back to reviewing the data from the morning's activities before Mr Lobart arrives at the control room. He usually inspects the report as soon as he enters the tuna farm. Despite all the automated verification and warning systems, he insists on additional manual checks on site.

When the door opens and the stocky figure of Albert Lobart blocks the incoming light, she has finished checking the whole network, but this is the first round of the day.

As she rushes to get the report ready, she feels his pressing stare behind her back. She knows he's often in a bad mood, so there must be a frowned forehead, angled eyebrows, and tightly pressed lips on his face.

"Is everything okay?" he asks without moving from the door.

"Yes, sir, everything is okay." She extends her hand, holding the electronic notepad with the latest downloaded report.

"Oh, happy birthday, Erin!"

"Thank you, sir," she replies, trying to sound upbeat.

Lobart walks down the steps, letting the sunshine flood into the room and blinding her momentarily. Erin keeps looking away as he grabs the notepad. She starts walking towards her desk, expecting he's about to leave the room, but the rattle of his boots stomping on the wooden floor warns her he's following her instead. Nonplussed, she turns around to face him.

"Listen, Erin … I want to warn you …" Lobart looks at her questioningly, as if she should know what he is about to say.

"About what?" she asks with a puzzled look.

"About your friendship with Sam—"

"We've been friends for a long time now."

"Just friends, eh? You know that Pat and I disapprove!"

Erin instinctively backs away, not only because he has startled her but also because she cannot stand the whiff of old dried tuna skin coming from his dirty overalls.

"I will dismiss Sam from the farm"—he steps towards Erin until his pointed finger is wavering a few millimetres from her nose—"if you go out with him again!"

"Why?" she protests, struggling to make sense of his irrational demand.

"I've no time for explanations now. Do what I say." Lobart sneers.

She feels the urge to confront him. But she soon composes herself and fakes total submission. "As you wish, sir," she says, nodding briefly and clasping her hands behind her back. She dares not mention that she and Sam had made plans to go out together this very evening.

"All right then … you can call me Dad," Lobart drawls while walking towards the exit.

He stops sharply in front of the steps to give her a final warning glare before making his way out. She avoids his hostile gaze and focuses instead on his worn-out sand-caked boots. The second she notices he's about to trip on the uneven steps, she stops short of warning him, but Lobart safely jumps up and out of the door at the last minute.

Erin feels a bit guilty that she wished he could have tripped and fallen over. But she soon dismisses her guilt, recounting his threatening words.

"Nothing will destroy my friendship with Sam," she reassures herself, talking under her breath, a steely glint of determination flashing in her eyes. "No one will stop me from seeing him, not even the Lobarts!"

# CHAPTER 4

# DISAPPEARANCE

*I wish something could happen that would*
*make her instantly disappear.*

Erin can hardly wait for her shift to finish, carefully checking every single node in the busy network. *The more I check, the quicker the time will pass*, she thinks. Much sooner than she expects, she hears the loud beep signalling the shift's end. It is five o'clock in the afternoon, time to hand over her tasks.

She has impatiently waited for a full three minutes, and at last, the next shift assistant has arrived. It's her former classmate, Stella, Sam's sister.

Stella walks past Erin without even looking at her, plunging onto the swivelling chair in front of the widescreen monitor. As Stella takes off her sun hat and shakes her head, her thick black curls pour over her shoulders. She reclines, finally glancing at Erin, arching her thin dark eyebrows and pouting her lips in scorn.

"Doing double shift today on your birthday, eh? Well, I suppose I'll have to fix what you didn't finish." Stella groans.

Erin lowers her head, briefly closing her eyes in disapproval.

Stella's attitude could not be more different from that of her brother, Sam. She is unwelcoming and rude. Her grudge and disdain make for an uneasy atmosphere around her presence. All the while, Erin wants to keep the peace. She's learned to ignore Stella's animosity since they were at school together, especially after that incident before leaving for university.

The scene flashes through Erin's mind for a few seconds. She was returning home from school when three girls from her class ran in front of her, blocking her path.

She stopped to avoid bumping into them, but one of the girls charged towards her, pushing her against the wooden fence along the footpath.

The girls mocked Erin, trying to intimidate her. As Erin tried to run away, Stella cut across her and slapped her angrily on her face. Erin felt a sharp pain on her cheek as the blow pushed her head briskly to one side. She tried to lift her hand to soothe her aching bruise, but the other girls grabbed her long braids and started pulling until she fell to the ground.

"Not so smart now, are you, Big Eyes?" Stella yelled. Her brows snapped together, and her mouth folded in a sour smirk.

Stella tried to slap her again, but Erin started to kick her legs in all directions.

First, Stella fell and then the other two.

Erin felt quite relieved and even impressed with her sudden burst of strength, but as she realised that somebody else was there helping her, she felt emboldened.

A boy was pulling the three girls up one by one and leading them away.

She felt so grateful when she recognised Sam. He turned to a stunned and aching Erin, still lying on the pavement, and extended his hand towards her, helping her off the ground.

As she grabbed his hand, she only managed to sit up against the fence, feeling dizzy and confused.

"Thank you, Sam. I'm so happy you came." Erin smiled at him in gratitude

But her face was soon veiled in sadness as the upsetting scenes rewound and replayed continually inside her mind. "Why would they do this to me?"

"Listen, Erin … they envy you because you're smart."

"Envy? What's envy?"

"Well, let's say that they would like to have something that you have, but they can't," Sam explained.

Erin tried to digest Sam's words as she stared at him, baffled.

"But that doesn't mean you need to change anything," he continued in a comforting tone. "You just need to know that there are those kinds of people about."

Erin nodded as she got up and shook the dust off her clothes. She smiled at Sam while arranging her dishevelled braids.

As he accompanied her home that evening, Erin told him she would never forget what a good friend he had been. Sam told her the same, and with a kiss on her bruised cheek, he added: "I'll be here when you come back from uni."

Erin has always wanted to tell Stella she's prepared to forgive her, but Stella has always kept a hostile mood towards her.

"Not much to do for the evening shift," Erin says as she strolls towards the exit. She doesn't want Stella to notice that she's in a hurry.

"I know Sam is taking you somewhere". Stella says in disdain. "You can start running now."

"That's none of your business!" Erin snaps as she hurriedly reaches the top of the stairs, slamming the door behind her.

As she starts running along the steel suspension bridge towards the coast, Erin bounces eagerly in long strides while the strong wind pushes her forward. She breathes in deeply, tasting the salty water droplets suspended in the air, her lungs flooding with the brackish aroma.

Stella keeps looking through the window until the fast-running figure shrinks to a small dot on the other end of the bridge. As she looks through the lookout telescope by the window, she spots her brother Sam running towards Erin.

"Ah, those two are inseparable," she mutters as she watches them jumping onto Sam's speedboat and setting off towards the cliffs. Seeing Erin sitting next to her brother, her resentment grows. "I never wanted my brother to be so close to that weird girl," she grumbles.

Stella tries hard to concentrate on her shift's tasks. Hours go by, but she keeps thinking about her brother and Erin. *I wish something could happen that would make her instantly disappear. And anything will do—a lightning strike, a shark attack, a sudden fireball.*

The phone rings insistently for a few seconds before Stella comes out of her damning stupor.

She perks up as she hears the worried voice of her father, Bill Sheppard, the maintenance manager at the tuna farm and a veteran member of the ARA's rescue brigades.

"Is Sam with you there? He should be picking you up," her father asks her as if expecting a positive answer.

Stella checks the time, and it's already ten o'clock. Sam is never late.

"No, Dad, he isn't." She checks the car park once again through the glass window.

"Did you see him today?"

"Yes, he met Erin after she finished the shift. They went in the direction of Diablo's cave, on Sam's boat."

"I've been calling him … but there's no response."

"What about Erin's parents?"

"Yes, I contacted them, but they've not heard from Erin either," Sheppard replies gloomily.

"Well, you shouldn't worry yet. They'll turn up soon! They must be somewhere close by … fooling around," Stella says in a fake encouraging tone.

*Surely, they're up to no good*, she thinks. But an uneasy thought lingers on, at the back of her mind.

"I'll come and get you home!" Sheppard says, this time sounding more annoyed than worried. "Wait for me!"

"Yeah, I bet he's home when we get there," Stella replies, trying to sound hopeful.

But later that night, the Sheppards keep waiting anxiously by their phones, with no news from Sam or Erin.

Right after midnight, Mr Lobart arrives.

"No news yet. For now, they are intent on hiding," Lobart announces as he looks at Sam's parents and sister with a disgruntled expression.

"It is so unusual for Sam." Martha Sheppard sits next to her daughter and hugs her. Mother and daughter are so much alike—the same curly black hair, long thin eyebrows, thin nose, and the same brown eyes covered in tears.

"Everything's going to be okay." Stella comforts her worried mother.

"We need to go now and check all the obvious places—even if we have to go inside Diablo's cave," Bill Sheppard states while putting his working boots on.

"I wonder why Erin was in such a hurry today," Stella wonders, looking probingly at her father. "She was in a hurry to meet Sam, and he waited for her by the coast … far from the control tower," she adds, purposely stressing her words.

"Hmmm." Lobart starts pacing around, looking down while gathering his thoughts.

"Hmmm, what?" Stella prompts him.

"Earlier today, I told Erin to stop seeing Sam—that Pat and I … well." He briefly gazes at Sam's parents one by one. "I was going to fire Sam from the farm if they continued seeing each other."

Everyone looks back at Lobart as if they have suddenly found their guilty suspect.

"Ah!" Martha exhales in astonishment and lurches back onto her sofa's backrest. Her husband comforts her, patting her shoulder before bitterly gazing at Lobart.

"So, they're hiding," Stella suggests. "Or they're eloping, or—"

"There's no point in guessing now," Lobart counters. "When we find them … we'll see."

Bill Sheppard folds his arms over his chest, frowning deeply at Lobart as if trying to channel all his irritation in a single glance. A burly man with a thick moustache and incisive gaze, Bill maintains a composure that unveils an uneasy self-restraint.

"Albert, it's about time you stop your paranoia about me trying to take over your job with the help of Sam and Erin—"

"Ah! That's what it is." Martha stands up, incredulously staring at Lobart. "Please tell me, Albert, that it's all been a misunderstanding—"

"Yeah, a misunderstanding," Lobart snaps. "But I tend to be right most of the time—"

"Let's call it a truce, Albert"—Bill briskly opens the front door—"for the sake of Sam and Erin."

"All right, let's go then," Lobart grudgingly agrees.

But their desperate search that night yields no further news. The next day, they set up search parties all across the island, their helicopters scouring everywhere inland and all around the coast, but they fail to find any clues of the pair's whereabouts. Even when the islanders extend their range inside the intricate cave systems, they find nothing after three days.

To make matters worse, the moment they start preparations to go deeper into Diablo's cave, beyond the second lake and on to the waterfall, an approaching storm compels them to abandon everything.

For a while, they had some hope that the violent winds would change direction and would miss the island altogether, but the zigzag path of the advancing typhoon is invariably pointing towards the rugged west coast.

The islanders rush to the secured underground shelters, but the Sheppards have joined the Lobarts in the tuna farm's control room. They reckon they have a better chance of spotting Sam and Erin from the high tower if the pair decide to come out from hiding.

As the wind brings in the strong smell of acidic rain, Sheppard and Lobart lock the shatterproof windows and doors. On the horizon, they can see the black clouds rolling over the agitated ocean, forming ever-increasing bulges as if preparing to engulf the whole island.

The bright lightning bolts fork through the clouds in random patterns as the sound of thunder vibrates through the supercharged atmosphere. The storm has arrived at their shores.

The reinforced steel tower is withstanding the brunt of the mighty two hundred and fifty kilometres per hour gales. Still, the howling winds and the constant deluge make the two anxious families fear that the thick metal trusses could begin to collapse after all.

"The control room will hold," Lobart reassures them.

But no sooner has he spoken than the ear-splitting thunder and its blinding lightning strike rip through the air as if the sky had cracked into smithereens.

They sit tight with their backs against the wall, looking at each other in sheer awe and then bury their heads between their knees as if trying to protect themselves from an impending collapse, even though they know the sturdy tower was built to endure this type of weather.

As they huddle together in their sleeping bags, the sturdy towering structure is keeping at bay the unyielding winds and battering waves. Despite their initial fears, they eventually share a comforting feeling of security as they fall asleep.

The following day, when they finally hear a pause in the bucketing rain, after a whole night of relentless pounding, they are relieved that, at last, the raging storm appears to be moving away.

Lobart climbs onto one of the desks to get a better view from the window. He reckons this must be the most powerful typhoon he has experienced in his whole life. Wiping off the misty stormproof glass panes, he tries to discern any details through the thinning fog, barely making out the ghostly outline of the imposing cliffs in the distance.

"At least we're in one piece," he says as he turns around to face the rest of the group, now gathered behind him.

"The storms are getting more frequent and more powerful." Martha sobs, fearing the worst for her son and Erin. "To think … if they got caught up in the tidal surge …"

"There's no point in getting so upset, Martha. They are young and fit. They know how to look after themselves." Pat tries to console her.

Lobart jumps down from the desk as Stella climbs up. She contemplates the desolate grey scene with her eyes fixed on the same place she last saw her brother take Erin.

"Stella, come on down." Sheppard urges her to take his hand. "There's nothing to see until the weather clears."

Stella gloomily nods as she prepares to take her father's hand, but before jumping down, she glances towards the window once more, as a deep orange glow in the corner of her eye catches her attention.

"What was that?" She strains her eyes and focuses on the glittering orange light coming from the black cliffs.

"Stella! You've got to come down. We're leaving!" Bill insists while Stella keeps staring into the distance.

She points towards the bright glow, but as she is about to ask her father to join her, the orange light goes out of her sight.

"Uh! I think I got a bit dizzy … I swear I saw a big bright orange light," she claims as she jumps from the desk.

"Maybe it was one of the rescue helicopters!" Stella tries to justify herself under her father's sceptical stare. "They should be resuming the search soon."

"Stella, the helicopter lights are green, not orange," Sheppard counters.

"Oh, forget it! It was the fog. I am so tired." Stella gives up, noticing the dismissive look on everyone's face.

The dwindling patting of the receding raindrops brings about an edgy aura of comfort as the emerging breaks in the clouds slowly restore their hopes to restart their search.

Lobart and Sheppard carefully sweep the ocean and the coast through the lookout telescopes, but all they can see is grim desolation.

As the group walks towards the exit doors and Mr Lobart unbolts the locking mechanism, all are eager to breathe in the fresh air.

Soon the fog starts to lift, and with renewed expectation, they watch as the helicopters fly along the coast, their roaring engines rattling and lifting their spirits. The ARA's rescue team is here to attend to the injured and repair the damages. Surely the special brigades can make the difference in finding Sam and Erin. That is the thought in everyone's mind.

But the storm is not done yet. The rain that follows lasts for two consecutive days, while it seems the whole region will soon be drowning in the sea.

As the rain falls like a thick, impenetrable curtain, swollen water streams rush down the hills and form new waterfalls, blocking the roads with dislodged rocks and mudslides.

The ARA has already classified the mighty storm ravaging the small but vital island of Tinian as a Level 1 Emergency, the highest level.

Most of the island's replanted trees have been mercilessly ripped off in mangled chunks and strewn across the landscape. The swollen water currents have carved new paths across the landscape, and the artificial reservoirs are now joined into a large single water basin.

The reinforced steel houses have fared better; they're still standing up in one piece amidst the waterlogged fields.

When the rain eventually stops and as the water levels start to subside, everyone steps out into the open to face a landscape that has been mostly uprooted and remodelled.

The sun's shimmering disc shines through the now thinning higher clouds, signalling the long-awaited break in the weather. The warming sunbeams disperse through the floating water droplets, forming a brightly coloured rainbow over the ocean as if celebrating the end of the storm.

Finally, after four days of disruption, the rescue operations can resume across the island. At the same time, preparations are underway for their next attempt at the cave system's most inaccessible site.

Now the last hope of finding Sam and Erin rests on the unlikely area of Diablo's cave's gorge. But their families and the ARA's rescuers haven't given up yet.

# CHAPTER 5

# CAPTURE

*Erin wondered if this was some afterlife experience and she and Sam were already dead.*

On the day of their disappearance, Erin was sitting next to Sam while he steered the boat at high speed.

"I'm taking you somewhere you've never seen before," he shouted over the roaring sound of the engine.

She eagerly smiled and nodded as if she already knew where they were going.

He welcomed her bubbly excitement; he wanted so much to tell her about his feelings. This would be the perfect time, the ideal place.

On the horizon, the black outline of Diablo's Point's majestic cliffs was getting closer by the second.

Erin was wholly absorbed, admiring the breathtaking landscape, while Sam kept watching her out of the corner of his eye. He kept admiring her long hair moulded by the wind as she untied her ponytail and tilted her head backwards.

For a brief moment, he lost concentration; his grip slipped from the steering, and the boat swerved briskly to one side, making Erin lose her balance.

"What was that?" she yelled as she firmly held on to her seat.

Sam managed to get the boat under control as he tried to find an excuse. "No worries. I thought I saw something in the water," he said in an apologetic tone.

Erin clasped her hands on the sidebars as the boat bounced over the rippling waters, her eyes now fixed on the approaching cliffs and the roosting birds flying overhead.

She looked up, admiring the sun's tenuous rays through the reddened clouds when suddenly she found herself passing under a high arch of piled-up rocks.

"You've gone through the arch!" she screamed, not taking her eyes off the tight rocky passage as the boat swerved into the open waters once again.

Sam was smiling proudly. This route was particularly tight.

There were several such arches along the cliff walls, flanking the entries of the coastal caves. As the waves continually bashed and eroded the craggy surface, it was quite dangerous to approach them, never mind passing under them.

"I've been practising." Sam cheered while purposely holding on to the steering wheel.

She gazed at him in reproach, but soon her eyes widened in anticipation as she realised they were nearing an even narrower archway.

"No, not this one." She screamed again at the sight of the implausible passage.

But there was nothing she could do to stop Sam whisking the boat through, with only millimetres to spare at each side. Erin was stunned by Sam's skilful manoeuvres.

He weaved his way through two more arches along the cliffs, in and out again, with such ease, Erin started to feel confident at last.

"I told you I've been practising," he reassured her.

They both burst into laughter, their hearts excitedly pounding as if they had been on a rollercoaster ride.

Sam sped off into the open waters and turned the boat around to face the cliffs yet again, but this time, he switched off the engine.

They were standing right in front of the largest cave entrance, watching the waves crashing ever more frequently on the jagged crevice.

"Diablo's cave!" she exclaimed.

"Aha!" He nodded as he started planning his entry strategy.

"You're not trying to go in there, are you?" Erin objected, but she realised that she was stating the obvious.

"You told me you always wanted to know what it was like inside—"

"But you know it's risky—"

"We're just going up to the second lake. Then we turn around," Sam assured her with an even more determined tone.

"We know it's a very long and deep cave—more than one kilometre deep. And then there are the passages to the waterfall." Erin tried to discourage him, but she could tell that Sam had already made his mind up.

"Only to the second lake. And we'll be out before you know it. I promise," Sam insisted.

"But it'll be dark in a few minutes. We may even see that bright sphere again." She tried to dissuade him, but Sam started the engines even before she finished talking.

Sam steered the boat towards the entrance, expertly keeping it away from the rough edges as he pushed through the choppy waves and rammed into the cave.

Erin held her breath when they came close to the sharp rocks, while Sam focused on keeping the boat dead straight through the craggy entrance. She kept her eyes partly closed as they went under the engulfing cave's mouth. As she looked back at the sea current rushing in and merging into the interior lake, she knew they had made it.

Sam stopped the engines and turned on the powerful spotlights, their white glow illuminating the spacious cavity. The rumbling sound from the crashing waves echoed all around the concave walls while a serene feeling invaded them.

"This is beautiful," Sam exclaimed, barely hiding his pride after his faultless rush through the hazardous entry.

"I thought it would be scarier … but it's peaceful." Erin marvelled at the capriciously carved interior and arching walls. She imagined being under the dome of a huge haunted cathedral.

"Now … we can go further into the second lake," Sam said in an inviting tone.

"Okay, let's go!" Erin cheered.

Sam quickly restarted the engine. Cautiously, he pressed ahead through the winding, unpredictable channel. At each bend, the basaltic cave revealed even more jagged columns and rock formations, moulded by nature over millions of years.

He skilfully steered the boat through the downward current, avoiding hitting the rocky edges, sometimes at the last minute. But as the cave walls were getting higher and the passages wider, he found it easier to advance.

As they reached the second, smaller lake, he turned off the engine and slumped on the side bench, proud of himself.

"There is something special about this place," he marvelled.

"I think this is the farthest we can go," Erin reminded him.

"I wanted to talk to you about something …" He said while holding her hands.

"What is it?" Erin looked at him hesitantly.

"Erin, we've been friends for years now. We know each other so well. But this friendship … for me … it has changed."

His words came out in spurts as he struggled with what he wanted to say. He felt a deep pain in his stomach, trying to anticipate her response. Erin smiled broadly at him, trying to calm his anxiety while searching deep within her soul. She knew that her feelings for him would never define themselves entirely. She'd always thought of him as her best friend, but nothing more. So, she said nothing, ending up staring at him with a blank expression.

"I missed you so much, Erin, while you were at uni." He held up her chin and tilted his head, trying to kiss her lips.

But at that instant, the boat violently rattled while sudden strong currents swept it away.

Sam grappled in vain to reach the controls as they both hit the floor. Like a fragile paper boat, the speedboat surged up and down, erratically swerving through the rushing waters.

"Are you okay, Erin?" Sam shouted as he hugged her, both crouching and leaning against the boat's sideboard.

"Shhh! Can you hear that noise?" Erin put one hand over Sam's lips.

Sam focused on the thundering rumble getting louder as they relentlessly moved downward.

"It's the waterfall!" They embraced and shivered as they screamed in fear.

Sam and Erin kept taking deep breaths through the relentless water surge splashing on their bodies, helplessly waiting for the inevitable end. As they could hardly open their eyes, the deafening noise warned them of their impending approach to the waterfall's edge.

As she gasped for more air, Erin suddenly realised water didn't clog her airways anymore. She breathed in even deeper to get as much air as she could, and when she finally could look around with her eyes wide open, she found herself surrounded by an all-pervasive, orange haze. She turned to face a wholly bewildered Sam; they smiled at each other, glad to be above water with their boat still in one piece.

Slowly they rose to their feet while exploring their surroundings.

But they were astonished when they realised that some unknown force was keeping the boat steady amidst the pounding fast-flowing currents.

"Are you okay? Hold on tight!" he shouted at the top of his voice. "I'll get you out of here!"

Erin wondered if this was some afterlife experience and she and Sam were already dead.

As they cautiously walked towards the bow, they baulked at the sight of the enormous black abyss in front of them, swallowing the tumbling waters. Still, their boat was holding on, propped up as if by magic.

They kept their eyes fixed on the dark gorge, not daring to move in case the boat gave way, blinking to try to clear their wet, weary eyes.

Their expectation grew as the haze became brighter and brighter, illuminating the plunging black walls and making the waterfall's edge sparkle. Then a low revving sound rising from the deep warned them that some sort of vehicle was about to appear.

*That sounds like a jet engine*, Sam thought as he hugged Erin even tighter.

They felt the temperature rise as a metallic object kept on breaking through the cascade, revealing its sleek wing-shaped body, three times the size of their boat. When it finally stopped, the alien craft triggered a sudden splash of bubbles, frothing around its bright orange rim lights.

It was then that the craft's curved top section turned transparent. Suddenly, they could start to define a sturdy figure sitting inside and staring back at them.

Sam instinctively tried to step back, but he found himself unable to make the slightest move. Erin waited as if she was wholly hypnotised. Everything seemed to be happening in slow motion.

They helplessly watched as the man jumped from his seat into the air and started to fly towards them, gliding through the transparent cockpit cover as it slid open.

Sam and Erin felt dizzy as a paralysing force took hold of their bodies. A dark cloud completely obscured their blurry vision until they finally lost consciousness and collapsed.

The man focused his full attention on Erin, crouching around her and inspecting her body from head to toe. He stroked her gently, wiping her wet skin and rearranging her dishevelled hair. He blew softly over her face, her cheeks regaining her rosy pink blush momentarily. As her chest heaved, her mouth briefly opened up to let go of a prolonged, gentle sigh.

"Shaillah!" The man exclaimed while carrying her in his arms as he stood up. Then, staring intensely at Erin, he placed her inside a transparent sack and hung it from his back. He soared into the waiting aircraft, its top cover turning an opaque white as he flew in. As the alien craft descended into the waterfall, the roaring engines gave off an intense orange flash while the down currents sparkled and splashed before swallowing it whole.

# CHAPTER 6

# HOPE

*Those kids … They must be here somewhere.*

Albert Lobart finds it difficult to stop thinking about the impending Diablo's cave operation due early the next morning.

He feels a strong urge to go back to the control room, delve once again into the video images captured by the rescue team, and check how the preparations are going.

He gets up from the dining room table and walks towards the kitchen door, briefly checking his phone for the latest ARA's news report on his way out. The warm wind blows through his thin, baggy nightclothes.

"Damn!" he screeches, realising he hasn't even changed into his working outfit, but he continues towards his vehicle and gets into the driving seat anyway. As his pickup truck's headlights illuminate the large backyard, he sees his wife's silhouette through the window.

"I won't be long," he shouts as he abruptly reverses his truck. He isn't sure if she has heard him.

Pat follows the truck's lights into the distance as it ploughs noisily up the farm road. *Why is he in such a hurry?* She wonders.

He speeds up on the narrow winding road, but his mind is focusing elsewhere. *What will we find in Diablo's cave?* He keeps asking himself.

The global appeals have come to nothing, bringing fake responses and concocted tales. The large cash reward has not even produced the slightest credible claim. All the while, Lobart is convinced they must be somewhere on the island, even in the unlikeliest of places.

The sight of the tuna farm's high steel gates makes him brake abruptly. As they open slowly, he is still imagining all kinds of outcomes, but the voice from the intercom breaks up his thoughts.

"Hi, Stella. Good, you're on shift tonight. I'm coming upstairs!" He squeezes his truck through the opening gap, coming to a sudden halt, right at the control room's entrance.

He slams the truck's door as he gets out and jumps onto the steel staircase, climbing up the steps so quickly that Stella is caught by surprise when he suddenly opens the door.

"Oh, Mr Lobart, any news?" She promptly gets up from her chair and walks towards him.

But he barges past her into the adjacent room where rows of wall-mounted screens display the rescue's wide-field images.

"I've been thinking all day, Stella," he mumbles without taking his eyes off the screens.

"I see that you have," she says in an ironic tone, bemused by his unkempt appearance but daring not to mention it.

"And the weather is on our side!" He waves his index finger in the air as he gets closer to one of the screens showing the roughened coastal area of Diablo's Point.

He taps on the touchscreen and stops the video images on Diablo's cave.

"The rescue team went in there … as far as they could," Stella reminds him.

"Not far enough!" He swings around to confront her.

"But my brother would not have taken Erin into the dangerous alleys," she contends.

"Those kids … They must be here somewhere," Lobart grumbles, staring back at the haunting black cliffs.

"What if they've travelled farther away? What if they've gone to LA somehow? Erin may have made some friends at uni." She raises her voice to attract his attention.

"No ... No. They're still on Tinian. And we must find them," he retorts, his unyielding tone making it clear he's not buying any of Stella's suggestions.

"What's next, then?" Stella replies in a resigned tone.

"I'll call your father. You can go back to your shift!" he orders her while dialling on his mobile phone.

"Hope you are right," Stella quips with a dismissive tone as she walks back into the control room.

As Lobart waits impatiently for his call to be answered, Bill Sheppard suddenly opens the control room's door, his phone still ringing in his overall pocket.

"I'm on my way to see John Sanders," Sheppard announces.

"About time! I'm coming with you!" Lobart blurts out while walking towards Sheppard.

"Okay, okay. Sanders and I are waiting for the order to set off. We'll need to search the numerous passages after the second lake."

"Numerous passages ... They could be in any of those," Lobart insists.

"The weather is easing. We'll finally find out once and for all," Sheppard states in a pessimistic tone.

"You still doubt, don't you?" Lobart says with a sneer.

"I've told Sam, in no uncertain terms, never to go far into that cave without me. He has never disobeyed me—"

"Till now!" Lobart contests.

"Okay, let's go. You're already late, Albert. You need to get changed!" Sheppard mocks a dishevelled Lobart, who keeps groaning as he looks for his working overalls in the control room's lockers.

"Stella, darling, your mum will pick you up tonight." Sheppard waves at his daughter as he walks out of the door.

"Good luck!" Stella nods at her father and then scowls at Lobart behind his back as he clumsily slides his overalls over his nightclothes while grumbling to himself.

Sheppard and Lobart are soon heading towards the nearest search and rescue base in Sheppard's pickup truck. As they arrive at the large harbour on the west of the island, they can see the ARA teams loading their equipment into the speedboats waiting by one of the piers.

They run towards the long grey building at the entrance of the overbuilt port terminal. Sheppard unlocks the gates and shouts Sanders's name as they make their way through the long path inside the vast aircraft hangar, walking past the five rescue helicopters parked in an orderly formation alongside each other.

As they reach the end of the aisle, they stop by the drones' wall shelf, waiting for John Sanders to join them.

If anyone can navigate the drones into the depths of Diablo's cave, it would be ARA Air Marshal John Sanders. Since leaving Tinian in his youth, he has worked worldwide in rescue operations; at the forefront of the ARA's most daring missions, he's found survivors in the most inaccessible places using these specialist drones. The experienced pilot has accumulated more than twenty thousand rescue flying hours in his fifteen years of service. The distinctive aircraft wings tattoo on his forearm shows a star for every thousand hours he has achieved.

"Let's start getting ready, Sanders," Sheppard says as the tall, lanky figure of John Sanders joins them, wearing his trademark blue-and-red ARA's flying uniform.

"Well … weather permitting," Sanders cautions.

"The wind is easing," Lobart notes while pointing at the weather channel on the wall-mounted widescreens.

"It can all change in an instant," Sanders retorts, but Lobart's obstinate glare won't budge.

Sanders picks up a shiny black helmet from the instruments bench and connects it to the computer, turning on the interior augmented reality displays.

"I'll set up the echolocation at the highest rate. This operation needs maximum precision," Sanders says while loading the entire Diablo's cave three-dimensional maps into the helmet's guiding system.

Lobart looks directly into Sanders's focused grey eyes as if checking for the pilot's readiness. "Excellent," Lobart says, nodding his head while patting Sanders on his shoulders.

"If they are there," Sanders stoically remarks, "we will find them."

"But that's the first part," Sheppard adds, his stark gaze forewarning Sanders of the challenges to come.

The men sit in front of the computer screens while Sanders logs into the ARA's Main Rescue Network site.

"State your request type and code," the ARA's voice-controlled assistant announces.

"ARA, rescue code is 2099-468. Requesting permission to proceed with the last stage of search and rescue."

"Waiting for authorisation," the voice replies, but then they hear nothing.

The extended silence does not deter them; the men know they face a long wait through the night.

After checking the drone's moving parts, echolocation trackers, and deep-range cameras, Sheppard and Sanders double-check every step of their carefully planned mission while an impatient Lobart keeps asking them questions. Unable to sleep, they wait for the zero hour.

# CHAPTER 7
# RESCUE

*All across the ARA's live stream channels,*
*the world watches in suspense.*

"Operation authorised," the computer's voice assistant announces, and the message "ARA ready" flashes on the wide monitor soon after the cloudless sunrise.

Sanders and Sheppard carry the drones into the rescue speedboat, waiting by the hangar pier. Sheppard has insisted on steering it himself. They're joined by two paramedics and one extra boat pilot, plus another boat carrying transmission equipment and ARA reporters.

Lobart eagerly waves them off, but they never look back. As they set off, all of their attention is directed ahead, towards Diablo's cave.

Everyone on the island is expectantly watching the search and rescue operation on the ARA live broadcast. Mr Lobart has called Pat, Martha, and Stella to join him at the control room as they all anxiously wait. The families hold their collective breath as they closely follow the live transmissions, wishing for the best but, deep down in their minds, preparing for the worst.

All across the ARA's live stream channels, the world watches in suspense as Sanders, Sheppard, and the rest of the team arrive at the cave entrance.

In seconds, Sheppard pushes through the receding waves, steering the speedboat cleanly through the rugged cave entrance. As he forges ahead, the adrenaline rush makes him feel stronger, surer of himself. The thought that he may be getting closer to his son makes him more determined with every metre he advances.

When they finally reach the second lake, Sheppard gets as close as possible to the central passage leading to the waterfall. The men moor the boat securely onto one of the rocky sides, tying the ropes to the wall's metal bolts installed there during the preparations. Once they're completely still, Sanders sends in the first drone.

They all watch in despair as the drone approaches too low and immediately hits the water, overturning and rolling downstream. But the second drone successfully passes through and flies unhindered over the current. Using his navigation helmet and remote controls, Sanders dextrously keeps the drone moving forwards, its spotlights reflecting on the rippling water surface, illuminating the dark interior and its numerous side alleys. He guides the drone along very slowly so as not to miss anything. It seems as if it takes hours to reach the end, deep into Diablo's cave's gorge.

He manages to keep the drone hovering on top of the plunging torrent, high enough to miss the spraying water jets and, at the same time, at a safe distance from the ceiling. He then sweeps the powerful bright spotlights in every angle, showing the swirling current being sucked into the mighty chasm. The thundering noise of the plunging waters builds up into the scene's gripping atmosphere.

"Well, there's nothing here," Sanders grumbles through the microphone as he daringly guides his drone as close as possible to the water's edge.

The last traces of hope are fast disappearing from everyone's mind as they keep staring at the bleak images transmitted from the drone.

"At least we tried everything." Martha sobs, hugging Stella while burying her head in her daughter's arms.

Pat Lobart stays motionless by her side while Albert breathes out impatiently.

Sanders tries one last time with the spotlights at full power. He slowly sweeps along the walls' rough surface, inspecting every illuminated recess in detail. He focuses on a small inlet before the waterfall's edge. Instinctively, he moves the drone in that direction.

"What are you doing, Sanders?" Lobart shouts, fearing the drone may hit the rocks, but the following image transmission soon stops him in his tracks.

There, tightly wedged between the pillars of yet another alleyway, the outline of Sam's speedboat is clearly visible.

The Lobarts' and Stella's cheers make Martha look again at the screen as Sanders carefully lowers the drone closer to the boat and into the deck area. The sight of Sam lying on the floor seems like an unbelievable miracle. It takes everyone a few seconds to finally take in what they're watching.

Sanders manages to land the drone near Sam and points the camera towards his upper body.

"He's alive!" Martha screams in joy as she notices Sam's chest slowly moving.

"Oh, I'm so happy for my dear brother!" Stella excitedly hugs her mother.

Sam seems to be alive but in a profound sleep. Everyone continues to be glued to the images of Sam breathing peacefully while unaware of his precarious position. They all assume Erin must also be somewhere inside.

Bill Sheppard double-checks the course he must now negotiate through the lateral passage. He closely inspects the alley's detailed map on the dashboard screen. It's a narrower route, its currents spilling on the waterfall channel through side openings, but it finishes at a dead end. He must make sure he steers his boat, avoiding crashing against Sam's and against the looming back wall.

As soon as they've untied the ropes, Sheppard revs up the engine and aims toward the tight entry. The crew barely has time to hold on to their seats as Sheppard skilfully swerves and rushes into the narrow archway, managing to nimbly scrape through.

The rescuers can now see far ahead, where Sam's speedboat is wedged. Sheppard steers the twin-propeller boat at an angle, gradually slowing it down as it advances, until he reaches the end.

Everyone watching from the island breaks out in loud cheers, welcoming the images transmitted from the rescuers' helmet cams. The sight of the two boats' sides gently touching and the men jumping onto Sam's speedboat seems like a far-fetched dream coming true.

Sheppard rushes towards his son, lifting his head while the paramedics give him oxygen.

To everyone's delight, Sam suddenly opens his tired eyes and then anxiously stares at his father's triumphant face as if trying to say something.

"Welcome back, son," Sheppard lifts his thumb high in the air as a sign of victory.

Martha runs towards one of the screens and kisses both her son and husband's images, Stella jumping by her side.

After a quick but thorough search inside the boat, a sombre-looking Sanders faces the cameras. "Sadly, we have not found any traces of Erin."

"How is that possible?" Pat Lobart mumbles, startled.

"Maybe she never went in with him," Stella hastily suggests.

"We'll go back in and find *her*," Lobart scowls and then walks out in a hurry.

"I don't know what to think, Pat," Martha comforts Mrs Lobart. "Let's wait for what Sam has to say."

The paramedics carefully carry Sam onto the waiting rescue boat, while Sheppard, utterly exhausted, hands it over to the other pilot. As they exit into the open seas, the rescue helicopter is waiting with its tethered basket in position. One of the paramedics fastens himself and Sam into the meshed metal seat. Overjoyed, Sheppard and Sanders watch as the cable steadily rolls up and its cargo reaches the cabin.

As the returning search party make their way into the island's port, hundreds of people who never missed a minute of the tense rescue mission eagerly welcome their heroes.

# CHAPTER 8

# RUMOURS

*Do you realise what it means? He took her!*

Sam can barely make out his mother's silhouette sitting by his bedside, but his blurred vision is getting clearer by the minute. As her familiar face comes into focus, he welcomes her gentle smile. He smiles back at her and briefly chuckles, his face relaxing into a contented expression.

Throughout the brief silence, he tries to memorise the startling turn of events in his puzzled mind. He recalls the fruitless arguments trying to convince everyone of his story, his calm demeanour increasingly changing into one filled with anguish.

"I'm not a liar," Sam protests.

"I believe you, son," Martha whispers in his ear as she squeezes him tightly and presses her wet cheeks against his. As she comforts him with her words of support, Sam calms down, and he breathes out a long resigned sigh.

But as he sees his father standing behind his mother, he stiffens his body and briskly pulls away from her to face Bill Sheppard with a pleading gaze. "What about you, Dad? Do you believe me? I know Stella does."

"Son, your mother, your sister, and I do believe you, but—" Sheppard pauses and then hesitantly adds, "The thing is … nothing makes sense."

"Nothing makes sense?" Martha flares up, "Well, you explain to me. How could he survive for days in that alley? Someone must have helped him, don't you agree? And what about the orange light that Stella saw, the same colour as what he describes."

"Coincidence? We've been through the story several times, Martha. He mentions this man flying towards them from the alien aircraft. How did he help our Sam?—"

"Stop! I don't want to start this argument again. The important thing is that our Sam is alive. Let's wait until he fully recovers and his memory is clearer," Martha retorts while tenderly stroking Sam's forehead.

"Recovering?" Sam frowns at his mother. "I feel fine."

"Well, the clinic's doctor will be checking you soon," she explains in a comforting tone.

"Any news about Erin? Have they found anything inside the cave?" he glumly asks as if already knowing the answer.

His parents' sombre faces say it all.

"Do you realise what it means? He took her. He took her!" Sam yells in frustration, jumping out of his bed and abruptly opening the blinds in the tall bay window.

But he's faced with a group of people leaning against the front iron gates, hectically focusing their cameras on him. Dazzled, he closes the blinds as quickly as he opened them.

"Who are they?" he asks, looking wholly perplexed while pointing at the window.

"They're reporters from the ARA," Bill explains. "They want to interview you."

"We told them you're not well. We're trying to keep them at bay," Martha says, walking towards her son and trying to hug him. "But they won't go away."

"Ah! You think the ARA will laugh at me, don't you?" Sam avoids his mother's arms, visibly upset.

"My dear," she continues in a soothing tone, "you have not completely recovered. You may feel all right now, but you've woken up from a very long sleep."

"Yes." Sheppard tries to calm down his son, putting his arms around Sam's shoulders. "It seems you are still under the influence of something—"

"How long have I been asleep?" Sam relents, dejectedly staring at his father.

"For the past fourteen hours," Sheppard calmly says while walking his son towards the bed, followed by Martha.

"By the way, all tests were negative. They didn't show any suspicious chemicals in your body. We're all baffled. What can be making you so drowsy?" Martha ponders.

As they sit and embrace one another, Sam recalls the last moments with Erin, painstakingly going through his memories once again. He tries but fails to come up with at least a shred of unrefutable evidence. He feels utterly hopeless, realising he's exhausted all means of trying to convince everyone that he's telling the truth.

"I remember fearing the worst as the boat surged ever closer to the waterfall … and then, suddenly the boat seemed to stop, held up by some force."

"But we found you in a completely different place," Bill tries to clarify.

"I've always said we were dragged into the current and then the boat suddenly stopped, right at the edge of the waterfall," Sam counters.

"We found the boat stuck, Sam, tightly wedged in between the rocks—on the side alley," Bill sternly replies, looking straight into Sam's eyes.

"Dad, why would I invent this?" Sam keeps firm as he holds his father's probing gaze. "This is what happened. An alien from the alien aircraft turned up from under the waterfall, took Erin, and left me on the boat. He must have moved it."

"Sam, who is going to believe such a story? You're in good health, with no evidence of not eating or drinking for eight days … How can we explain what you've been doing all that time? You say the alien kept you immobilised until we found you … but how? And why? Do you want to know the latest rumours going around? Sheppard resignedly says as if he has entirely run out of ideas.

"Do you believe those rumours?" Sam challenges his parents with a deep frown on his face.

"No, absolutely not!" Martha hurriedly replies.

"What are they saying?" Sam asks despondently, sitting upright and folding his arms on his chest.

"They've been saying," Bill starts explaining in a dismissive tone, making it evident that he doesn't believe it either, "that you prepared everything to take Erin into Diablo's cave's dead-end channel, and you kept her hidden against her will. But as she kept rejecting you … you killed her and threw all the evidence … and her body … over the waterfall. Then you waited for rescue, as you knew I would eventually go there looking for you."

Sam throws himself back against the bed's headrest. "That doesn't make any sense!" he protests.

"To them, it makes more sense than the alien story, son," Martha sombrely adds.

"But why would I want to kill Erin?" Sam insists, sitting up straight and punching the bed with his clenched fists. "I love her."

However implausible his story seems to be, Sam's parents do believe him. But they're not sure if anybody else will.

"We believe you, son. We believe you!" Martha and Bill keep telling Sam as they huddle around him.

"We must go back there, to Diablo's cave. He'll come back," Sam pleads with his father.

"We are already there. The ARA is setting up closed-circuit cameras. They've found nothing so far," Sheppard replies after checking his phone for any missed messages.

"He'll come back," Sam snaps. "He will!"

"Answer me this question, Sam. Why did you go as far as the second lake?" Bill scolds him.

"It was very strange," Sam mumbles and then pauses while staring into the distance as if in deep thought.

"What?" Bill urges him.

"There was this power beyond my control … pushing me. I can't fully explain it." Sam reclines onto the pillows in a helpless gesture, realising that, yet again, he's saying something nobody else will believe.

His dispirited demeanour soon disappears as the nurse enters the room. *I must show them I have fully recovered. I must find Erin soon*, he firmly tells himself.

After a clean bill of health from the clinic, the Sheppards take their son back home, deciding to avoid any contact with anyone else outside their family, at least until the day of the court hearing.

# PART II

# CHAPTER 9
# AWAKENING

*Welcome to your ancestors' world, Shaillah.*

As Erin wakes up and slowly opens her eyes, an intense glow hurts her pupils. She covers her face with her hands and tries to peer through the narrow slit between her fingers, but she cannot focus on anything.

She takes a deep breath, but the rushing cold air numbs her throat. Next, she tries to get up, but as she does, her body flips backwards, and she realises she's floating in mid-air. Aimlessly spinning, she cries out for help, but no matter how hard she tries, she cannot hear her screams.

Erin tries to work out how she ended up trapped inside this icy bubble. She remembers standing by Sam's side, utterly mystified by a mysterious figure flying towards them.

*Is he keeping me captive? Am I alive … or dead? And where is Sam?* This last thought makes her open her eyelids as much as she can stand it, desperately looking and reaching out for her best friend through the thick haze, to no avail.

As she starts to fear that she's alone, her despair changes into full expectation when the all-pervading haze starts to dissipate, and the blinding white light progressively fades. Her body stops spinning but then starts shaking, her heartbeat pounding hard in her aching chest. Still, she tries to control herself to confront whatever she will encounter when the foggy shroud finally clears.

At last, she welcomes the fresh air warming her body as the unfamiliar surroundings gradually start to take shape in front of her.

Erin marvels at the striking view of a startled, bleary-eyed girl floating off the floor and looking directly at her from the back of the room. *I'm looking at my own reflection.* She watches herself blink several times while her mouth stays wide open. The girl on the life-size three-dimensional image looks as stunned as she feels.

To the right of her gleaming body, a bright red heart pounds at the same rhythm as her pulse, and a translucent brain flashes with random blue sparks. Rows of intricate symbols fill the rest of the space, rotating while glowing in different colours and brightness.

Three tall men are staring closely at the ethereal projection while talking among themselves. She immediately recognises one of them as the one who appeared on the waterfall. His sturdy body, distinctive white hair, and black glossy uniform stand out against the brightly coloured picture. *Oh, he looks just like the mysterious soldier. I guess I'll be waking up soon.*

She next tries to extend her feet to touch the floor, and as she does, she's thrilled she can stand up at last. She straightens her back and bends her knees and elbows, crouching and standing up; her newly found self-control brings her some comfort, and she momentarily forgets about the strangers, concentrating on her body instead.

She keeps all her attention on the life-size image of herself. She twists and turns, inspecting her tight white bodysuit and the high velvet boots wrapping comfortably around her feet. Her eyes are shining with a deep purple glow, and her long blonde hair has now turned a glossy silver-white.

Suddenly, the men's tall bodies block her view, making her shudder. Erin can feel the pressure of their stare as they stand a short distance in front of her. She tries to move away and as she desperately screams, this time, she can hear her shrieks echoing through the high vaulted chamber.

But the men are hardly perturbed by her frightened reaction, keeping a patient guard as if knowing it's a matter of time before she calms down.

As she instinctively searches for an exit, she notices her vital signs chaotically changing on the holographic projection, her rapidly pulsating heart, her constantly flashing brain. But then she starts feeling inexplicably calmed; her pulse suddenly steadies, and her sparkling brain signals fizzle out. Soon, she finds herself quietly staring at the waiting men as if expecting their next order.

One of the men steps forwards while warmly smiling at her. As she slowly makes out his welcoming face, she feels even more sedated.

He goes down on one knee, maintaining his hypnotic gaze as if inviting her to get closer. She feels an irresistible urge to run to him. As she looks straight into his piercing emerald-green eyes, her fascination overpowers her caution.

She feels her heartbeat racing once again. Even if she tries she cannot breathe, as she realises that, in front of her, is the man of her dreams. She desperately wants to touch him, to feel him; she needs to know that he is real.

As she runs towards him, she feels her body breaking through the invisible sheath that has been keeping her captive. In a fleeting second, she finds herself leaning against his chest, looking down on him, while he is wrapping his arms around her waist. She breathes in deeply, filling her lungs with his alluring scent; she can taste it.

He keeps perfectly still and allows Erin to inspect him for as longs as she wants. She is intrigued by his exotic looks, puzzled by his magnetic aura. His thick dark eyebrows join together over the long thin nose. When he momentarily blinks, the glow from his pupils flashes through lush dark eyelashes. His slick silver hair flows over his thick neck and falls over his forehead in a jagged fringe. Her fingers play with his hair as she strokes his face, pressing hard on his cheeks and jawbones. *Oh, he is real!*

He moves one arm behind his back and brings about a crystalline pyramid-shaped object, perfectly balanced on the palm of his hand. The sharp-edged piece shines at the edges with a fuzzy iridescent light, and as it starts to rotate slowly, Erin recognises the letters of the alphabet randomly appearing on each side in a bright red colour.

The man speaks slowly in a gravelly voice. She listens carefully, trying to understand in vain what he's saying. But then she notices the translated words are being formed from each letter, right on the pyramid's surface: "Welcome to your ancestors' world, Shaillah."

"Shaillah?" She frowns.

"Seij, Shaillah" (Yes, Shaillah). He declares while withdrawing his hand from under the pyramid and letting it float and rotate in between them, displaying the name "Shaillah" on all its sides.

She tries to touch the pyramid, anticipating a cold sensation from the glassy surface, but the sudden electric discharge makes her jolt.

"No, no," she protests, shaking her head firmly. "My name is Erin. What is yours?"

The man wryly smiles at her sharp response. He stands up, his broad shoulders rising above her head. He puts one hand over his chest, briefly bowing his head, as he says in a mellow voice, "My name is Rothwen."

Erin looks up at him, her mouth wide open in surprise as she hears the words in perfect English. "So, you also speak English," she marvels.

"It's not a big deal, Shaillah. You'll soon be speaking our language as well."

She backs away from him, gathering her thoughts; a lost and bewildered look flashes across her face. Then she realises that the two other men are inquisitively looking at her as well.

"Meet our supreme commander, Kuzhma-Or, and our chief scientist, Athguer," Rothwen announces, ignoring her baffled expression.

"Kuzhma-Or, Athguer," she repeats as she looks at each of them in turn.

Athguer is wearing a navy bodysuit with a high open collar around his neck. His trimmed silver-streaked hair and beard are impeccably combed back in straight lines, exuding a zest for perfection.

Kuzhma-Or's highly decorated uniform gives him a compelling dominating appearance. His thick white eyebrows and rectangular beard stand out against his black glossy attire.

The hefty commander acknowledges Shaillah with a brief nod, while Athguer keeps looking at her, narrowing his eyes in a studious stare.

"Unda ye, Shaillah," Kuzhma-Or orders while turning around and briskly walking towards the glossy ebony table running through the back of the vast room, in stark contrast with the pure white polished walls.

She reads the translation on the floating pyramid's side: "Follow me, Shaillah."

She repeats to herself, *Unda ye, Unda ye*, and she has the impression that she has heard those words before. *Maybe in my dreams?* She wonders.

As Kuzhma-Or walks away, the pyramid follows him, floating along and gliding over the table. He lounges back on his tall chair at the head of the table while stroking the glitzy gemstones adorning the golden hand rest.

Rothwen waits patiently by Erin, as she still dares not move. She knows her only option is to obey them, but she buys herself some time while inspecting the strange but intriguing multichromatic view quickly changing in front of her.

Athguer returns to the flickering three-dimensional projection, analysing the packed rows of symbols as he strolls back and forth, totally consumed in his thoughts.

With a sharp glance, Kuzhma-Or orders Rothwen to join him at the glossy table. Rothwen takes Erin by the hand, leading her to sit opposite him while facing the imposing commander and the colourful images. Erin sits on top of her crossed legs, stretching out her body to make herself look taller. She looks up at the men in an expectant pose while checking approvingly on her body's reflection.

"Seya, Shaillah" (Welcome, Shaillah)! "Your awakening has long been awaited … by us all," Kuzhma-Or says, opening his arms in a welcoming gesture, his booming voice resounding all around the concave walls.

She starts to read the translated words on the pyramid, but she finds herself understanding every word, even before she finishes. All the while, she keeps glancing at Kuzhma-Or and Rothwen, trying to ascertain their intentions.

The glossy tabletop slides open at its centre, and two tall black goblets rise from within the gap, their rims bubbling up with a bluish effervescent foam.

"Drink, Shaillah. It will energise your tired body," Rothwen encourages her, placing a goblet between her hesitant hands.

She cautiously smells the bubbles popping up as she nervously holds the cold thin glass stem. She sticks her tongue out, touching the frothy top. As she tastes the refreshing liquid, a rush of energy flows through her body. The taste and feel are so enticing that she tilts the goblet over her mouth and keeps it there until the last drop is gone. As she places the empty glass back on the table, she looks at each man in defiance.

"Who are you? And why have you brought me here? Where is Sam? I want to go back home," she demands, with such impetus that she is even taken aback by her bold move.

But the men hardly blink.

Kuzhma-Or leans forwards and clears his throat. Then he speaks calmly in perfect English while stressing his words. "Shaillah, you should know the Rom-Ghenshar world is your real home."

She can't tell whether Kuzhma-Or is threatening her or warning her, but she finds the tone of his voice very convincing. Still, she can't bring herself to believe him.

"Rom … Ghenshar? What kind of world? And why do you keep calling me Shaillah?"

"Rom means *power*, Ghenshar, *glory*. Shaillah is your real name, the name given to you by your creators. We all come from our vast, beautiful, and indomitable Rom-Ghenshar world." Kuzhma-Or continues unabated, completely disregarding Erin's rebellious mood.

Rothwen is subtly smiling as he keeps scrutinising every gesture she makes.

"You have Rom-Ghenshar blood and cells now," Kuzhma-Or declares, swaying one arm in the air. "Your transition will soon be complete. Nothing of your inferior human genes will remain. You will think as we think, act as we act, dare as we dare."

Erin's mind is racing as she strives to make sense of what she's hearing. She promptly concludes that this must be another of her recurring dreams. She tries with all her inner strength to wake up and be in the comfort of her bedroom, even if that means hearing Mrs Lobart's nagging voice again.

She attempts to stand up from her chair in a bid to run away, but her body hardly moves. Feeling powerless, she wants to scream in fear once more.

Noticing her despair, Rothwen uses his telepathic mind to calm her down. He induces his pervasive brainwave field on her mind, disconnecting her overexcited neurons and bringing her back into a relaxed state.

Rothwen offers her another goblet of the sweet, energising drink, and she feels a numb sensation overpowering her thoughts. This time, she doesn't hesitate and gulps it down in one go.

"Rom-Ghenshar, eh? And from what continent is this?" She sarcastically asks as she puts the empty goblet back on the table.

"Shaillah," Kuzhma-Or calmly replies while stroking his beard, "we come from no continent at all. We come not from this planet but from much, much farther away."

"How f-far?" she stutters, trying to withhold her sarcasm.

"It's thousands of light-years away, on the opposite side of our galaxy, our beautiful Senyeraikh" (Milky Way). "Humans' feeble tools have not even found it yet." Kuzhma-Or pauses as Erin dumbfoundedly stares at him.

"Then … it would take you thousands of years to get here, even travelling at the speed of light … How could you possibly make it? Or do you use wormholes?" Erin contests.

The men burst into loud rapturous laughter while Erin shows her impatience, biting her lips, her face turning red in frustration.

"Impulsive!" Kuzhma-Or lifts one eyebrow as he glances at Rothwen, who can't keep his eyes off Erin's firm stance.

She catches a glimpse of Rothwen's long-drawn, admiring gaze, and her entire body shivers.

"Daring!" Rothwen exclaims, his whole face beaming in unrepressed satisfaction.

"Shaillah, I would say not everyone would agree with your calculations," Kuzhma-Or remarks with a dismissive tone.

She throws herself back onto her seat in a bout of resignation and dejection. *Anyway, all nightmares must come to an end.*

Athguer walks towards the table, ceremoniously folding his arms as he announces, "She is progressing so quickly. I can confirm she's ready!"

"And about time too. Brilliant, Athguer!" Kuzhma-Or cheers, briskly standing up and gesturing for Rothwen to follow him.

"I can tell she's ready, even without looking at the data," Rothwen quips while walking towards Kuzhma-Or and Athguer.

The men animatedly converse while pointing at the bright pictures and symbols. Erin is attentively watching them out of the corner of her eye. *Kuzhma-Or seems so dominant. How did I dare confront him? Athguer looks serious and aloof. But Rothwen—he is so handsome.*

She straightens up in her seat as she sees Rothwen walking towards her. As he holds her dainty hands, the warmth of his palms makes her feel protected, and for that, she feels grateful. A gentle smile spreads across her face, her tense muscles slowly relaxing as she keeps gazing at him.

"Shaillah, I only ask for your patience," Rothwen tells her in a soothing tone as he slowly lifts her off her seat. "Let me take you—"

"Where to?" She looks around the vast white-walled room, wondering where he would be taking her.

Rothwen sharply nods at Kuzhma-Or, and to Erin's astonishment, the sturdy commander starts disintegrating in front of her eyes. In a flash, he has completely gone. But before she can recover from her shock, she next sees Athguer vanishing in front of her eyes. She tightly holds Rothwen's hands, thinking he would disappear too.

"They were only body copies, Shaillah" You'll soon meet them in the flesh when we reach our domain. And that's where I'm taking you."

"Will we comc back?"

"Ensheren" (Definitely)!

"Wait!" Erin pleads, clutching Rothwen's hands as firmly as she can. "Where's Sam? How long have I been here?"

"We've been taking good care of you for a few days. As for your friend … he's safe. He'll return to his family very soon."

Erin shudders as the impressive sight of Diablo's waterfall bursts into view right in front of her, its thundering roar reverberating through the whole chamber. She covers her mouth with her hands, holding her breath as she notices Sam's boat wedged in the side alley. As she sees Sam lying on the deck, peacefully sleeping, she smiles with relief, but then she worries. She reaches out, trying to touch him, but her hand goes through a sheath of gleaming particles.

"Why have you done this?" she mouths in despair. All the memories of her last minutes with Sam flash through her mind, and she fears for his life.

As Rothwen turns the vivid images off with a thought-command, her anguish grows. She confronts him with a reproaching glare.

"How long since you brought me here?"

"Exactly eight Earth days," Rothwen calmly replies. "But don't worry. He's been kept in hibernation. He'll be all right until they find him."

"Promise me he'll be okay."

"I promise ..."

She looks at Rothwen warily as he pulls her against his broad chest and embraces her in a bear hug. His electrifying grasp makes her feel as if her blood is evaporating away.

"Shaillah ... trust me!" He stresses his words while running his thick fingers over her cheeks.

"You kidnapped me. You're holding my friend against his will. How can I ever trust you?" she protests while wrestling within his arms.

But Rothwen holds her steady while intensely gazing at her. "Look at me! Look at me!" he demands while pulling her face closer to him until their noses touch. "You must trust me!" He keeps a firm hold until she timidly looks back at him.

She fakes a complacent smile as she tries to stay collected. But deep inside, she feels frail and overpowered by his presence. Her skin is covered in goosebumps. Her trembling body betrays her fragile state, even though she tries to appear defiant.

Rothwen keeps tightening his grip, his pupils widening around a brightening glow. She repeatedly blinks, trying to withstand the burning sensation at the back of her eyes, until she has to close them tightly. Blinded and confused, she concentrates on her breathing. Every time she feels the air rushing through her lungs, every time she smells him, she is relieved to know she's still alive.

*Any moment now, my heart will stop beating*, she fears. But soon, she is overcome with such ecstasy that she finds herself wishing the enthralling embrace would never end.

"You see?" Rothwen speaks in a mellow voice as he loosens his grip. "You cannot escape from my embrace. You see? But I'd never harm you. You can open your eyes now."

Erin slowly opens her trembling eyelids as she breathes in and out, resting her hands on Rothwen's chest while he keeps looking at her with a proud smile.

"Good!" Rothwen smugly says. "Be patient and listen to me. This is as hard for me as it is for you. We're both out of our comfort zones. But I had to bring you here. It all started when you moved to the island. I couldn't stop watching you—"

"How did you watch me?"

"I can see every single point of this planet from anywhere, every place, at any time. I used to watch you while you were asleep or even when you were out and about," Rothwen says while softly caressing her forehead.

"I saw you in my dreams." She gazes at him, delving into his unmistakably chiselled features as he continues talking to her.

"For a while, I thought Zula could be right. I might've been going through an 'irrational phase', but I felt so torn as you grew up. You would be swimming alone, and you'd be looking at me but without seeing me, and I'd be caressing your hair but without touching you. You were in that forbidden boundary I should've never crossed. But in all this time, there hasn't been a moment when I've stopped thinking about you."

Erin's pupils sparkle under the copious tears flooding her eyelids and spilling over her cheeks. "I never stopped thinking about you either. I couldn't wait to close my eyes at night to see you in my dreams. Why didn't you just turn up?"

"I was denying it to myself every time. I thought this feeling would end as suddenly as it had started. But instead, it got stronger!"

"It got stronger for me too—"

"That much I knew. That's why I made your friend bring you to me—the night of your sixteenth birthday and not a second later, when your body was ready to bring you into my world."

"You could have taken me from anywhere, anytime. Why did you do it when I was with him?"

"He happened to be in my path. Shaillah. You'll find out when you get to know me. I do things my way."

"Who are you?" she demands while expectantly gazing at him.

Rothwen gently wipes away her tears, his eyes glinting with unashamed desire. "Right now, Shaillah, I'm nothing more than your humble servant."

## CHAPTER 10

# THE PASSAGE

*As the twin suns rise, your life will begin anew.*

"Look closely at the data, Shaillah. What do you see?" Rothwen asks.

"I see unintelligible symbols." Mesmerised, she stares at the packed matrix of three-dimensional glyphs, each one forming a unique geometrical shape, perfectly aligned throughout the volume of a giant cube, floating over her.

"They describe your biological fingerprint." He explains, "each edge, angle, and colour combination defines your molecular signature in every cell type."

"Why are you showing me this?" she asks without taking her eyes off the glowing image, as more finely drawn details keep revealing themselves.

Rothwen points at another block of symbols starting to form next to the first one. The cubes move closer together and merge, every edge and node brightening as they superimpose onto each other. She watches the symbols blinking against the dark background, every pulse pounding on her puzzled mind.

"As you can see, every signature code in each block closely match!" Rothwen explains, "There are some black markers on the incompatible zones, but we can deal with those later."

"And the second block is?"

"The Rom-Ghenshar biological fingerprint!"

"So, my body ... is now different. It was hijacked—changed—without my permission?" She stares reproachingly at Rothwen.

"This is not an option, Shaillah," he impassively replies. "It's long been decided."

Erin struggles to gather her thoughts as Rothwen speaks, but the more she tries to comprehend, the more confused she feels. She purses her lips while tilting her head backwards in despair. Rothwen places her hands on his chest as he slowly takes her towards the back of the room.

"Let me take you into our world, Shaillah. Then—and only then—you'll understand why you are here." He pulls her by one hand and leads her into a downward flood-lit corridor.

*There's no use in struggling anymore. I'm exhausted,* she thinks while breathing in deeply the thick, salty air. She resigns herself to follow him wherever he is taking her.

The long steep path seems to converge into a luminous point in the distance. *It looks like the entrance into another chamber,* she thinks. As they descend along the aisle, the bright green surroundings make her close her eyes, and the thickening atmosphere makes her gasp for air. Every few steps, she peeps through her eyelids, closing them tightly again.

"Shaillah, you are doing well. We are nearly there," he encourages as he leads her farther down, checking on her from time to time.

"Where are we?" she moans, tiptoeing behind him.

"Shaillah, you are entering our world."

"Don't call me Shaillah. My name is Erin," she protests between breaths.

"Erin in the past, Shaillah from now on," he counters.

She wheezes loudly to let him know she's feeling very uncomfortable.

"You may struggle now. But you'll be fine. I see your body is soon adapting to our atmosphere."

"What's your atmosphere anyway?" She fumbles her hands out of his grasp, feeling she cannot walk any further.

"Just a few more steps, and we reach our first gate." He gently takes her hands, pulling her towards him, keeping a close watch on her reaction in case they have to turn back.

When Rothwen has her against his chest, he holds her within his strong arms as they sit on the floor. She buries her face under his shoulder.

"The ionised oxygen in our high-pressure atmosphere produces this green light and would destroy any foreign cell. Your body must absorb these higher energy levels before settling down."

Rothwen keeps her in a protecting embrace while stroking her back and reassuring her. "You're doing well, my brave Shaillah."

Eventually, she feels her lungs expanding, supercharged with the rushing energising air. At last, she can start breathing deeply, unrestrained. When she opens her eyes, the surrounding aquamarine reflections bring her a soothing feeling.

A beautiful underwater world fills her field of view, its deep, dense waters confined behind a concave transparent wall. Odd-looking fish with pointed serrated teeth and prickly fins, large-tentacled octopuses and cuttlefish, long-legged spiny crabs and colourful jellyfish swim erratically on the other side; their bodies sometimes crashing against the thick glass and then disappearing back into the dark background.

"Extraordinary!" she exclaims as she sits up straight, her face beaming in fascination. "I've never seen so many sea creatures at once!"

"They live down in these deep trenches," he explains, "and they're attracted to the light."

"Where are we?"

"Right at the bottom of the Pacific Ocean," he replies while she excitedly runs towards the all encircling underwater world.

She presses her hands against the smooth surface while walking along the curved glass barrier, closely inspecting the sea creatures' peculiar bodies. Rothwen doesn't interrupt her, watching her childish moves and admiring her curiosity.

She jumps high to reach the biggest jellyfish as if she is competing to be more agile than them. Rothwen smiles, allowing himself some respite. He knows she is at ease, at least for now. All her fears and uncertainties are far from her mind. But it's no time to relax for him. The crucial tests are fast approaching as he prepares to take her through the most challenging passages yet.

At last, she manages to jump at the same height as any jellyfish that approaches. She is surprised at how nimble her muscles feel, never imagining she could be this fast.

"See what I can do?" She proudly shows off.

"I think you're ready to go even farther," he enticingly gazes at her, catching her as she falls from her last leap.

"To your domain?" she asks as he gently sets her down.

"Our domain, Shaillah. A whole new world. And our journey begins here."

"It seems there's no way out of here," she muses while looking around.

"Are you sure? Shaillah, prepare to enter into your new world. We are going to pass through three gates—the gates that only a Rom-Ghenshar can enter. And the first one is here."

"I don't see any gates," she says in a dismissive tone.

"Each gate takes us closer to our destination," Rothwen continues, completely ignoring her scorn. "Each one links into the next, like one-way locks." He bends down and sweeps the floor with his index finger, revealing a thick circular line around them. As he completes the circle, he stands up and holds her by her waist. The area under their feet suddenly judders and rises with a clicking sound before it starts descending directly into a tunnel, dragging them down.

She presses her head against his chest as they accelerate downwards, and a swirling feeling of weightlessness makes her stomach churn.

"Don't be afraid," Rothwen reassures her. "You're doing fine. We are going down slowly as your body gets used to our atmosphere."

"Slowly?" She ponders. It feels to her like they're hurtling down through an abyss.

"Yes, slowly. We go faster in our crafts."

"It's very dark now," she complains. "All I can see is your dark figure."

"Yes, we're going down the deepest sea trenches. You call them the Marianas."

"How far down?"

"Stay still!" he whispers, tightening his protective hug around her.

As they continue shuttling down, Erin has completely lost the notion of time. Now and then, she sticks out her head and peers through the surrounding blackness, before hiding it again under his arms.

At last, she senses they are grinding to a halt as she starts discerning clearer patterns in her field of vision. The gleaming outlines of tall tapering pillars covered in stacks of mother-of-pearl rings shine through the undulating currents of a crystal-clear ocean.

"What are those towers?" She points towards the group of height-defying structures, rising imposingly from their sturdy metal trusses and surrounding an immense pearly white dome.

"Ah! you can see now into our infrared band!" Rothwen exclaims, his heartbeat racing in sheer expectation. All that he meticulously planned and hoped for is now only two steps away. "The towers?" he asks, appearing somewhat indifferent, "they are our robotics workshops." Then, pointing ahead, he proudly adds, "We are going into the dome!"

Erin smiles as she looks back at Rothwen, relieved that, at last, their destination is within reach. Still, his hot-blooded yearning gaze pierces like a dagger right through her heart. The charged air sparkles as they keep staring at each other in an alluring hypnotising spell.

"Can I kiss you?" he whispers.

Her eyes glaze with uncontrolled desire as their lips are drawn to each other, fusing their bodies in a long-awaited kiss.

"I never felt like this before." She gasps through a short pause, her pupils darting back and forth, longing for more.

"Me neither," he admits.

"Rothwen, it feels like we're meant to be together."

"Every time you pass through one of our gates, Shaillah, you get closer to me," he boasts, and then he kisses her for even longer, even more passionately.

The taste of him reminds her of her favourite cinnamon flakes; she engulfs herself in his sweetened musk, squeezing his face to make sure she is not dreaming.

A sudden jolt makes them break apart as the whole tunnel starts to vibrate with a humming sound.

"What's that?" She asks, startled.

"Our second gate has arrived. It's one of our scouting crafts," he replies as Erin notices the arrowhead-shaped craft rising from the bottom of the tunnel, its orange spotlights continually flashing.

"Now, once inside our scouting-craft, you will be wholly within our environment. Then there's one more gate to go. And we can celebrate your first successful transition." He announces, his voice barely concealing his excitement.

The panel under their feet slides open, and they both fall into their seats. As the craft exits from the vertical tunnel and shoots towards the glistening, imposing compound, Shaillah expectantly looks ahead through the transparent deck while Rothwen keeps checking on her.

*Well, it was sometimes frightening, but I've made it here,* she thinks, feeling pleased with herself.

"You made it here because you are a Rom-Ghenshar," Rothwen says.

Erin gives Rothwen a puzzled look, then frowns. She finds it both surprising and annoying that he knows exactly what she is thinking.

*So, I am now a Rom-Ghenshar. Why did this happen?* she thinks.

"It happened because I made it happen," he boasts.

"Are you spying on my thoughts?" she protests.

"We all interconnect via our thoughts—on our fine-tuned brain network," he explains to an increasingly frustrated Erin. "We can control their frequency and intensity, even choosing when to turn them off and on."

"So that's how you're controlling me, is it?" she grumbles as she wriggles on her seat.

But Rothwen holds her arms down, keeping her firmly in her place. "It is how it is," he bluntly replies, his eyes flashing in a warning glare. "You'll get to know how it works ... very soon. Don't move."

"I don't know what to think anymore," she resignedly tilts her head back.

Suddenly, she hears a constant buzzing inside her head, getting louder and louder. Her forehead throbs with an intense quickening pulse; she closes her eyes tightly, fearing her head is about to explode. She presses her hands firmly over her ears as they pop and feel about to burst with a high-pitched whistling sound.

Rothwen keeps a close impatient watch on her. He knows this passage will be swift, but it's the most dangerous yet. Any second now, he will know whether the third and final step has succeeded, and with its success will come Shaillah's first transition into his world.

As the intense humming finally disappears, an uncanny sense of tranquillity runs through her entire body. She feels as if she's in a completely different state of mind, calmed and self-assured. She slowly looks back at Rothwen, and their eyes lock in flares of relief, triumph, and joy.

*That was the third gate, Shaillah.* She hears Rothwen's voice clearly inside her head, but she is sure Rothwen did not open his mouth. *You've joined our brain network. Your brain has successfully tuned into our high frequencies. Only we, Rom-Ghenshars, can connect to this network.*

As Erin realises that she can clearly understand what he's thinking, she feels overjoyed by her new powers.

*I can read your thoughts.* She relishes in her newly found ability, her face glowing with a satisfied smile.

"We are connected. We are like one. The long wait is over!" Rothwen cheers, drawing her from her seat into his lap and hugging her tightly.

The lovers share their feelings and wishes without uttering a word while their fast-moving craft sifts through the towers and breaks seamlessly through the pressure-levelling shield and into the supple concave dome's wall, grinding to a halt just off the sandy surface.

As the cockpit cover slides open over their heads, Erin stands up and welcomes the refreshing ocean smell. The swirling breeze caresses her face and hair as she eagerly scans the fascinating landscape under a tenuous radiance. *Like transcending into a new dimension, I'm changing fast. I can feel it. It's a new me … Shaillah.*

*Seya en* (Welcome back).

*Suan enjie* (Always victorious).

Rothwen and Shaillah hear the messages from Kuzhma-Or and Athguer as they jump out of the craft and onto the moist sand.

She contemplates the stretching outline of rocky outcrops and rolling hills at each side of a vast shimmering pink ocean. "A sea within a sea within a sea," she marvels.

The foamy waves keep pounding on the gravelled coast, rattling the tiny colourful gems peppering the shifting ground.

"What are we waiting for?" she asks as Rothwen stands motionless, purposely looking into the distance.

"Just wait," he urges her.

As the shimmering mist glistens in rainbow-like hues, her expectation grows. With her polarised pupils, she focuses on a emerging glow breaking through the horizon. The bright, thin arc of a yellow disc floods the sky with its warm shafts of light, piercing through the thinning clouds. As the billowing globe keeps rising, it seems to want to pull the ocean up with it. When it finally hangs cleanly over the floodlit waters, the flickering rays of a second smaller red sun paint the horizon in deep crimson hues.

The two suns steadily ascend on the brightening opalescent sky, aligning in a perfect diagonal while burning the dense morning mist. A band of multicolour lines spread over the ocean surface as two beautiful broad double rainbows intersect across the rolling hills.

As Shaillah keeps admiring the unfolding colour-changing scene, a deep feeling of belonging overcomes her. *This is your new world, Shaillah,* she thinks while her mind is swept in a whirl of emotions.

She pulls Rothwen's hand to make him look back at her.

"So beautiful!" she cheers as she impulsively jumps up onto his hips.

"I wanted you to admire the twin sunrise of Rom and Ghenshar," Rothwen tells her with a proud smile.

He holds her up to his face and starts kissing her while he tells her through his thoughts, *As the twin suns rise, your life begins anew.*

The suns' rays shine through their moving lips as if the glimmering shafts want to steal a share of their passion. The incoming tide reaches up to his knees, but they are oblivious to the swell. They are drowning in their irrepressible desire. Time goes by, and the twin suns keep rising; the school of flying lyshars skim their fluttering wings over the sea's surface, but their shrieks go unheard, their presence unnoticed. All Rothwen and Shaillah can hear is the thumping echo of their racing hearts.

## CHAPTER 11

# THE REPLICA

*Thank you, dear Zula. And however hard to believe,*
*thank you for showing me who I am.*

Rothwen is resting by the scattered boulders on the seashore, taking stock of his endeavour. Today, whatever the perils and unknowns, he wouldn't have it any other way; of that, he is sure. But what the future may bring—of that, he is not so sure.

He sends his last thought-message to Zula-Or, the Rom-Ghenshars' high counsellor: *I was tired of the desolate wanderings. I needed something to shake up my demons, something to keep me from fighting against myself.*

*You always have what you want, Rothwen, and this is no different,* Zula-Or replies from her ethereal gem-studded garden.

Rothwen looks at Shaillah's angelic face as she soundly sleeps, her head lying snuggly against his bare chest.

*No, my dear Zula … this is different,* he counters.

Shaillah rolls open her drowsy eyes as she stirs within Rothwen's arms. Her mind is blank and her vision blurred, but the swooshing sound of the ocean and the warmth from his body soon take her out of her slumber.

"What time is it?" she mumbles, stretching out her arms and legs.

"Time?" Rothwen wryly smiles. "The time is now."

"Now?"

"Yes. Now. Free yourself from any time constraints, Shaillah, for it's an illusion. There is *artificial local time*, and there are *entangled space-time frames*." Rothwen pauses and smiles at Shaillah puzzled face. "The frames that we twist and bring together so we can change space and time … at our will. That's how we can travel instantly across our beautiful universe."

"How do you twist them and bring them together?"

"In many ways—virtual tunnelling, vacuum energy, supergravity. It all depends on how fast and far we want to go."

"Interesting. When can I see it?" Shaillah ponders as she finds her balance while standing up, feeling sluggish from her long sleep.

"Sooner than you think," he assures her.

Shaillah checks herself and then her surroundings, scanning the immense horizon. The two suns shine low in the sky, painting the wispy clouds in swathes of orange and cherry hues. She reminds herself of where she was before falling asleep, gasping for air in an endless kiss, melting inside Rothwen's arms. She turns around to look down at him, smiling childishly.

"You are still here." She chuckles, her voice wobbling in a mixture of awe and joy as she throws herself over his shoulders and hugs him tightly, as if making sure he won't disappear again like in her dreams.

"Yes, I'm still here. We made it—together!" Rothwen exclaims as he stands up in front of her, holding her hands and admiring her svelte figure. "You look amazing—after all you've been through. I must say, you're definitely made for this world."

Shaillah's face beams with sheer self-confidence.

"Now, let me put this on—your utility belt." Rothwen draws a glistening band from within his thick belt and wraps it around her waist. He firmly clasps the buckle at the front, its central jewel flashing as it clicks and locks up.

"This is your primary control," Rothwen explains, rubbing on the trapezium-shaped buckle. "It depends on which edge your touch. But you can also use your mind commands—when you're ready."

Shaillah swings her waist around, inspecting the beautifully decorated belt. A golden mesh runs along its strap forming rhomboid patterns, each section framing a central iridescent gem, flashing in step as she turns.

"The most important three functions are here," Rothwen continues. "The buckle's gem deploys your biomagnetic shield; the right and left edges are your flying controls; the top and bottom edges tune your electrostatic field. And it all responds to your unique fingerprint or your unique brainwave transmission frequency."

She frowns, looking inquisitively at Rothwen, who continues enthusiastically explaining.

"And some useful features of your shield—you can make it match any background, you can fine-tune its strength, you can change … Well, the possibilities are endless."

"I can't wait to try all this," she exclaims, admiring her belt's colourful gems and radiant central buckle.

"You won't have to wait long," he says, fastening up his tight vest and turning around onto the hill behind them.

They climb up the rocky path hand in hand, and as the whole striking scenery comes into full view, Shaillah feels as though this eerie fascinating landscape is opening its invisible doors to her. There lies her new world, mysterious and uncertain, but she is determined to conquer it, whatever it takes.

From the hilltop, she marvels at the sprawling ocean under the vast domed sky, its winding shores broken up by the scattered rolling hills and jagged rock pools. The entire scenery looks wild and unpredictable, but its most prominent feature makes it look singularly perfect and wondrous.

A massive crystalline rock stands over two stories high in the middle of the ocean, under a flat-topped hexagonal platform. All around the rugged sides, thick golden pillars rise and crisscross each other in a diamond lattice, towering over the platform while reflecting the sunrays in all the rainbow colours.

"It's the command base, our temporary quarters," Rothwen explains.

"Temporary?"

"Yes, we're just passing. We never spend much time here. The robots build and maintain the site for when we need it."

"Passing? The undersea tunnels, the towers, the dome, the base?" she ponders.

"Shaillah, press and hold the sides of your buckle to activate your antigravity field," he tells her, grabbing her hand and jumping with her into the air.

As Shaillah presses on her buckle sides, Rothwen lets her go free. To her astonishment, she is now floating by his side, hovering over the mesmerising ocean.

She breathes in the aromatic, marine scent of the alien atmosphere at every turn. The vaulted sky seems to be stretching farther away as they keep flying. The unusual but strangely familiar views play inside her mind like déjà vu. *I must have seen this before, the glistening coastal hills, the magnificent twin suns, and this multicoloured ocean.* She concentrates hard as she tries to recollect her memories. *For some reason, I feel as though I've been here before.*

She feels as light as the fluffiest feather, free to move in any way she pleases. She touches each edge of her buckle, playing with her gliding controls. She rolls; she dives and swoops; she giggles with pure joy, relishing in her unbounded freedom. From time to time, she glances at Rothwen, who, with a reassuring gaze, encourages her increasingly bolder moves.

Rothwen gets close to her, wrapping his arms around her waist and guiding her towards the distinctive multi-pillared structure. As they get close to the platform's golden guard rails, he glides over the top and stands her softly on the polished floor.

Looking around, she feels dwarfed by the vastness of the glistening hexagonal platform and the six pairs of rising pillars at each of its sides. Rising high off the floor, she sees that each set of pillars converge into gaping archways, each framing a dark beckoning entrance. She looks up, following the golden tapering edges, until her eyes are stuck on the hexagonal skylight at the very top of the dome's zenith. She reckons this must be the very centre of the enormous compound, the point of no return for her; and this thought unsettles her.

She looks back at Rothwen, her concerned expression asking a thousand questions, but she only manages to say timidly, "Is this the end of our journey?"

"It's only the beginning, Shaillah, the very beginning," Rothwen states as he starts walking towards one of the high archways directly in front of him. "There's so much for you to see and learn."

Rothwen grabs her hand and makes her walk towards the foggy entrance. Once inside, a greyish glow softly lights up the space around her, but she cannot see any walls or borders. It's as if she is standing on an eerie floating cloud.

"You will learn how to navigate these corridors. It doesn't matter which one you enter, they all interconnect and lead to any of our chambers. Think about your destination and the space-tunnel will take you," he explains.

She was sure they weren't moving, but soon she finds herself standing in the middle of a purple-lit room. She sees Rothwen walking towards what she thinks is the back wall. But as she follows him and stands beside him, she jolts backwards as the tips of her boots bend over the edge of the floor. She loses any sense of space or direction while looking into the infinite dark void in front of her; even the purple glow suddenly stops at the sharp boundary.

Before she can even organise her thoughts, a whirl of fine particles starts to fill the impenetrable blackness, shining through a fast-thickening fog, all flashing in a constant rhythm. She struggles to recognise the emerging shapes within the flickering haze. But suddenly, the crisp three-dimensional sight of towering, jagged structures come into sharp focus.

The intricate height-defying constructions rise and intersect over long chains of rocky islands, sometimes forming bridges, sometimes forming tall needle-like towers, scattering across a swirling crimson ocean.

"Do you like our world?" Rothwen asks.

But Shaillah can hardly speak. She is so spellbound by the meandering, elaborate buildings that she doesn't notice Rothwen pushing her forwards until the whole setting completely encircles them.

"We are now inside the quasi-reality chamber. You may feel a bit dizzy, but it will soon pass."

Shaillah tries to figure out precisely where she is. It's as though the grid of geometrically shaped columns and sinuous sculptures have wholly engulfed her, and suddenly, she finds herself floating inside the very place she thought was a mere imaging projection. *Am I inside a hologram?* she asks herself.

"We come here when we want to feel close to home. I want you to experience how it feels like, to help you understand who you are. And I want you to meet our most admired venerable high counsellor, Zula-Or. She cares about you very much."

Shaillah keeps gazing at him with her eyes wide open while he continues talking, unabated.

"Of course, she lives far away—on our beautiful planet Rom-Enjie. But we can reach her—right there." He leads her in between the voluptuous buildings, gliding through intricately decorated pearl-encrusted columns.

She watches the inhabitants strolling in all directions, sometimes flying off towards the sky. They all share similar body shapes and features as if they were all part of the same family, donning elegant bodysuits made of shiny, silvery fabrics. They seem utterly unaware of Rothwen's and Shaillah's presence even if they pass close by. Rothwen explains that only when invoking the virtual tunnelling inside the quasi-world can they contact the entangled space-time frame's residents.

As they leave behind the heavily built areas, they enter a greener landscape filled with exuberant spiky vegetation growing on the smooth hills' backdrop. Soon, Rothwen heads towards a conspicuously tall spiral-shaped tower.

"This is Zula-Or's favourite retreat. She wants you to see it," Rothwen explains as they land in front of the imposing helical structure. Rothwen touches the blinking circle of light on the smooth white wall, causing a packet of rippling waves to spread outwards on its surface, its wobbly area progressively turning into a spotless mirror.

Shaillah smiles at the vivid reflection of herself appearing in front of her. She inspects her long silver hair, bright purple pupils, deep red lips, and smooth rosy skin.

"Fascinating!" she marvels, admiring the graceful, confident young girl looking directly at her.

"Walk through this virtual gateway. You will find Zula-Or at the other end." Rothwen rushes his words as he pushes her forwards against the giant mirror.

She hardly has time to react as her whole body passes through the quivering surface. As a piercing cold sensation numbs her skin, she suddenly finds herself at the centre of a warm cavernous vault.

"Welcome home, Shaillah!" A honeyed voice greets her as she discerns an elegant spritely figure walking towards her.

The elegant woman is wearing a long flowing white tunic embroidered in tiny red crystals; an elaborate crown of red glassy petals sits tightly over her head. As she walks, the stunning pink diamond hanging on her chest catches Shaillah's attention. Swirling from its gilded necklace, the beautiful stone incessantly sparkles through its flower-shaped golden mount.

"Zula-Or proudly welcomes you," the woman says as she opens up her arms. "I feel so privileged, my dear child."

Shaillah stays motionless, intently looking at Zula-Or, marvelled by her radiant graceful presence and attire. The lady's supple and firm complexion shows a smooth pale skin; her long eyelashes and thin eyebrows frame a sharp gaze from her blue almond-shaped eyes, giving her a smart truthful aura. The curly tips of her thick braided white hair almost touch the glossy floor.

"Come, Shaillah, come. I want to show you our special place." Zula-Or warmly smiles while holding Shaillah's hand and guiding her into the widening corridor.

As they stroll deep into the spacious half-lit room, Shaillah can feel the lady's radiant skin through her palms, energising her body. They tread over a downwards spiral of floating steps, their path illuminated by rainbow-coloured crystal chandeliers. As they reach the bottom, they walk through the rows of flowering bushes lining up the shores of a central shimmering lagoon. The bright shrubberies' vivid reflections blend onto the undulant waters, forming random flashing strokes as if a mysterious artist was busily conjuring a final masterpiece on an animated canvas.

The iridescent garden stretches far and wide—as far as the eye can see—packed with bulbous, spiky bushes covered in a multitude of colourful crystalline blossoms. *So many flowers; it's a wonder the stems don't break,* Shaillah thinks.

"Of course, these are not flowers as you know them. They are fast-growing precious gems," Zula-Or explains as they both stop by the gleaming lakeshore.

"Tell me, my dear child, do you still miss your previous home?"

"I do!" Shaillah hastily replies as if she had been thinking about it all the time, but she immediately doubts herself.

Zula-Or raises her chin as a nostalgic streak flashes through her sharp, glistening eyes. Then she adds in a melancholic tone, "When I was very young, I also missed my home. But I was too far away, and of course, we did not have the means we have now."

Zula-Or pauses, looking back at Shaillah to make sure she's listening attentively. "Back then, we had discovered planet Earth's riches, and we did not waste any time in settling down. We went, and we stayed. We showed the humans how to find the vast deposits of diamonds and precious metals. We taught them how to build magnificent sky-high monuments. For a time, we lived in harmony. We even interbred. But it was not to last. Humans became very controlling and eventually saw us as a threat. They started killing anyone of Rom-Ghenshar descent as they tried to eliminate every trace of our civilisation.

"So, we had no other alternative but to flee for our lives, but not before emptying all their precious mines and taking away all the tools we had given them. We unleashed massive wildfires and then endless floods. We thought they would never recover. We returned to our mother planet, licking our wounds but wealthier and wiser, and we swore that one day we'd be back."

Zula-Or's face beams in a triumphant glare. "And now, after ten thousand Earth years, we are ready to fulfil the dream of our ancestors. We have been closely observing the humans. We know their weak and strong points very well. We've prepared everything. Now we're ready. But this time, it will be unlike anything they have ever seen. We've grown stronger, smarter, invincible. We are immortals."

Zula-Or's self-conceited grin changes into an impatient grimace as she adds, "Of course, we would've finished our mission long ago. But we were held back by the unexpected—let's also say non-negotiable—demand. We had to change and delay all our plans so we could bring *you* into our world first, lest we incur the rage of one of our finest space warriors—oh no!—our finest."

Zula-Or pauses as she notices the look of disbelief on Shaillah's face.

"I s-see," Shaillah stutters. "Why me?"

"The strangeness of our universe often conspires to thwart even the most carefully planned mission. Nobody could predict it. But as soon as Rothwen saw you … and knowing where you come from—"

"Where do I come from? Please tell me now—"

"Listen, Shaillah, you have regained what is rightfully yours. Your Rom-Ghenshar ancestry was always within you. We only needed to activate it."

"I don't understand," she mumbles.

"My sweet child, you were … artificially created."

Shaillah's heart sinks. She covers her mouth with her hands whilst closing her eyes and shaking her head, refusing to believe Zula-Or's words.

Zula-Or grabs Shaillah firmly by her chin and shakes her face until she opens her eyes. Then she stares intensely at Shaillah while, with her other hand, she takes one of her crystal petals off the back of her headpiece. Suddenly Shaillah finds herself trapped in Zula-Or's arms as she feels a sharp blade against her neck, slowly cutting into the flesh.

Shaillah helplessly watches as she is immobilised while her blood drips in a steady thread onto the floor. *At any time soon, I will faint*, she fears. But then she realises she does not feel any pain, and she is not even feeling in the slightest bit dizzy.

Zula-Or takes the blade out of Shaillah's slashed skin. Immediately, Shaillah covers her bleeding neck with her hands, but she is wholly astounded to feel her wound sticking together and healing under her fingertips.

"Does it hurt? Do you feel weak at all?" Zula-Or probes while placing the red crystal blade back into her bristly crown.

Shaillah shakes her head.

"That's because you have our rapidly regenerating high-energy supercells. They would starve of oxygen in Earth's weak atmosphere."

"Who created me?" Shaillah asks timidly while caressing her healed neck.

"I designed you, Shaillah. You are very special, one of a kind. Our Chief Scientist Athguer, sculpted your genes to perfection. You are the most advanced hybrid replica we ever created. I'm so proud of you."

"Why do you do this?" Shaillah asks, completely baffled.

"We design all types of replicas, place them in different planets as fertilised eggs, and check their progress from time to time. So, we did the same with humans, studying them as they are born and develop in their environment, getting to know them intimately, changing them, and controlling them. But when we started with you, we decided to embed Rom-Ghenshar supercells into your body. It had an amazing effect. Look at you!"

"It's all too hard to believe right now." She sobs.

"Don't cry, Shaillah. You have now this amazing opportunity to get to know who you are and to realise your potential. You'll soon understand your abilities and power. I admire you so much." Zula-Or praises her.

Shaillah looks down while in deep thoughts as Zula-Or softly caresses her face and wipes away the tears, giving time for Shaillah to come to terms with her real self while inspecting her closely.

"Your beauty and strength are as evident as the radiance of this gem-studded garden. Your indomitable soul shines through, my dear Shaillah." Zula-Or proudly says as she keeps staring at a disconcerted Shaillah.

While evoking the past aeons of her life, Zula-Or can't help but draw striking similarities between herself and Shaillah.

"Shaillah, Shaillah." She repeats her new name as if trying to get used to it, encouraged by Zula-Or's warm and uplifting gaze.

"Yes, correct. Perfect!" Zula-Or holds Shaillah's shoulders, energizing Shaillah's body with her all-pervasive vigour. "You will soon get used to it. With every passing moment, you will become one of us—the most advanced civilisation in our universe."

Zula-Or's vibrant tone and revitalizing aura slowly help Shaillah let go of her vanishing past and embrace her inevitable future. The more she dwells on it, the more she comes to accept her heritage and her new life.

Shaillah's eyes glisten with profound confidence as her newly found identity and sense of belonging lifts her spirits.

"What about you? Who created you?" Shaillah brazenly asks.

Zula-Or smiles widely before bursting into ecstatic laughter. She straightens up her body in a self-satisfied and flaunting posture.

"I am one of the *Oi Renski*" (Originals), "my dear child," she announces pompously, but then she adds in a sombre tone, "Although … I was once mortally wounded by a human."

Zula-Or composes herself while looking defiantly into the distance. "I managed to survive. Our experts worked tirelessly on me. They regenerated every cell in my body from its original fragments, copying and reloading them into new ones. So I survived with all my features and thoughts intact.

"There is a distinguished race of originals, those who have lived for aeons. We are revered for our wisdom. We append the -Or to our names, but you can call me Zula." The lady talks to Shaillah in a mellow voice while hugging her tightly.

Then Zula-Or takes off her dazzling pink diamond necklace and places it around Shaillah's neck. "Here! My sweet child, my gift to you. Wear it always. It'll give you energy, help you on your journey."

Shaillah clutches the brilliant pink diamond now hanging on her chest, feeling its radiating energy enter through her palms and run through her body. "Thank you, dear Zula. And however hard to believe, thank you for showing me who I am." Shaillah gratefully smiles and then puts her hands together, bowing to the wise lady.

"I am your shelter, your guardian. Come to me whenever you need me," Zula-Or reassures her.

As Shaillah looks back into Zula-Or's radiant pupils, they share a deep connection, as if a long-time separated mother and daughter have suddenly found each other.

"What about Rothwen?" Shaillah abruptly asks as if her words have escaped from her mouth unintentionally.

"What about him?" Zula-Or snaps, looking inquisitively at Shaillah.

"Oh, I can hear your desperate fluttering heart! There's one thing you can never do, my dear child. You can never hide your feelings from me. I know all about this attraction between you two and a mighty one at that. It has disrupted all our plans. We tried to stop him, but he would not relent. While you were growing up among the humans, he would not lose sight of you. And he would keep visiting your place more often than he would want to admit."

"I feel so different when I'm with him," she confesses, unable to control her quivering voice or stop her cheeks from blushing. "He makes me feel special. Is he a replica too?"

"What he is—and you should never forget it—is an elite space warrior, a tireless invincible soldier. He never settles anywhere. For him, this mission is a mere insignificant chapter in his unending list of victories and adventures." Zula-Or raises her long arched eyebrows in a warning gesture.

"Then I may also be a small adventure for him," Shaillah ponders, an uneasy glare flashing through her face.

"Hard to tell. He is unpredictable. He can be alluring, but he can also be as icy and unforgiving as a dead star. Don't be fooled by his charm."

"I won't!" she says firmly, holding her head high and stroking her diamond to absorb its uplifting energy.

"My advice for you, my dear child—be yourself." Zula-Or's cautionary words fade into a distant echo as Shaillah's body starts spinning.

She extends her arms, trying in vain to stop the whirling motion that is inexorably and progressively pulling her back as she is sucked into a cold all-absorbing vacuum.

# CHAPTER 12

# LONG-LOST PASSION

*Tell me how you feel, Shaillah. Do you feel your skin burning?*

Shaillah closes her eyes firmly, counting down the seconds as the powerful suction force takes hold of her. Suddenly, she feels a warm breeze bringing a sweet, calming fragrance. As she slowly opens her eyes, she's relieved to find herself back in the same quiet purple-lit room, her body resting flat on the polished floor. The memories of her passage into the dreamlike landscape where she met Zula-Or spin inside her head like a far-fetched fuzzy illusion.

As she tries to get up, she hears a tinkling rattle under her chest. She fumbles around with her fingers until she feels the edges of her gilded pendant.

"Oh, it was real!" She rejoices as she contemplates the brilliant shafts of lights reflecting on her hands.

"How was Zula, the wisest lady in our vast Rom-Ghenshar empire?"

As she hears Rothwen's voice, she tries to get up but immediately lets herself fall, realising Rothwen is sitting on the floor in front of her. She sits up while briefly looking back into the gaping blackness, hardly believing she has returned from that bottomless abyss.

"Revealing. Our venerable councillor, Zula-Or, helped me understand and accept my true ancestry, and she gave me this gorgeous diamond." Shaillah lifts the beautifully crafted gemstone from her chest.

"Oh, she gave you the Quark-Star diamond! One of her most prized possessions. Zula must like you very much," Rothwen exclaims, fully realising that the unique gift is Zula-Or's message of acceptance for Shaillah.

Shaillah keeps admiring the flickering stone—so many facets, so many colourful sparks. *Like my own rapidly untangling life*, she thinks.

"You definitely made an impression on her. Zula-Or can tell how special you are. And she is a very wise lady." Rothwen adds while lifting Shaillah's chin and gazing enticingly at her.

"I see the desire in your eyes. She warned me about you," Shaillah says hesitantly.

"She did?" Rothwen grins while clutching her hands inside his broad palms. "True, she is right to warn you. I don't have a glittering record, so to speak. But only I know how I feel. Only I know why you are here—now. Nothing could change my mind, not even Kuzhma-Or or Zula-Or or any other *Oi Renski*. It was a long-fought battle. Of course, they had to give in at some point—"

"I see."

"As I started to feel something new, something unusual … it hit me like a paralysing flare, but I wanted more."

"Why unusual?"

"For us, very unusual. We care for victories and riches, skill and precision, perfect results. Everything else is irrelevant, inconvenient. So, in our quest for perfection, some useless traits and feelings were edited out of our genes."

"For example?"

"Fear, pain, guilt, and …" Rothwen stops as if struggling for words.

He caresses her forehead while gazing intensely at her as if looking for an answer.

"Tell me how you feel, Shaillah. Do you feel your skin burning when we are close?"

"Yes, very much!"

"That's exactly how I feel. I think this feeling can't be bad if it makes my heart beat faster."

"What makes you feel like this?"

"Not what, Shaillah … but who." Rothwen fervently says while drawing her face closer towards him.

She looks deep into his sharp green eyes, enthralled, imagining that she is swimming into his pupils.

"Perhaps, a dormant trait was always lurking inside me, waiting to be awakened. Or sometimes space warriors need something to thump their bleak soul," Rothwen ponders.

They speak in a mixed language without even noticing if it is human or Rom-Ghenshar.

He places her hand over his heart while sliding his hand under her pink diamond pendant and over her heart.

"Is this feeling what humans call 'passion'?" he asks.

"I think so," she murmurs, stroking his warm hand.

They feel their exhilarating heartbeats pulsating through their veins as they desperately kiss in an electrifying embrace. Shaillah's shivering body flutters against his strong muscles, and an overwhelming sensation invades him, that same feeling that he cannot entirely shake off, no matter how hard he tries.

"Is there anything stronger than passion?" he asks as he kisses her again and again, in between words.

"Yes. It is called *love*."

"What's it like?"

"I don't know. But I've seen it in movies and read it in books. It can kill, or it can heal. It's so strong it can make you lose your mind."

"Whatever this is between us, it's certainly strong. When it was time to bring you into our world, I told Zula, 'She will be with me.' She dismissed it outright, saying, 'It will never work out between a replica and a space warrior.'"

"And what do you think?"

"I won't pretend it'll be easy," he concedes. "But you're not an ordinary replica. There's something about you that makes me feel very different. That's why I asked Athguer not to change your memories or your emotions. And I'm ready to see where it'll take us."

"What can you do to me? It seems like you can change my body any way you like," she reproaches him.

"Shaillah, there wasn't another option." Rothwen brings her head against his chest and kisses her forehead. "There were necessary things I had to do to bring you here. I had to make those decisions, tough decisions, for us to be together. I cannot explain everything right now. But I can promise you this—once your transition is complete, no one will ever change you again, without your permission."

"If that's what it takes to be together," she whispers, "then so be it. It was meant to be."

"Yes, it was—even if it meant breaking all the rules, taking all the risks."

"How come?"

"As a rule, we never bring replicas from other planets into our domain. We study them, change them, control them—*in their environment.* That is why I have to break all the rules for you."

"And the risks?"

"We had never turned a hybrid replica into our race fully. I had Athguer's word that it would work. He is a genius, but there were no guarantees."

"I see," Shaillah ponders, a nervous glare flashing through her face. "What would have happened if it'd failed?"

"We would've returned you—back to your waiting friend. And you would've never known anything about it."

Shaillah opens her mouth wide in astonishment, her mind racing through countless what-if thoughts.

"But that was the easy part," Rothwen continues. "If it succeeded, we didn't know if your body would be strong enough to withstand the entrance into our dense atmosphere and connect to our brain network. I have to give it to Athguer. He did this first part of the transition to perfection."

"First part?"

"Yes, there's a second part. It will give you superpowers. But don't worry about it. You are already a Rom-Ghenshar. It won't be as risky as before," Rothwen reassures her.

"I feel numbed," Shaillah mumbles while in deep thought, playing back her perilous journey inside her mind.

"That's why I was with you every step of the way. We could've sent one of our guardian robots, but I decided I had to bring you in, personally. I was prepared for anything, Shaillah. If you had shown the slightest weakness, I would have asked Athguer to try again until we succeeded," he says in a resolute tone.

"I'm pleased it went better than expected." She breathes out a sigh of relief and pauses as if checking her inner thoughts. Then she adds in a nostalgic tone, "But I still miss home."

"That's normal. Something you and I must deal with. But now, embrace your new life. Together, we can venture on to greater things."

Rothwen jumps up, his glossy boots creaking on the polished floor. Then taking Shaillah's hands, he pulls her up as he announces, "Let me show you. I have a special present for you!"

He leads her out of the purple room and into the space-tunnel enclosure. Soon they're crossing the high gaping archway and walking around the hexagonal platform by the golden balustrades. She admires the captivating landscape as she leans over the top rails. The glimmering yellow sun is slowly starting to set against the pink-orange sky as the restless ocean waves keep breaking into foamy whirls over the rugged shoreline.

She gazes at the broad-winged manta ray-like creatures skimming the water surface, then soaring so high into the sky that she cannot tell if they are some kind of alien bird or flying fish.

"They're neither. They're our own species, called *lyshars*," Rothwen explains. "They're preparing for the sunset … they always mate at sunset."

Shaillah watches as the lyshars flip over and pair up, their bellies touching. Then they dive as one and disappear into the sea, splashing through the water's crimson sunset reflections.

"So beautiful," she exclaims.

Rothwen, standing behind her, caresses her shoulders. "Yes, they pair up for life—unlike us, Rom-Ghenshars," he remarks in a derisory tone.

"Humans do. Well, most of them do."

"Yes, they got it all wrong. I prefer to be free, go wherever I want, be with whomever I want, and so on."

As the sky darkens and the last feeble sun rays drown behind the horizon, Shaillah wonders about the destiny that awaits her. But surely, it's impossible now to turn back—not that she wants to. Despite all her heartaches and misgivings, all she wants now is to be with Rothwen. She hardens up inside while coldly responding, "So do I."

He pulls her away from the balcony, making her walk past the central hall and into another arched passage, eventually stopping in front of a curved silver-coloured door, its top panel decorated in distinctive crinkled pictographs.

"Now, you can use your unique brainwave frequency to open this door," Rothwen tells her, his tone encouraging. "Concentrate and give it the command to open."

Shaillah hesitates momentarily, altogether doubting herself. Then she tries it.

To her surprise, the graphics' wavy lines start unravelling and reassembling into new shapes. She gleefully stares at the newly formed symbols, spelling her name in the Rom-Ghenshar language. Then the door slides open, silently and slowly, letting the bright lights from the inside flood the entrance.

"It takes practice, but you will soon learn how to use your brainwaves for everything," Rothwen explains as they enter the brightly lit space.

A crystal–clear, azure swimming pool glistens at the centre of the room, extending up to the overhanging balcony at the end. On either side of the pool, stylish cream and gold sofas furnish the aisles, surrounded by ornate golden vases holding her favourite gem-studded blossoms from Zula-Or's garden. "How beautiful!" She marvels. As they walk through the elegant decor, she admires the unique garments, colourful make-up sets, and precious jewellery showing through the glass doors and corner tables.

"This is your private smartroom, Shaillah, all decorated and stocked up by Zula for you. She wanted to spoil you."

"For me?" she asks in complete awe.

"Your sleeping suite is at the back, by the balcony, overlooking your private lake. There're plenty of refreshments and entertainment gadgets, all your favourites. And if you need anything else … think about it."

"Why didn't she tell me? I should've thanked her," Shaillah laments, overwhelmed by so much extravagance.

"You'll have plenty of time to thank Zula. But for now, find your way around, discover, enjoy."

Shaillah looks up at the rows of elegant dresses gleaming through the transparent doors of the aisle-long walk-in wardrobe. She extends her hand to reach one. And as she does, the doors open. She takes one of the gold-embroidered tunics, rubbing her fingers on the silky fabric. She slides it over her body while excitedly checking herself in the free-standing tall oval mirrors.

Rothwen's approving expression turns into an attentive frown as he receives a thought-message from Kuzhma-Or.

"Must leave now. I'll be coming for you later tonight. We'll be meeting Kuzhma-Or and Athguer in the flesh. Get ready," he says in a hurry as he kisses her briefly on her lips.

Shaillah chews on her bottom lip as she watches Rothwen walk away. She relishes the taste of him in her mouth. It dawns on her that, for the first time since she entered this tantalising alien world, she is looking forward to the future and can't wait until he gets back.

"This could be my downfall, but I've fallen for you … Rothwen!" She exclaims as a deep shiver runs down her spine. An intense yearning for him envelops her, she attempts to fight it off, but she can't escape it, challenging her self-control. Then she realizes that she is revelling in her cravings. She runs while undressing and dives into the pool. Underwater, she imagines he is swiftly swimming towards her. She thinks she is dreaming while awake, feeling his arms wrapping around her body. She closes her eyes tightly, wishing she wouldn't stop dreaming anytime soon.

# CHAPTER 13

# THE CONQUERORS

*After every star system we conquer, there is always another … and another.*

Supreme Commander Kuzhma-Or is leaning over the central platform's large golden balcony, casting his admiring gaze over the vast ocean. To his side, Rothwen seems to be wholly absorbed, looking up into the night sky.

As the packed starry heaven reflects over the darkened waters, it seems as though the entire visible universe has come to descend over one single place. Still, as if the beautiful, mesmerising spectacle was not enough, the resplendent reddened disc of a giant moon peeks out from the mercurial horizon, tinting the moving waters with a blood-lit spill.

Kuzhma-Or keeps immersing himself in the magnificent scenery, stirring up memories of his precious home planet. Only the sound of the pounding waves rippling on the gravelled shore below interrupts his thoughts. His piercing eyes dart from one star to another, sometimes resting on some of the distant worlds he has already conquered. He slowly nods, poised in self-assurance, inflating his chest as he breathes in the intensely mineral-charged air.

"Nowhere is more beautiful than our world. When we finish our next daring mission in Ankjeshur" (Omega Centauri), "the magnificent supercluster, we must return to our homeland on an extended visit. I must stop wandering about—"

"Stop? The great Kuzhma-Or stopping?" Rothwen bursts out in laughter.

Kuzhma-Or's face toughens. He clutches and pulls on the balcony's golden rails as if wanting to uproot it altogether. *How could I be thinking about stopping?* But his brief ill-temper soon dissipates, and he ends up joining Rothwen in his hilarious rapture, their bursts of laughter resonating throughout the vaulted archways.

"Ah, the Rom-Ghenshar spirit never rests!" Kuzhma-Or roars as he gives a final admiring glance towards the rising moon and starts walking away.

"Suan enjie" (Always victorious), Rothwen cheers, pushing hard on the guard rails with his knuckles before following Kuzhma-Or into the archway.

As they make their way into the UniverseScope's long corridors, Kuzhma-Or shares his thoughts, opening up his broadcasting brain frequency: *Can you remind me, Rothwen, why we left this planet until now? We know it will be effortless, and there are still vast reaches to claim.*

Rothwen tunes into Kuzhma-Or's transmission frequency as he replies, *It's on our way to Omega Centauri. We wanted to finish an easy target before embarking on our most difficult mission yet, especially after the challenges of the dying pulsar with its orbiting triple planets.*

"Yes, it was brilliant how you dismantled the whole magnetosphere with our unstoppable destroyer-crafts." Kuzhma-Or's gloats, his face glowing with infinite satisfaction. There's nothing more he enjoys than remembering past victories while preparing for the next.

The supreme commander and his faithful master navigator have been on more adventures together than they can recount in a single night of celebration. They are the vanguard of the Rom-Ghenshar expeditions, the ones who go on the forefront and always return with nothing less than total victory, setting up the subjugated domains for the subsequent all-out Rom-Ghenshar occupation.

For this particular mission on planet Earth, they built the underground Rom-Ghenshar command base, painstakingly duplicating the landscape of their cherished planet, Rom-Enjie. Their vast army of self-replicating robots dug and shaped the virgin rocks, moulding them into a sumptuous multi-pillared fortress at the centre of an artificial ocean. They recreated their oxygen-rich watery environment, sculpting their living quarters to their planet's likeness, replicating their native ecosystem. From their impregnable fortress, they could come and go as they liked, spy on any earthlings as much as they wanted, and prepare their takeover of the completely unaware inhabitants. Humans could never detect their all-pervasive impenetrable non-baryonic shields.

"After every star system we conquer, there is always another … and another," Kuzhma-Or boasts.

At the end of the long aisle, they can see Athguer walking over the sparkling high podium, closely inspecting the massive platform extending wall-to-wall beneath his feet.

Athguer rushes to greet them as they climb onto the platform's gleaming steps.

"Everything is going as expected," Athguer announces as Kuzhma-Or and Rothwen pace all around the glassy stage, sometimes briefly stopping to concentrate on a particular place.

Kuzhma-Or glances at the bustling images springing up across the translucent surface as he walks over the glittering display. A subtle smile of approval slightly softens his usually stern expression. Through the UniverseScope's multi-focusing layers, they have a complete, unimpeded view of what's happening above ground on the planet, at any location they choose to stand on. Not only can they see it and hear it; they can precisely control it at their will.

"All the robots are on standby," Rothwen adds.

"Indeed," Athguer confirms.

"I got the signal from the Grand Fleet. They're expecting my order to assemble outside the Oort Cloud," Kuzhma-Or announces, looking proudly at Rothwen.

"You can give the order, Yei Boishen" (My Commander). "I've finished programming their routes."

"Shewe" (Very well). "That's what I most admire about you, Rothwen. You're always ahead of the game—so precise, so efficient. Are you sure you are not a robot?"

Rothwen and Athguer burst out in laughter, and Kuzhma-Or promptly joins them as they gather jovially around one another. Even in the middle of all their planning, they always find an excuse for some relaxing humour, however short-lived.

"Finally, we can go ahead with the last stage of our plans"—Kuzhma-Or breaks his laughter with an uneasy gaze at Rothwen—"after we had to change it all because of your unrelenting demand."

"A small delay and change of plans won't interfere with our grand scheme," Rothwen snaps.

"But I must say, Rothwen, your perseverance is unparalleled, only closely matched by your blind obsession with that human replica."

"Her name is Shaillah!" Rothwen seethes, his bottled-up anger flaring through his narrowing eyes.

Kuzhma-Or lifts his hand in a calming gesture. "I now understand, Rothwen, thinking about it. She may be one of those short-term trophies you usually claim … and then discard."

"I take what I want when I want. And I may deal with the consequences later," Rothwen blurts out.

"We know, we know, Rothwen. You also want to feel how we used to feel, to forget the coldness of our souls, even temporarily," Athguer intervenes, trying to defuse the rising tension.

"Cut out the rhetoric, Athguer. I don't need your sympathy," Rothwen directs a scolding gaze at Athguer while stepping back from them.

Kuzhma-Or walks forwards, confronting Rothwen's simmering expression. Then he adds in a slightly conciliatory tone, "Remember, my distinguished master navigator, our iron hearts are what gives us our power."

"I brought her here. It will be my decision what to do with her. Leave me alone!" Rothwen fumes, walking along the glassy surface in an exasperated gait.

"Are you sure she will be able to withstand it down here? You know I will test her," Kuzhma-Or warns.

Rothwen suddenly stops and turns around to challenge Kuzhma-Or's doubting gaze as he vows, "I'll train her. She learns fast!"

Kuzhma-Or can see the raw determination in Rothwen's undaunting glare, but he can't stop himself from riling Rothwen further. "Even for the Grand Fleet expedition?" the supreme commander asks ironically, raising his thick white eyebrows.

"I haven't thought that far ahead yet, My Commander," Rothwen replies nonchalantly as he jumps off the high platform. "And you know me. I'm a space warrior. I'd rather travel alone."

Kuzhma-Or folds his arms, his sceptical face flaring in a dismissive smirk, as Rothwen impassively looks up to him.

"Permission to leave, My Commander," Rothwen calmly asks.

Kuzhma-Or is used to his master navigator's dark moods and shifting obsessions, and there's no point in opposing him any longer for something that will surely pass, he promptly concludes. So, with a brief nod, he lets Rothwen go. The headstrong master navigator solemnly bows to his supreme commander before turning around and walking into the aisle.

"Rothwen is always pushing his boundaries," Athguer notes.

As Rothwen walks away, he feels their sceptical stare and listens to their doubtful thoughts, but the seemingly implausible is precisely what his restless spirit craves. Before going out of view, he turns around and defiantly warns them, "I will be bringing Shaillah to our fest tonight. She is with me now. You should treat her fairly."

## CHAPTER 14

# THE CHANT OF HONOUR

*You disarmed me with your deadly weapon.*
*Will you take me in your army?*

*Being underwater is like being embraced by my ancient home,* Shaillah thinks as she relishes her exhilarating freedom, swimming up and down the depths of her smartroom's crystalline pool. She moves through the fragranced waters as clustered bubbles shape her path; she speeds up and then slows down, playing with the frothy trails her wild strokes leave behind. The purifying liquid cleans and moisturises her skin as the smouldering purple spotlights, flickering like candles from the bottom, uplift her spirit.

She doesn't want to get out of the pool, but she has to. Rothwen may be coming for her soon. As she climbs the exit steps, a silvery footstool moves towards her and stops right at the pool's edge. She takes the fluffy white gown folded neatly on the top, and as she wraps it around her body, the radiating warmth gently dries her body and long hair.

Walking towards her balcony, Shaillah glances at the oversized white corner bed, and she can't resist diving onto the lustrous bedding, plunging under the pile of feathery cushions. She rolls in between the sheets and pillows, chuckling girlishly, until she finally lays back, her eyes barely showing under the ruffled bundled silk linen. She stares at the fuzzy neon-like light strips covering the ceiling, dimming as she closes her eyes or brightening if she opens them. She suddenly feels hungry.

As she hears the clatter of plates and cutlery, her attention turns to the far end of the room. She rushes towards the opposite glass console table. But by the time she reaches it, her favourite dishes are all stylishly presented, as if they have been served from behind the wall by a master chef. *Be careful what you think, Shaillah,* she jokes to herself while dipping her fingers through the chocolate desserts first and licking her fingertips as the creamy meringue melts inside her mouth. She eats and drinks as she hears the rumble of the distinctive Rom-Ghenshars' laughter resounding nearby. *I must get ready for Rothwen.* She thinks to herself as she enters the side aisle, her heart throbbing with excitement.

Shaillah strolls by the high transparent doors, admiring the beautiful garments changing in colour and style as she advances. Each one she sees is to her liking. Stopping at the walk-in wardrobe's entrance, she contemplates the neat long shelves full of clothes, accessories, and fanciful shoes. She picks the first silk undergarments she sees, and as she puts them on, she spots the gold-embroidered tunic lying on the floor by the side of her belt. She remembers the admiring look on Rothwen's face when she first tried it on. "It has to be this one." She slides the silky, glittering piece over her body and straps her belt around her waist.

She lounges on one of the cream and gold canape sofas, thinking about the tall, elegant boots she liked in the walk-in wardrobe. "I think I have time for a small treat," she reckons. One of the wandering footstools springs into action and soon approaches with the glossy high-heeled boots she was thinking about. *I could get used to this.* She giggles.

In front of one of the dressing table's oval mirrors, she stares at the colouring sticks, creams, and powders lined up in neatly organised rows. It's hard to choose which ones to use. But she has to finish her make-up quickly. Rothwen is at her door, calling her. As she puts on her pink diamond pendant, the sparkling gem competes with the glow of her pupils, shining under the rosy eyeshadow and the overextended black eyeliner. She rushes to comb her hair, and as she grabs the pearl-covered hairbrush, she notices a delicately braided ruby wreath under the glass top. She regally places it over her forehead while thinking that the beautiful diadem seems to have been made especially for her. Her plump lips gleam under the creamy red tint as she smiles at the mirror.

She runs towards the entrance. And as the door slides open, she bluntly stops right in front of a stunned Rothwen who is staring at her, spellbound. Shaillah's elegant presence overcomes his senses. For as long as he remembers, he has never felt so vulnerable. In his mind, the images of his glorious victories pale into insignificance under the hypnotising splendour of her figure. This battleground is new for him, one he has barely prepared for. He must conquer this new rival, subjugate it to his will. But for now, he is prepared to let her dominate him.

Her hair is floating softly over her shoulders, blown by the incoming breeze, enveloping him in her enticing aroma. He is not used to feeling so helpless, so he stubbornly fights against the overriding force, making him feel weak at the knees. He bites his tongue and swallows hard. He can't get enough of her curvy figure, piercing through her elegant tunic. He clutches his hands until they swell and redden with his sweltering blood, but he eventually relents. He briskly pulls her against his chest, their eyes locking into an intense devouring stare.

He basks in the glow of her enthralling pupils. "You disarmed me with your deadly weapon. Will you take me in your army?"

"I'm not a soldier," she says while tenderly caressing his face.

"But you will be," he pledges in his deep husky voice. "You will be."

She holds her breath while he draws her into a tight embrace, the air around them sparkling with the runaway energy of their churning desire. He keeps fighting against himself, overcoming the wave of irrepressible lust taking hold of him. As he lets go of his embrace, he feels a powerful tension working against him, as if he was trying to rip apart the poles of a powerful magnet. Shaillah is still leaning on one of his open arms, her body trembling in an expectant pose.

Rothwen glides his hand over her cheek and then down to her chest and waist, savouring every touch. "Oh, you are beautiful … dangerously beautiful." He exhales while ecstatically looking at her. "My obsession … my insatiable obsession."

But his admiring gaze suddenly turns into a sombre glare as he adds grudgingly, "I must take you now. They are waiting for us."

He makes her stand in front of him as he speaks to her. "Listen to me carefully, Shaillah. Forget about your pure earthly feelings when you meet our supreme commander and our eminent chief scientist. They will be looking for something to disqualify you. But you show them. Show them your fearless, invincible Rom-Ghenshar spirit!"

A self-assured smile springs on her face as she keeps staring at him, her eyes beaming with a determined, unyielding glow as if she was already preparing for the announced battle. "I can do this," she declares in a firm tone.

Rothwen presses his face against hers while his steely gaze pierces deep inside her pupils, searching for her inner fire. In the burning furnace of her soul, Rothwen finds the fighter inside her breaking free, embracing him. "I know you can." He takes her by her hand, leading her towards the central hexagonal hall and into one of the golden archways.

"How're you doing?" Rothwen checks on her as the space-tunnel take them down into the deepest underground chambers.

She nods confidently, even though she does not know what to expect.

"Let us enter our very own UniverseScope's arena," he announces as they step into a long wide corridor, the blue light strips at each side intensely flashing at their every step.

Rothwen's thudding footsteps and the click of her high heels echo across the haunting space.

She breathes in the dense atmosphere's heavy metallic scent, expectantly looking around her. The high ceiling and concave walls shimmer with bright stereoscopic images of alien spaceships and bizarre celestial bodies. Suddenly, the aisle opens up into a vast double-sided arena, packed with impassive attentive onlookers, sitting in orderly rows on the slanting terraces. At first, she thinks they are real people, but then she notices their jointed body parts and glistening metallic skin. They have two primary eyes, gleaming in a bright green colour over their pointed noses and thin mouths, but they also have a row of smaller eyes extending in a circle around their oval heads. Blinking in succession, the robots' watchful eyes are tracking her every move as she walks by.

Rothwen clutches her hand reassuringly while explaining through their tuned thoughts, *They are our guardian robots. Keep walking. Don't look at them.*

As they make their way through the large amphitheatre, under the watchful gaze of the motionless robots, Shaillah looks up at the intricate floating images. She is sure she can read and follow the history of the

Rom-Ghenshar conquests and victories in the painstakingly decorated scenes.

Rothwen keeps urging her, *Look ahead!*

When she finally discerns the impressive figure of Kuzhma-Or, majestically sat on top of a high golden throne, she feels a sudden jolt of awe and anticipation. The intense pain in her chest makes her feel as though her heart is grinding to a halt, but she promptly manages to compose herself and bring her heartbeat under control. With every step she advances, her confidence grows, encouraged by Rothwen's praising words.

Rothwen stops at a short distance from the supreme commander, resting his arm over Shaillah's shoulder and making her bow briefly as a sign of respect.

Kuzhma-Or leans forward while his gleaming black helmet barely moves. The glittering throne stands over the glassy platform, making him look even taller, even more imposing. She feels the pressure of his invasive stare all over her body. Still, she manages to stay firm, controlling her nerves, in time to confront Athguer, who has appeared by Kuzhma-Or's side while intensely observing her. They are both looking for any sign of weakness, any sign of fear or hesitation.

Kuzhma-Or raises his chin and his long thin lips ripple as he recognises Zula-Or's Quark-Star diamond sparkling on Shaillah's chest, the unmistakable signal of approval from the high counsellor herself.

"Zula told me you have visited her. I can see she is very pleased with you," the supreme commander admits somewhat reluctantly.

"I feel privileged to have met our distinguished wise lady, Zula-Or," Shaillah calmly replies.

"Shewe" (Very well). Kuzhma-Or keeps looking at Shaillah, slowly nodding while stroking his glossy white beard.

At the same time, Athguer lets a subtle proud smile escape from his usual hermetic expression.

No one is speaking a word, but they are all mind-conversing. She keeps hearing phrases inside her head, their meanings getting more apparent as she starts deciphering their words of judgement.

"Soyelani, Yei Boishen" (I am ready, My Commander), she proudly announces.

Kuzhma-Or raises his thick eyebrows at Shaillah's resolute and self-assured stance. "I see that Rothwen is very pleased with you as well," he concedes, his prying gaze steady. He bends his sturdy body even further towards her. The shiny images of the two suns distinctively etched on his backrest flash in front of her eyes.

"Come, Shaillah." He beckons her by briskly moving his head as he stands up from his golden throne.

Rothwen gently pushes her towards the platform, making her climb the glistening steps.

Suddenly, Shaillah finds herself standing over an endless dark background, bristling with the bright swirls of infinite star clusters. She doesn't dare make a move, lost in the vastness of the fascinating cosmos unravelling at her feet.

Kuzhma-Or's face beams with an arrogant smile as he watches her dazzled reaction. "That's right. We all wonder at the riches of the universe. We all want some of it. Watch as I am standing on your local zone," he boasts as he pompously opens his arms while ordering her to come closer.

Shaillah slowly moves forwards, her eyes fixated on the floor. As she steps on a star point, the view under her boot focuses and zooms in on that particular region. She stops at a prudent distance from the supreme commander, still staring at the multitude of glittering celestial bodies moving towards her, their sizes growing against the starry background.

But as she feels Kuzhma-Or's powerful presence stirring the air around her, she can't help but lift her head. Her eyes slowly follow the tall, sturdy figure blocking her path. Starting from his ebony boots, she inspects the highly decorated uniform and the intricately braided belt, studded in multicolour gemstones. A thick golden pendant in the shape of an arrow-like ring-bound spaceship hangs from his broad shoulders. Sweeping over his white-silver beard, she confronts his piercing, overpowering gaze.

Their gazes are locked in a silent duel. Shaillah is looking for acceptance with an unwavering stare, while Kuzhma-Or's prying eyes are still trying to find even the slightest imperceptible hesitancy.

He points at the colourful view zooming in under her feet; she follows his finger hovering over the yellow sun and its familiarly shaped planets. She immediately knows she is beholding her own solar system.

"Just another star at our disposal. We ignored it for aeons as we extended our grip around more challenging star-studded regions in our beautiful Senyeraikh" (Milky Way). "But not anymore. Now we are here, and we must take what is rightfully ours. There will be no respite, no withdrawal." Kuzhma-Or's pupils contract and widen, flashing with a fearsome glare as he speaks in a vengeful tone.

Shaillah hardly reacts to Kuzhma-Or's foreboding words. She knows she can't flinch in the least, and she feels proud of herself, as she puts one arm across her chest while cheering, "Suan enjie Rom-Ghenshar."

She looks out for Rothwen through the corner of her eye, and she gleefully smiles as she sees him walking towards her.

"Impressive!" Kuzhma-Or cheers as he turns to his chief scientist. "What do you think, Athguer?"

"Perfect, she looks perfect," Athguer boasts while walking towards them with an all-triumphant grin.

Then Athguer takes both of Shaillah's hands and holds them tightly against his chest while noting in a sceptical tone, "She should not only have our greatness in her looks, but also she must have our unbreakable spirit. I perceive something deep in her mind that still hasn't settled down … It's troublesome."

Shaillah swiftly withdraws her hands from Athguer's grasp while firmly staring at him. "I'll prove you wrong!" she ripostes, her face beaming in sheer conviction.

Athguer is taken aback by her impulsive response, his eyes widening in admiration as his eyebrows flash up.

"Save your qualms for the lab, Athguer!" Rothwen objects. "She is as ready as she can be … for now."

"Let Shaillah go back to the humans and announce our first meeting to inform them of our reasonable terms. We'll see if she lives up to our expectations. And we'll see how the humans react," Kuzhma-Or intervenes in his typical commanding tone.

Kuzhma-Or's words take Rothwen by surprise. The thought of Shaillah returning to the humans unnerves him.

But as he is about to protest the order, Shaillah's response leaves him speechless: "It'll be my honour to take your message to the humans," she declares in a resolute tone as she bows to Kuzhma-Or and Athguer.

"Ai Rom-Ojserahni sen Rom-Ghenshar" (All the universe's power to the Rom-Ghenshars), Kuzhma-Or booms while the rising beat of a haunting melody starts echoing through the vaulted walls.

"Ai Rom-Ojserahni sen Rom-Ghenshar," Athguer repeats, nodding and glancing first at Shaillah and then at Rothwen, inviting them to join.

Rothwen's exasperated gaze gradually changes into one of reluctant concession as Shaillah turns to face him with a reassuring smile while sending her thoughts to him: *I'm doing it for us.*

"Ai Rom-Ojserahni sen Rom-Ghenshar," Rothwen finally cheers as they all come together in a tight circle.

"Ai Rom-Ojserahni sen Rom-Ghenshar," Shaillah exclaims, standing proudly next to Rothwen.

Kuzhma-Or firmly crosses his hands over his chest as Rothwen does the same in their solemn army salute. Then a rotating glowing sphere starts to descend from the high ceiling.

"And now for the Rom-Ghenshar Chant of Honour: 'Unshe, Rom-Ghenshar, unshe'" (Forever, Rom-Ghenshar, forever). Kuzhma-Or raises his powerful voice while, with a single glance, he sends an order to his guardian robots.

The packed formation of robots stands up at once and starts singing, making the whole place vibrate as if its foundations are about to give way.

"Unshe, Rom-Ghenshar, unshe," they all sing as one.

As the booming voices resonate ever louder, echoing and amplifying all across the vaulted chamber, the expanding sphere fills the whole space around them, revealing the vivid, colourful holographic scenes, showing passages of their past victories and conquests in ever-increasing details.

Shaillah feels moved by the exhilarating showcase and the contagious, emotionally charged rhythm. Her face lights up with sheer excitement as Rothwen proudly stares at her. Any thoughts about her past she manages to keep well away from her mind while she keeps singing.

"Unda ye. Anse kori. Unda ye. Suan enkleerm, suan enjie Rom-Ghenshar" (Follow me. Never stop. Follow me. Always advancing, always victorious Rom-Ghenshar).

# CHAPTER 15

# SURRENDER

*I'll be unbreakable, impossible to bend, and hard to ignore.*

The sight and sound of distant worlds engulfed in exploding fireballs and the roaring booms of accelerating spaceships piercing through infinite space like incandescent rays of doom repeatedly flash in Shaillah's mind after the long series of glittering ceremonies. All she wants to do now is to go back to her smartroom and plunge into the pool.

As Kuzhma-Or, Rothwen, and Athguer gather around yet another point on the UniverseScope's viewing platform, she slowly walks towards the steps. One of the guardian robots moves forwards and extend his spindly arm to help her as she starts going down. She agreeably smiles while resting her hand on his silvery limb, allowing him to lead her down onto the aisle.

As she closely inspects the robot, she realises the android is imitating her every move, even her facial expressions. Even when she blinks, his multiple eyes blink all at the same time.

"That'll be all, thank you!" she says as she reaches the bottom of the steps.

"Thank you!" the robot replies in perfect English before retreating to his place.

*Spooky that the robots react to my thoughts and commands*, she thinks. *I'd better not attract their attention too much.*

She strolls through the long central aisle, looking around the dazzling overhanging showcase. This time, she gets to see and recognise more details. The vivid scenes of victory parades mixed with those of ravaged worlds disconcert her, but she keeps looking for something in particular.

Eventually, she recognises the images of ancient Earth's cities, choking under billowing smoke clouds, drowning under devastating flood waves, their magnificent fortresses and cities destroyed. In the background, the roaring spaceships filled with the injured and the dying desperately flee the apocalyptic scenes, exactly as Zula-Or had described to her. At the bottom of the harrowing pictures, she can read one of the Rom-Ghenshar battle slogans, depicted in bold red symbols: "Those who once suffered immense agony turned into invincible warriors."

With her gaze fixated above, she swirls around while exhaling a hastened breath as she makes her way out of the arena. Looking back, she contemplates the rows of floating imageries converging at the centre of the impressive golden throne. The Rom-Ghenshars' extravagant show of power shakes up her mind and troubles her.

*He brought me into this world of unimaginable forces and awe-inspiring might. Chaos and destruction are threatening my precious planet. My heart may falter, but my resolve and spirit will stand firm, for I'll never give up on the human race!*

As she enters the space-tunnel's shadowy confines, she wishes to be at the central platform's guard rails, and then she waits.

The refreshing ocean smell welcomes her as she walks through the arching columns. She opens her arms as she hurls herself towards the top rails and lets her body dangle, balancing on her belly. She imagines flying over the rustling ocean as she takes the whole view of the starry night sky all to herself.

As she looks to her left, the sight of four moons stretching over the horizon takes her breath away. In decreasing diameters, the arched yellow moons zigzag through a tenuous dusty band. She follows their multiple reflections on the water, intertwining through the waves and sudden whirlpools, stirring her tangled restless thoughts.

She jumps back onto the floor and starts walking towards another archway while staring back at the braided moons for as long as she can. As she arrives at her aisle, she stops in her tracks when she sees Rothwen, looking at her as if he had been waiting for a long time. He is leaning on his back with his arms folded on his chest, pressing one of his heels against her front door. She runs towards him.

She gasps. “How did you get here before me?”

“I know all the shortcuts within this maze.”

She tilts her head to one side, her contrived expression trying to hide her delight. As her door opens, she pushes through, bumping purposely against his shoulder. He starts walking by her side, but she barely acknowledges his presence.

“I thought to come and see you, since you are thinking about me,” he tells her smugly, trying to shift her icy demeanour.

“No, I wasn’t,” she protests.

“Yes, you were,” he insists.

She suddenly stops to face him with a scolding gaze, pursing her lips. “I’m so tired, Rothwen, of you reading my thoughts.”

He tries to caress her hair, but she bluntly avoids his touch with a swift jerk of her head.

“You will get to control your thoughts precisely. I will show you,” he calmly says, ignoring her rebuff.

She softens her stance and half-smiles, then starts walking away as he closely follows her.

She confronts him. “I’ve seen what you’re capable of. What are your plans for this humble planet?”

“We’ve come peacefully. We do not use our past tactics—anymore. Of course, it all depends on the humans. If they don’t provoke us … Have they changed their ways? We’ll see.”

“You say you are coming peacefully, but I’ve seen the zest for revenge in Kuzhma-Or’s and Zula-Or’s eyes—”

“They cannot forget what happened. But things have changed. We’ve grown merciful and wiser.”

She runs towards her overhanging balcony, rushing through the opening glass doors and onto the golden railings. As she leans forwards and looks up at the sky, her eyes fill up with the gleaming beams of the rising arched four moons.

"Oh, glorious universe, let the mighty Rom-Ghenshars' leniency prevail. Let them, in their infinite wisdom, be generous," she pleads, her voice breaking in a deep emotional sigh.

Rothwen stands behind her, wrapping his arms around her shoulders while pressing her back tightly against his chest. He breathes in deeply through her hair, filling his powerful lungs with her delicate aroma. "Shaillah, you need to stop thinking so much about the humans. You are one of us now," he murmurs in his drawn-out husky voice.

"But I still have human feelings."

"And that's what makes you unique. But you have to learn to control your emotions. I will show you."

She turns around to resist him, but when her hands fall on his bare muscular chest, under his open jacket, she struggles to control her runaway desire. "So … you are my personal trainer now," she says in an ironic tone while trying to keep her composure.

"Something like that." His eyes mischievously sparkle as he notices her flustered reaction.

She stares warily at him, making up a hardened face as she manages to say in a defiant tone, "Don't think you can control me like one of your robots. I'm a free spirit. I'm like this diamond"—she briefly dangles her pink diamond in front of his eyes—"but not because of its perfect cut and dazzling glow. I'll be unbreakable, impossible to bend, and hard to ignore."

He caresses her neck with both hands while looking intensely at her and subtly smiling. "Challenge accepted, Shaillah." He simmers, holding her chin and drawing her face close to his.

His wild passionate kisses burn through her tongue like melting treacle. Stopping for breath, she looks deep into his eyes, trying to decipher his thoughts. "What do you want from me? Are you using me for your dark desires?" She questions him as her heart keeps pounding uncontrollably.

He breathes out an impatient sigh, a seething glare flashing from his pupils. "Maybe you should ask yourself why I've changed all my plans so I could bring you into my world—when, in the end, you'll decide whether to run away from me."

"Will I?"

"You'll be as free as a Rom-Ghenshar space traveller," he promises in a solemn tone.

"What about my memories and my emotions? Will I ever forget my past?"

Rothwen keeps staring at her, narrowing his eyes as he mulls over his answer. Then, softly caressing her forehead, he whispers, "Not for now. But as much as I like the way you are, you'll have to make this decision as well … eventually."

She slowly slides her hands over his eyes, down his nose, and across his partly opened mouth. At this moment, she cannot think why she would possibly consider running away or forgetting him, ever. "Yes, I've been thinking a lot about you, Rothwen. But I'm not sure if all these feelings are mine or … made up by you."

"It's all coming from you." Rothwen's face muscles tighten as he speaks in a tense, single-minded tone. "What would I gain by making this up? I'd certainly be making a fool of myself."

Shaillah's whole body shudders. She can discern the truth in the intensity of his words. His lingering gaze, filled with raw devouring passion, wins her over as she feels all her defence barriers crumbling down, one by one.

"Shaillah, all I can say to you now is this—this magnetic attraction binding us together, it's so strong that I can't fight it. It goes against my will, and I know it controls yours. So why fight it? Why discard it? Let's welcome it now, if it's so amazing."

She throws her head back in abandonment as he runs his kisses up her neck while she mumbles in a fake protest, "No, No, Rothwen."

He wildly runs his hands over her body, pulling off all her clothes, her pieces of jewellery clinking on the floor. In no time, all their garments end up floating on the pool while their boots sink to the bottom.

They slide down the balcony's inner wall, dropping on the marble floor. Barely noticing the hard, cold surface, she lies on her back as he matches her body form. Rubbing her hands over his chest, all she wants is to surrender as he rolls her up within his arms. *Again, he is right. Why fight it if it's so amazing?* she thinks while running her fingers down Rothwen's spine as he draws her in even closer. Pupils against pupils, they keep kissing, relishing in each other's breath. It feels unstoppable and all-consuming, so enthralling in ways that words could never describe.

The resplendent moonlight shines over the balcony, bathing the room in a serene golden glow. Still, for them, everything around magically disappears while they make love, all throughout the long night.

# PART III

# CHAPTER 16

# THE VISITOR

*You want to know the truth of what happened,*
*my friend. I will show you.*

Sam is sitting at the centre of the small room, his arms spread alongside the table. He's staring aimlessly at the opposite wall while his thoughts are wandering from scene to scene far back through the years since he first met Erin. It's been a month since he was rescued, a long tortuous month of despair and regret but, most of all, of stiff determination of sticking by his story.

The memories of her beautiful smile bring him comfort and joy. He soon turns sombre again, though, at the realisation that he is now being accused, not only of having caused her disappearance but also, worse still, of her death. He buries his head into his hands; the thought of being found guilty is too much for his tortured mind to take in.

He hears the door open behind him, but he hardly moves. Sam knows who's entering the room. He knows the man who has questioned him endlessly, and now he's prepared to face him again, on the eve of his last day in court. He knows he will be giving his defence lawyer the same answers, no matter how incredible, to the same questions, no matter how unusual.

The story of Erin's disappearance and Sam's unwavering explanation of the alien abduction has seized the public's imagination. Conspiracy theories abound about the ARA's cover-ups and denials at the growing reports of even more UFO (Unidentified Flying Objects) sightings. Everyone is feeling nervous and suspicious.

World-renowned Jack Wray is an exceptional defence lawyer and private detective. He has managed to unmask even the most elusive fraudsters throughout his extensive career, dispelling the most unravelling mysteries and conspiracies, however challenging. Brimming with confidence, he has always come out on top of tricky situations; he would stop at nothing to achieve his goal; the more complicated the case, the more obscure, the more intriguing, the better for him.

That's why he didn't hesitate to contact the Sheppard family to offer his services. When the news spread all over the world's media with headlines such as "Innocent Girl Gone: Murdered by Monster or Abducted by Aliens?" and "Where is Erin Lobart? Mystery Baffle Islanders. Suspect Named", he knew he was the right man for the job.

All over the world, the media showed photos of Erin's demure figure, contrasting with the distant moody expression of Sam's serious face. Everyone had already reached the most apparent conclusion—without a doubt, he had murdered her; justice must be done!

Wray calmly sits opposite Sam and carefully places his suitcase by his side on the floor while sliding his thick sunglasses over his bald head. He focuses his sharp dark brown eyes on a disgruntled Sam while clearing his throat to attract his attention.

Sam finally lifts his face from within his hands with a glare of infinite resignation, as if he has given into whatever destiny might bring.

"I will go straight to the point, Sam," Wray announces in a defeatist tone. "It doesn't look good."

Sam nods slightly, looking down in a daze.

"The evidence presented by the prosecutor is so damaging, for the first time in my forty-year career, I find myself with the most unimaginable prospect of a defeat." Wray tightly presses his lips in frustration, waiting for Sam to respond.

"You shouldn't have taken on this case in the first place. Why did you?" Sam retorted despondently, still looking down onto the floor.

"First, I was intrigued. Then the contradictions lured me. But after I spoke to you, I was convinced that I could help you because—"

"Because of what?" Sam snaps, lifting his head and making eye contact with Wray, albeit dejectedly.

"Because I believed you, Sam. I do believe you truly loved her. I could see it in your eyes, deep down to the bottom of your soul. Every time you spoke about her, your eyes glowed with passion, your cheeks bloomed in bright red patches, and your voice never failed to tremble with anguish. Every time you recounted your story—"

"And do you believe what they've said about me in the hearing?"

Wray opens his suitcase and takes out his digital notebook. The screen comes to life with high-contrast images and bold texts showing the latest news headlines. He scrolls through until finding the content he was looking for—the summary of all the witnesses' accounts.

"Let me read some of the damning testimony now," Wray says, pausing to look directly at Sam before continuing with a gloomy voice. "Sam was always pursuing Erin. He often waited for her after school or after finishing her shift at the tuna farm and then accompanied her to her house. He once confessed to me that he was besotted with her. Still, he was frustrated that he never saw any inviting gesture from her. He said he had waited long enough to have her and that he would not wait any longer. He said his feelings were so strong for her, he couldn't live without her. The day they disappeared, I noticed he was very nervous. He even arrived at work later than usual.

"We all laughed at Sam. He looked like a clown, like a small puppy around Erin. And it was plain to see she didn't want anything to do with him, but he was fascinated with her.

"Sam used to practise boat surfing on the dangerous coast. He told me one day he would enter the Diablo's cave and get close to the treacherous waterfall, and he wanted to impress someone, someone very special to him."

"Sam told me, if he could not have Erin, then no one ever would. He said he would do anything on Earth to make sure she would be his. These are his exact words: 'I'm prepared to even kill for her love.'"

Wray finishes reading and gazes closely at Sam for a few more seconds, as if trying to decipher every muscle movement on his face.

"The things people say looking for the limelight—and after so much bad press about you." Wray shake his head dismissively.

"I know I'm fascinated with her. I love her so much, but she was never interested, despite our close friendship. I was very frustrated. I probably said something similar. But I never meant it seriously."

Sam stands up, glaring at his lawyer, who leans back in his chair, waving his hands to try to calm his client down.

"I love her. I still love her," Sam insists. "And I'd never kill her."

"Okay, okay, but you need to realise that no one will believe this story about the alien man flying towards you while keeping the boat perfectly still at the waterfall's edge, then taking Erin away with him." Wray tries hard but cannot keep himself from sounding very sceptical.

"He must have taken her. I fainted before I could see what he did …"

As Sam lounges himself back into his seat, the lawyer strokes his bristly black moustache before continuing.

"Sorry, but it's hard to follow this story, never mind taking it seriously."

"I am very sorry too, as I have no proof, no witness, no compelling evidence," Sam replies in a sad whisper.

"I see only one option," Wray says, leaning over the table and trying to sound upbeat. "Tomorrow, you must prove to the entire court and the world what you said to me. Write your final plea as a proclamation of love, and let's hope that Judge Abiko, so profoundly touched by your testimony, shows some leniency."

Sam slowly nods with a bitter look of defeat in his eyes. Deep inside his mind, he has come to accept that nobody will ever believe him.

"Don't give up," Wray reassures him while patting his shoulders. "If you are telling the truth, then it's worth fighting for it."

"Okay, I'll do it. I'll write something—that is, if they want to hear my testimony after the last witness from the prosecution gives evidence," he glumly replies.

"Sam, concentrate on what you have to say. I'll handle Professor Khan and Ms Porter. Deal?"

This time, Sam nods with a flashing smile and a slight expression of confidence that finally pleases Wray.

"Let's get ready for tomorrow, as all we have is today," the lawyer concludes in an uplifting tone, putting away his notebook and grabbing his suitcase. "Don't ever lose hope if you are telling the truth," Wray firmly says, looking straight into Sam's eyes before closing the door.

That night, Sam pours his soul out into his lengthy self-defence testimony. He writes the whole story—since he first met Erin until the last minute he saw her alive. Reading his words repeatedly, he realises that his writing resembles something more of a fatal epitaph, a dire capitulation of a failed wasted young life.

"I am entirely to blame for taking her there, and now she's gone … she's probably dead. First, I should pay for what I've done, but never for being a coward, never for being a liar. This tragedy is solely my own making, so I should get the punishment for what is entirely my fault.

"How can I make this right? How can I make this entire nightmare disappear as if it has never happened?" he keeps asking himself.

He starts twisting his bed sheet into the sturdiest rope he can make and then ties it tightly around his neck, pulling away at each side as firmly as he can. The throbbing pain pushes through his sweaty forehead; he shivers as his pounding pulse knives through his swollen temples, but he keeps pulling even harder. As his vision becomes blurry, he starts hallucinating and hearing double-echoed voices from afar while he aimlessly stares at the ceiling.

*Only when I am gone will this whole madness come to an end. I must find somewhere to hang from.*

Suddenly, he hears the cell door opening, and then he feels his neck burning. As he tries to grab the twisted sheet, it disintegrates into charring embers. He turns towards the door, dazed and bewildered, his eyes stinging as he opens them wide.

A sprightly figure is standing in front of him. His heart jolts as if nearly coming out his chest, and his jaw drops in disbelief.

There, in front of him, is the sweet welcoming smile of his dear friend Erin. He can discern the shape of her body as it softly glows against the darkened walls.

"Are you real?" he mouths very slowly.

"Yes, Sam. It's me, Erin." She puts her hands on her chest while smiling even wider.

"Oh Erin!" He jumps off the bed and runs towards her.

But as he extends his arms to touch her, he cannot feel her, his fingers sliding down an invisible barrier.

"I cannot even touch you. I cannot feel you. But I can feel this subtle energy coming from you. What is this barrier stopping me?"

"It is my body-shield," she starts explaining as she gently pushes him onto his bed and makes him sit down next to her.

"At least I can sense your presence … so I guess you're real," he says hesitantly, his eyes fixated on her.

"My biomagnetic shield …" she pauses, trying to find the right words to explain. "It protects me from this atmosphere."

From Sam's puzzled expression, she can tell it will be quite challenging to make him understand everything she wants to say to him.

"I've come to get you out of here. And there was no need for that," she scolds, pointing at his bruised neck as she grabs the rope's remnants and burns them with her gloved hands.

"I thought you were dead." He moans. "I felt so helpless, so inadequate."

"I understand." She looks sympathetically at him. "But now you see I have returned. You're not a liar. It did happen. What you saw—it was real."

"You certainly came at the right time. What took you so long?"

"I was learning to use my new body. Training to be a true Rom-Ghenshar."

"A what?"

"I am one of them, Sam, a Rom-Ghenshar, as it happens … they created me."

"Ha! they created you …" Sam frowns at her in distrust. "How do I know you're Erin, anyway? You look similar, but you're not the same. Your hair is white. Your pupils glow too brightly. You even look taller."

"Ask me a question only you and I would know the answer to," she dares him.

"What did you tell me when I tried to kiss you?" he asks her, trying as hard as he can to conceal his anxiety.

"I didn't have time to respond. The currents dragged the boat away."

"Answer me now, Erin," Sam pleads. "I've been waiting for your answer since then."

"It doesn't matter anymore," she whispers, turning her face away from him and looking down. "I'm not the same girl you used to know."

"In what way?" he asks her in dismay.

"I mean …" She hesitates, looking poignantly at him. "It will never work."

"Yeah. So he took you, changed you, Erin. Now he owns you—"

"But you'll always be my best friend, that's for sure!" She cheerfully says, but Sam's face is only getting gloomier.

"What has he done to you? Who are these aliens?" he grumbles, standing up and leaning against the wall with his head down, his arms folded as in complete denial.

"Remember that late afternoon when we both saw a bright sphere briefly appear over the sea?" she says while standing in front of him and lifting his chin, making him look back at her.

As she speaks to him, Sam starts to realise that she must be, indeed, Erin. He can no longer ignore the unmistakable tone of her voice, her subtle gestures and mannerisms.

She keeps talking as if she hasn't noticed his trembling lips, his paler complexion, or his drifting gaze.

"You asked me never to tell anyone, to keep it a secret, didn't you? It was nearly dusk, and the sun was setting—"

"Enough, Erin, enough! Why did he take you?" He bursts out.

"Calm down. I can explain, but it will take time for you to understand."

Sam exhales a long, deep resigned breath as he stares at her in utter abdication. "I give up," he relents, walking sombrely around the room. "Do whatever you want, Erin. Explain everything. I suppose we have all night, so you can tell me all about it. But first, tell me, how did you find me?"

"We can find anyone anywhere on the planet. I followed you closely. I was planning to come to the hearing tomorrow. But I couldn't wait any longer."

"How did you get in here?" Sam gulps, his confusion growing by the second.

"Well, I asked them to give me all the security codes and … they duly obliged. The guards will do anything I ask them to," she replies, a smug grin flashing through her face.

"Oh, really?" Sam retorts in a markedly sarcastic tone. "Then, let's get out of here right now!"

Erin nods enthusiastically. At least something she said has managed to cheer him up. She opens the door, inviting him to follow her.

They exit the cell, walk down the stairs leading to the main hall, and open the double exit doors without anyone making the slightest attempt to stop them, even when Sam makes funny faces at the guards. They both giggle and jump in joy as they finally run out of the court building.

She continues to guide him through the high-security gates, which she promptly opens on their arrival. Sam suddenly stops at the sight of the large police presence, makeshift campsites, reporters, and onlookers staying outside, waiting for the hearing. He tries to turn around, but Shaillah holds him firmly by the arm.

"They can't see you. I'm protecting you," she assures him.

"How?" Sam looks at her open-mouthed, completely baffled.

"Well … Part of my shield is surrounding you, and I am controlling their minds so they can only see or hear what I want them to …"

"Can I learn that trick? That's why I requested to stay here. I was tired of being hounded by them," he grumbles.

"Well, they won't do that from now on."

Sam smiles gratefully at her. For the first time in a while, he's feeling relieved, even uplifted.

"Where are we going now?" he impatiently asks as they reach the edge of town.

"You want to know the truth of what happened, my friend. I will show you."

She finds an isolated spot amidst the grassy hills and sits on the ground, inviting Sam to sit beside her. He follows her command automatically, not even attempting to imagine what will happen next.

He has never felt so intrigued and so bewildered at the same time as he watches a thick gyrating light column starting to form in mid-air.

He continuously rubs his eyes until the pain stops him. Still, he finds himself in the same place, sitting next to Erin, watching the most unbelievable light spectacle. *If this isn't a dream, it must be a life-changing event*, he says to himself.

The luminous column gives way to swirling bands of floating particles, spreading far out and gradually forming a sprawling translucent haze, filling the entire space in front of them.

He can see the images starting to build throughout the fluctuating medium, eventually creating a three-dimensional hologram.

"I will show you what happened in this time-slice hologram," she explains, "so you can understand why I'm here at all."

Her spirited voice vibrates inside his numbed head, making him jump out of his stupor. "Where is all this coming from?" Sam wonders.

Then he notices the stones on her belt's strap, flashing in a nonstop sequence. *It must be coming from her belt*, he reckons.

She briefly nods at him, confirming his thoughts, and then points towards the ethereal scenes.

He stares at the shifting shapes constantly swirling in front of him as more defined patterns emerge within the hazy flow. He can't take his eyes off the hypnotizing spectacle, not even for a second.

Sam starts to discern the edges of a giant translucent bubble floating off the gleaming floor at the centre of a vast white-walled chamber. He holds his breath when the full view comes into sharp focus in an instant. The curled body of a girl starts stretching out inside. As the bubble's outer layer starts turning more transparent, he immediately recognises Erin's long white hair floating around her body as she slowly opens her eyes.

Sam is so entranced with the vivid images that he starts to believe they are real. He impulsively runs towards the bubble, trying to break it with his hands in an attempt to reach Erin. He aimlessly slices the air around him with his fists, hardly noticing that he's only in the middle of a light field.

Shaillah patiently allows him to burn all his anger and frustration until he finally drops on the ground, his resolve crushed. She stands up and runs towards him. As she inspects him, he briefly glances at her but soon looks away, unable to contain his embarrassment and disappointment.

"You can't get into the time-slice," she calmly explains.

"Arrgh," he groans, lying flat on the ground and clutching his stomach, trying to stop the sinking feeling invading his tired body. "I'm feeling sick."

"Sam, please be strong for me," she pleads while grabbing him from under his arms and helping him stand up.

"So that's where he took you, did he? Who is he?" he says, twisting his mouth in ridicule.

"He's just a soldier," Shaillah says sharply.

"A soldier … a soldier," Sam ponders, staring intensely at her as if trying to gauge what she's thinking. But Shaillah's emotionless expression keeps adding to his misery.

"How many are there?" he sneers.

"Just three. The others are our supreme commander and our chief scientist."

"Am I supposed to believe that? A commander with one soldier?"

"The Rom-Ghenshars, we are from another star system, thousands of light-years away … See?" She points back at the images, ignoring his sarcastic tone.

Two diagonal suns hang solemnly on a pink-orange sky. They shine onto a vast multicoloured ocean, its frothy waves pounding off the intricate metallic bases of imposing interwoven sculptures, rising mightily from rocky outcrops and breaking through the high, dense clouds.

"Rom and Ghenshar are the names of our two suns," she continues, hardly containing her admiration as she points at each star in turn. "The bigger, the yellow one is Rom; the smaller red star is Ghenshar. Rom means *power*; Ghenshar means *glory*."

The vivid image slowly changes into another, like a three-dimensional slide show, each visual setting unveiling a fascinatingly vibrant alien world.

"Immense deep oceans mostly cover our planet. We build our cities on top of the rocky islands, but we also have vast undersea and underground constructions—all interconnected by space-tunnels." She enthusiastically describes every scene as Sam watches, awestruck.

Height-defying structures linked by arched hanging bridges spread across the vast interconnected cities. The gem-studded shorelines reflect the twin suns' rays in a multitude of colours. Over the ocean surface, schools of giant lyshars glide majestically in perfectly choreographed zigzag patterns.

"Our land is rich in diamond and precious minerals," she continues, trying to break into Sam's perplexed silence.

"This is all very well, but why did they want you? What do you do?" he blurts out as if all his patience has finally run out.

"Well, let's say, my dear Sam, I'm their messenger."

"And what do they want? What's their message?"

"You'll find out soon."

"Erin, you're making it difficult, aren't you? Why don't you tell me right now?" he shouts while kicking hard on the ground with his heels.

"All right, all right, that's enough for today," she says apologetically, gently holding his arm and making him walk beside her.

As the images disappear in a flash, Sam seems to calm down.

"I've come to help you," she says in a reassuring tone. "Let's return to your room now. We have to finish this. I'll go to the hearing tomorrow."

Sam nods in resignation as he strolls by her side. *Somehow, I feel compelled to do whatever she tells me to.* He thinks to himself.

They enter the court building, walking through the aisles without being stopped. Sam is amused as he gives a military salute to the officers, but they do not react in the slightest.

Back in his cell, Shaillah carefully places Sam onto his bed and makes him fall into a deep sleep. As she wraps the bed covers snuggly around his body, she softly pats him on the chest and blows his curly hair gently off his forehead.

"You rest now, my dear friend. Tomorrow will be an interesting day."

Shaillah closes the heavy cell door and races down the stairs like a fleeting ghost. She exits the outside gates, passing in front of the night guard, who sips unwittingly at his cup of coffee.

Out in the open, she saunters through the fields with her arms fully open while her gleeful eyes stay fixed on the starry sky. "So far and yet so close," she says to herself as she glances through the constellations, taking her time to admire the glittering starlit night. She watches the prominent Orion's stars appearing on the horizon, then focuses on the less conspicuous Eridani system, waving its dim pearly wreath right off the bright star Rigel. She watches each faint point of light on its wavy river-like pattern, feeling as if her ancestral home is calling on her, and she is responding. All the while, she cannot stop thinking about Rothwen.

The approaching scouting-craft interrupts her thoughts. As the craft smoothly brakes to a halt and silently hovers by her side, she swiftly boards it, flying through the opening top cabin.

In a fleeting second, the craft jets off vertically and disappears into the night, leaving behind a bright orange trail that soon dissipates across the sky. The groups of puzzled onlookers calling the police that night will be flatly dismissed and told to stop drinking.

## CHAPTER 17

# THE WITNESS

*Professor Khan, please explain. What is the probability of intelligent life existing on another planet and visiting us, here, on planet Earth?*

The court hearing is being broadcast live across the world, on all major news channels. At the top of the highest buildings, giant screens show the images transmitted from the courtroom while the latest headlines roll underneath.

Judge Abiko solemnly enters the room and takes his seat at the podium. A stocky man with a serious round face and short grey beard, his impassive expression demands total respect. He orders his papers while looking around the courtroom over his thin glasses, channelling all his authority through his piercing narrowed eyes as he tells everyone to be seated. He speaks in a firm tone as he describes the day's proceedings and asks the prosecutor to call his last witness.

Ms Porter, the chief prosecutor, is a lady of a strong-minded demeanour. Behind her black-rimmed glasses, her steely brown eyes briefly focus on Sam with a frosty look before calling her star witness. Even the heavy make-up and thick mascara can't smooth out her stern face; her flattened hair pulled tightly back in a bun makes her look even harsher.

Professor Mishu Khan takes the witness stand and readily stares at the packed gallery as if he's about to start another of his famous scientific lectures.

As emeritus professor of the World's Institute for Science and Space Exploration (WISSE, or WIZE as it is most commonly known), he is the leading expert for the prosecution. He has dedicated most of his professional life to researching one of the most crucial questions scientists and laymen alike have ever asked: Are we alone in the universe? He has gained a worldwide reputation for his outstanding work in biocosmology, being the first man to discover life-essential amino acids in warming coalescing molecular clouds.

His face is partially covered by his bushy white beard and thick sideburns, as if trying to hide the all-pervading wrinkles. His small, beady eyes give off a flash of vitality and strength that is in complete contrast to his ageing complexion. He's wearing a navy blue overall with red trims. Over his left top pocket, a thick red badge, topped with a glossy golden star, boasts of his high position in the WIZE organisation.

Sam holds the professor's scolding gaze as the revered scientist is about to speak. He remembers the famous Khan's lectures on the science programs, but never in his wildest dreams did he imagine that he would be confronting him one day, contradicting his every word.

"The data from our high orbit surveillance satellites show," Khan explains in a confident tone, "that there has never been a positive irrefutable evidence of an alien spaceship, ever." He raises his voice even louder on the word "ever".

"Thank you, Professor Khan. Please explain. What is the probability of our survey satellites missing such an event?" Ms Porter asks.

"Zero," Khan confidently replies, looking straight at the judge, "our specialized Near Earth Objects satellite network scans the space around us in all frequencies of the electromagnetic spectrum, constantly analysing and identifying every signal, every second. I may add … I have dedicated most of my life to studying life as we know it. With our powerful optical, infrared, and radio telescopes, we've acquired a vast amount of data in our extensive research. So far, all we have to show for it is the presence of stable life-essential amino acids in distant molecular clouds."

"Objection, Your Honour," Wray protests. "How can we be so sure? Maybe we haven't detected it yet because we do not have the right means to do it. The alien technology may be so different from ours that it is impossible to identify it."

"Sustained!" Judge Abiko replies instantly.

"Let me bring to your attention, Your Honour, another matter that is equally as important," Ms Porter continues, unabated. "Professor Khan, please explain, what is the probability of intelligent life existing on another planet and visiting us, here, on planet Earth? What is the probability that these aliens may be similar to humans?"

A brief suspenseful silence seems to spread across the crowded courtroom, all eyes now fixed on Professor Khan, who appears to be thinking hard on his best answer.

"Our best cosmic statisticians have concluded that it would be virtually impossible for intelligent life to evolve the same way somewhere else. Even here on Earth, where the conditions are perfect, how come only one species, us, has evolved advanced intelligence? In our cosmic backyard, on the Orion spiral arm, suppose that solar systems with habitable planets are abundant, for the sake of argument.

"We know it would take us a considerable number of lifetimes, with our current technology, to get to any of our closest stars. For example, it would take us tens of thousands of years to get to our nearest star, Proxima Centauri, at around four light-years away. And to reach the exoplanets around the star Wolf 359, we would have to travel double that distance. So, if any alien makes it here, first they have to be an extraordinarily advanced civilisation, able to warp space or travel close to the speed of light. They would've, by now, let their presence be known, or we would've, by now, detected some trace of their advanced technology, at least. As for the probability of intelligent life living on another planet and visiting us, I can answer this with another question."

Khan stops for a second to look across the expectant audience. Then he adds in a sarcastic tone, "Where are they?"

A rumble of sceptical laughter ripples through the entire room.

"Order, order!" Judge Abiko leans forward, hammering impatiently on the table.

Sam purses his lips to stop himself from contradicting Professor Khan. *Erin is right. There's only one way of making them believe me. We have to show them*, he says to himself.

"Any further questions?" Judge Abiko asks the prosecutor.

"No, Your Honour," she replies and then proceeds to walk ostentatiously to her seat after scolding Wray with a searing gaze.

"Let's hear the defence's closing statement next," the judge orders as Professor Khan leaves the stand and takes a seat in the very front row of the packed courtroom.

Jack Wray clears his throat before speaking. "Your Honour, thank you very much for your patience during this most unusual court hearing. I appeal to your wildest imagination, to your profound ability of thinking outside the box. The question we must carefully consider is the following: Why would Sam Sheppard, a kind, fun-loving teenager, kill the girl he loves? Even if she were to reject him, why would he do it? Could it be that, in a sudden rage, he lost his mind? No, no, and no! As we all know, Sam Sheppard is a normal decent stable young man and that he would never contemplate such a crime. And I think that he would be the best one to convince you of that." He extends his hand towards Sam, beckoning to approach him.

Sam saunters towards the witness box, looking directly into Professor Khan's eyes and then into Judge Abiko's.

"Objection, Your Honour." Ms Porter runs towards the podium. "We have not been instructed of the defendant taking the stand."

Judge Abiko looks intensely into Sam's supplicant gaze. He finds the youngster's silent plea impossible to reject. By the persistent way Sam is looking at him, the experienced judge can sense that something significant is about to happen.

"Overruled! Let Sam Sheppard speak," the judge orders, nodding at Sam and not even bothering to acknowledge Ms Porter's presence by his podium.

Sam smiles and gratefully bows his head to the judge. For the first time today, his uptight demeanour has changed into a confident one. He stares at the public and then at his tearful mother, Martha, and his anxious sister, Stella, nodding slightly at them in a comforting gesture. Then he looks at his father, with a forewarning glare flashing across his face.

"Thank you, Your Honour," Sam finally says, his voice breaking through the dead silence of the expectant audience. "Perhaps I can introduce you to a special witness …"

Everyone, even Ms Porter, is holding his or her breath in anticipation.

At this very moment, when the courtroom appears to be frozen in time, the double entrance doors creak and abruptly open wide, giving way to a bright white beam flooding the central aisle. Everyone gasps as an elegant, veiled woman walks amid the light shaft toward the podium—everyone, that is, except Sam, because he knows perfectly well who the unexpected visitor is.

The white veil disintegrates around her, revealing her svelte figure gleaming in a white bodysuit. The purple glint from her almond-shaped eyes immediately grabs the audience's complete attention.

She nods in turn as she encounters every disconcerted stare and then she says in a vibrant voice, "My name was Erin, but I'm not dead."

"Erin!" Mr Lobart screams in disbelief as he runs towards her, making his way through the standing public and pushing everyone away in a desperate attempt to reach her before anyone else. "Is it really you?" Lobart staggers, stretching his arms towards her but stumbling onto the floor before he can reach her.

Every muscle in his face knots up in exasperation as he tries to understand what has stopped him. Then Pat Lobart tries to get close to Shaillah, but she too is pushed back as if she has bumped into an invisible barrier. Judge Abiko stands up behind his podium, hardly believing that Erin Lobart has suddenly appeared in front of him. Ms Porter's face has turned so pale, she seems about to faint. Professor Khan is stroking his beard as he struggles to find an explanation for what he is witnessing while Jack Wray can hardly move from his seat, startled. "I'll be damned," he grumbles. "So he was telling the truth."

Several people leave their seats, congregating along the aisle and close to the seemingly invisible wall surrounding Shaillah. Sam makes his way through the startled group until he reaches the dividing edge, and to everyone's bafflement, he is allowed to go through and stand next to Shaillah. They both look directly at the judge, who seems completely lost for words.

Martha tries to reach her son, but all she can do is sweep her hands over the invisible wall surrounding him.

"Erin! Stop this game, please," Martha pleads, fearing for what could happen to Sam.

"Do not dare harm him," Stella shrieks in a threatening tone.

"Sam is perfectly okay, and he is telling the truth," Shaillah replies calmly. "I've been away. But I've returned to bring you a message."

"What message?" shouts Professor Khan, who has joined Judge Abiko at the podium.

"On behalf of the Rom-Ghenshars. They are here and want to let you know about their plans … as soon as possible," Shaillah declares.

"Is this a joke? A new kind of alien abduction scam?" shouts Ms Porter.

The impatient audience seems to have had enough and breaks out in a turmoil of protestation, everyone demanding to know what is happening and trying to get a better view of Shaillah in any way they can.

"Order, order!" Judge Abiko shouts over the noisy crowd, eventually managing to get the courtroom under control. "Let Erin Lobart speak."

"Thank you, Your Honour". Shaillah smiles at Judge Abiko. Then she looks around the courtroom as she speaks in an uplifting tone. "The Rom-Ghenshars have come from very far away from within our galaxy. Humans must feel fortunate that they have chosen to visit this planet and even offer their friendship and assistance."

"Who are these people? The Rom … whatever?" Ms Porter disgruntledly asks amid the grumbles and murmurs of collective incredulity.

"We, the Rom-Ghenshars, have now come full circle from a distant past. Today is the day of a new beginning when vast distances are erased and faraway worlds are reunited. We have come to start a new era, to forge a new destiny. Let us work together—for a brighter future."

Shaillah raises one fist in the air in a triumphant gesture, but the multitude around her hardly moves, staring at her in complete awe. She looks at Sam with a proud reassuring smile, but he is also in absolute shock.

Realizing that everyone is struggling to believe her words, she starts walking towards the exit, pushing Sam in front of her. As they step forwards, the crowd has to make way to the impenetrable protecting shield.

When they reach the exit doors, she looks back and announces, "You have heard what I had to say. And I will repeat it until no doubt remains."

Then pushing Sam onto the waiting scouting-craft hovering over the pavement outside, she adds, "Now, it's time to set Sam free."

As Shaillah enters the cockpit, a puzzled Sam is scratching his head while inspecting the dynamic flickering dashboard. A constant stream of multicoloured symbols springs up and flashes above the glowing screens, weaving into a network of intertwined pathways.

"Wow, Erin. And you drive this?" Sam asks, astounded, his eyes wildly moving around, unable to focus on anything.

"Oh, It's quite easy. All routes are programmed in advance. I only need to activate the sequences from my brain. Like this!"

The swift vertical jolt makes Sam fall on his seat. As the engines roar amid a fast-scattering white mist, they fly over the townhouses and then out over the country roads, trailed by the line of chasing police cars and helicopters. The sleek aircraft frequently decelerates to maintain a constant leading gap with its pursuers, as if not wanting to disappear from their sight.

It soon becomes quite clear where they are all heading—towards the Lobarts' farm.

# CHAPTER 18

# THE SIEGE

*And are you still going to tell me that you are not human?*

As the scouting-craft gently lands on the farm's backyard, Shaillah jumps out onto the grass and rushes towards the kitchen door, breaking open the lock with a swift but intense electric discharge from her body shield. A startled Sam follows her cautiously, keeping a safe distance.

An overexcited Blazer greets them as they go in, jumping at her repeatedly every time he is knocked back, trying to reach her.

"So, Blazer seems to recognise you all right," Sam notes while the dog keeps jumping towards her.

She points at her wooden chair, guiding her dog to stand on it and ordering him to be quiet. Blazer immediately stops panting and shaking, sitting perfectly still and looking at her, whining as if wholly hypnotised.

As Sam watches her guiding Blazer, her giggles and sighs of joy bring back memories of the Erin he knew so well and loved so deeply. *It's Erin! It's her*, he repeats to himself.

"Are you still doubting it?" she reprimands him.

"N-n-no," he stammers, wondering how she could know what he is thinking.

The whirring of the helicopters rattles through the air, and the squeaking of the braking cars vibrates through the ground. Sam rushes to one of the front windows and looks towards the farm's road through the spaced wooden fence panels. Astonished, he sees several vehicles trying to approach the farmhouse from different directions, only to grind to a halt a few metres away from the fence as if stopped by an invisible barrier.

No matter how hard they try, the drivers are unable to make their cars advance any further. Likewise, the pilots cannot make their helicopters descend past a certain height, eventually giving up and landing farther away, beyond the parked vehicles of the islanders and ARA personnel.

Albert Lobart drives his pickup truck right up to the row of police cars parked at each side of the road leading to his farm's front gates. He asks Patricia to get out, and as soon as she does, he accelerates and weaves his way through the gaps between the cars. His mad dash doesn't last long, as his truck crashes and grinds to a halt against the invisible barrier, provoking a sudden lightning strike against the bonnet. He falls flat over the steering wheel.

Two police officers run to him, finding him completely unconscious. As the officers quickly carry Lobart's non-responsive body towards a waiting police car, Martha and Bill Sheppard approach them. They watch in disbelief as the officers lay a lifeless Albert Lobart on the backseats while despairing at how their son might be faring inside the farmhouse.

Pat Lobart arrives as the vehicle speeds off.

"Oh, Patricia," Martha shouts, running towards a dazzled Mrs Lobart, "he's badly bruised. He crashed against the barrier, no wonder."

"What barrier?" Patricia growls in disconcert.

"Listen, everyone." The voice of J. J. Walker, the island's police section captain, resounds over the rowdy congregation. "Do not approach the farm from any direction. Stay clear of this area. I repeat—stay clear."

It's not long before news of the day's events spread across the island, and many of its residents and visitors rush towards the site. The police and ARA brigades start to surround the area and set up a police cordon, keeping the curious people at what they consider a safe distance, fifty metres away from the farm's perimeter fence.

"Are you ready to come out now, children?" shouts Captain Walker through the loudspeaker, stressing the word "children" in a sarcastic tone.

But to no avail. No one is responding from the farmhouse.

Martha Sheppard runs towards the captain and asks him to let her speak to her son. He reluctantly hands the loudspeaker to her.

"Sam, Sam, it's your mother. Please talk to us, darling." She tries several times, but her desperate plea is unanswered.

"I'm afraid we'll have to wait until they decide to come out," Walker concludes. "Let's hope it's not too long."

Walker grabs his binoculars and scours the farmhouse's large front lawn and wide porch, eventually spotting Sam standing by one of the front windows.

"Ah! Mrs Sheppard, I can see your son. He seems okay." The captain smiles at Martha, but even then, he cannot conceal his concern.

Bill Sheppard takes the binoculars from the captain's hands and points in the same direction. He finds his son standing by the window, looking directly at him.

Bill passes the binoculars onto Martha, but Sam has disappeared from view by the time she focuses on the window.

Shaillah has taken him out of the line of sight and into the backyard once again. Blazer follows them obediently, walking close to Shaillah's feet.

"Did you see your parents?" she asks.

"Sure, I did."

"Why didn't you wave at them?"

"I'm so confused, Erin. Was it you stopping me?

"Yes, I was. Just wanted to show you how I can control you. But don't worry. You'll be with them soon."

"Will you please stop all this? What are you trying to do?" As he tries to touch her shoulders, he is struck by a swift electrical discharge and has to let go swiftly.

"What the hell?" he shouts, looking at her, astonished, "Okay, I suppose I have to believe all your weirdness. I have no choice."

She keeps nodding at him, reaffirming his words. "I'm not Erin anymore, Sam. If you call me by my real name, it will be easier for you to accept our new reality. My name is Shaillah."

"Oh sure. And why have you brought me here, Shaillah?" Sam emphasises her name in the most sarcastic tone he can muster while bowing to her in a derisive gesture.

"I wanted to say sorry … and maybe goodbye," she replies in a dead-serious tone as Sam straightens up his body and looks back at her with a dumbfounded expression.

"But I don't want to say goodbye, Erin," he protests. "You can be whatever you want to be. I'll always be here for you. I'll change if I have to—"

"This cannot be. We must say goodbye. I belong to them—the Rom-Ghenshars," she replies in an unyielding tone.

She takes his hands and then puts them close to her chest. He feels his palms getting hot as subtle electric pulses come off her shield, but he holds on firm, fighting his intense emotions as he notices her glimmering tears.

"I see the sadness in your face. And are you still going to tell me that you are not human? that you feel nothing for me?" he vehemently asks her.

"True, I still do have some human emotions. But every day, I feel more different. Every day, I feel closer to them."

"Damn them, whoever they are!" Sam can barely contain his frustration, but he manages to stay composed as he vows: "I promise you, I'll never leave you. You can say goodbye as many times as you like. But I'll always be here for you—anytime you need me."

As he tries to hug her, the sudden discharge pushes him back, reminding him that he cannot even touch her.

"And for the record," he adds downheartedly, "did I ever tell you that I love you?"

She slowly shakes her head while looking directly at him and pressing her index finger against her mouth to discourage him from talking.

But Sam keeps a persistent, albeit dejected gaze. "I've always loved you since the day we met," he declares, trying to sound firm, but the anguish in his voice betrays his crushing despair.

"Don't say anything else. There's no point. Goodbye, my dear friend. Thank you for everything," she sombrely replies.

All the memories flicker through Sam's mind like a flipped deck of cards. Still, the revolving images suddenly stop right in the middle of this moment—the moment that he must accept that something profound, way beyond his control, has come to separate them.

"Go back to your family now. Tell them everything will be all right—as long as they don't try to attack us. We bring a message of peace and friendship." As she speaks to him, her face changes into a blank, distant expression.

Slowly stepping backwards, he approaches the front door, feeling as though he is moving away from a vanishing mirage. Her words seem to be coming from very far away. Her image is getting ever blurrier, in double vision.

As he appears on the farm's porch, the armed guards instinctively point their weapons at a petrified Sam, who raises his arms in the air while Captain Walker repeatedly shouts through the loudspeakers, "Don't shoot!"

A tense atmosphere sets in as Sam steps onto the front lawn while nervously glancing at the armed guards, who immediately lay down their weapons. He makes his way to the front gates in a dash. A loud cheer comes from the crowd trying to get a better view behind the police cordon as Sam appears outside the fence and rushes towards his parents.

At that moment, taking advantage of the guards' full attention on Sam, Pat Lobart runs towards the farmhouse, attempting to push through the front gate from where Sam had walked out. Two of the armed guards go after her, trying to stop her, but she runs with even more impetus as she manages to go past the invisible line and through the gate. As Pat reaches the porch of her house, thinking she is about to pass through the open front door, she crashes against the barrier that has now formed just outside the building walls.

"Erin, Erin, you will pay dearly if you don't come out right now!" Pat Lobart shouts as she pounds her fists against the invisible barrier over her front door.

Suddenly, Mrs Lobart collapses, hit by a bolt of lightning. When the guards cautiously approach, they find her unconscious, as was the case with her husband.

Shaillah watches in sorrow from the living room's window. Her mind is in disarray, as she is about to let go of everything she cherished and trusted, her best friend and her beloved pet dog and horses. But as hard as it feels now, she understands there is no other way. She must dismiss any past emotions and possessions, no matter how strong, no matter how precious.

She goes back to the kitchen, reminding herself she'll be there for the very last time. She grabs her favourite coffee mug and then lets go of the handle. The cup shatters into tiny pieces against the stone floor. "As my past life is ending," she mumbles.

As she enters her room, her heart misses a beat. "Why does it feel so strange? It doesn't seem like it's my room anymore." She stares blankly at her half-made bed, reflected on her wood-framed wall mirror.

She picks up her hairbrush and pulls off some of her old hair from the bristles. Looking at herself in the mirror, she compares it to her now silvery tresses.

She has the unnerving sensation that she is now an intruder in her room. She throws the hairbrush on the floor and walks out into the backyard, running towards the stables while trying to dismiss her conflicting thoughts, Blazer following her everywhere. She glances at the parked cars and helicopters waiting beyond the rear fence while their occupants, not daring to make a move, keenly stare at her through their binoculars.

She opens the large wooden stable doors, and her two horses immediately recognise her, kicking and neighing as she approaches them.

"Go, my dear friends, be free," she says as she opens the fence gates, letting them run out into the open countryside, galloping past the baffled onlookers.

Once back inside the kitchen, she cannot contain her tears as Blazer is jumping at her, trying to lick her face. But she must move on.

As much as she tries, however, she can't keep ignoring Blazer's insistent gaze and sorrowful whining. "Oh, my dear Blazer, how can I ever give you up?" Turning off her shield momentarily to be close to him, she picks him up from the floor and strokes his smooth hair and velvety ears, rubbing her fingers on his belly while Blazer happily licks her nose.

As she finds a brief moment of solace playing with her beloved dog, everyone outside is waiting for her next move. No one dares approach the farmhouse fence, even though they know the impenetrable dangerous barrier has reformed further back.

Sam is sitting next to Captain Walker, inside the police car, his parents and sister at the back.

"I suppose she'll come out eventually, don't you think?" Walker comments hesitantly.

"We have to wait. Don't do anything silly like the Lobarts." Sam stresses his words, turning around to face his parents. Then firmly staring at Walker, he adds, "From what I've seen so far, she has some powers far beyond what we can control or even understand."

"What did she do? What did she tell you?" Walker asks while staring probingly at Sam.

"She wanted to say goodbye." Sam tries to contain his quivering voice, so he changes the subject. "But she also said that she brings a message from the aliens—something like they are friendly, and they are ready to talk to us."

"I don't see anything friendly about her!" Stella quips.

"The aliens … eh?" Walker rolls his eyes in mockery.

"Come on, Walker, you have to start taking this very seriously. Look at what happened in the courtroom, and look at what has happened to the Lobarts. Right now, we're all waiting here, at her mercy. She obviously has some powers we cannot yet understand," Bill Sheppard interjects.

"Everything has an explanation, Mr Sheppard," Walker replies, looking incisively at Sheppard. "But it must be a credible explanation."

"She can create electric fields. And she can control it with her thoughts," Sam eagerly explains. "When I tried to touch her, I could feel sparks all over my body."

"As you seem to know her better than most, what do you suggest we do next?" Walker finally relents.

"We need to hear what she has to say first," Sam suggests.

The captain's face shows he remains hesitant.

"Ah! And she can listen to my thoughts … even control my actions," Sam adds as the captain twists his mouth in a dismissive gesture.

Their conversation is suddenly interrupted by a knock on the windscreen. Walker opens his door and jumps out of the car to greet an anxious Professor Khan, who has come to see him, accompanied by a group of ARA's soldiers. The heavily armed, uniformed men, stone-faced, take up their positions in front of the police line, their weapons at the ready.

"What is this? Ready to go to war?" Walker says with scorn while extending his hand to the professor.

"How're you doing, Mr Walker?" Khan responds, ignoring the captain's irony and not shaking his hand. "We've come to find out once and for all what is going on. We need to get that girl, Erin."

"I see. Easier said than done," Walker replies in a sceptical tone, immensely annoying Khan.

"We have come prepared. The ARA's Space Defence team is here, our specialist rescue robots are here, and General Stewart is leading the task force. We are ready!"

"Well, first things first. How are you going to get her out of there?" Walker says sarcastically, pointing at the farmhouse.

The large stone and steel building seems eerily quiet and uninhabited. An uncanny peace lingers in the front lawn as the sunset looms, the grass bending under a soft breeze. Behind the police cordon, the onlookers' clatter sharply contrasts with the ghostly farm's scene.

Several soldier units have arrived, displacing the people farther and taking positions close to the surrounding fence. Behind the police and soldier units, the world's media have now managed to set up their broadcasting camps, while a large group of onlookers are still refusing to go home.

"We have to convince her to come out. Then we'll surround her. Where is her friend?" Khan wonders, looking through the driver's window.

But Sam, who has been listening through the partially open car windows, promptly gets out of the car, only to bump against the guards' tight circle. Khan walks towards him while shaking his head. He puts one arm on Sam's shoulders, trying to calm him down, but Sam backs off and tries in vain to run away again.

"Listen, boy, you'd better help. Or she will end up dead, dead!"

"You know what is dead, Professor Khan? Your plan, Professor Khan! You'll never catch her. You'll never succeed," Sam firmly states.

"Let me tell you something, Sam. Mr and Mrs Lobart are now critically ill in hospital. Who's going to be next? That girl, Erin, is a danger to us all—"

"The Lobarts brought it upon themselves. What about me? She has never harmed me," Sam remarks.

"Because she is using you. Can't you see that? She is using you," Khan ripostes.

Sam's expression changes from upset to confused. *Could it be that she is using me for some yet unknown lethal purpose?* He feels afraid. As he stares up at the sky, the buzzing sound of the surveying drones fills the air. His mind is clouded with the frightening thought that Erin might not be his friend but, instead, his deadly enemy.

His vision blacks out, and he feels as if he's about to faint. As he tumbles, his father's arms hold him firm, preventing him from falling flat on the ground as Stella runs towards him, staring pitifully at him.

"Oh, my dear brother, what has she done to you?" She sighs while hugging him tightly.

"I am so confused," Sam mumbles, "so confused."

Stella keeps staring at him with a sympathetic, thoughtful gaze, trying to comfort him while stroking his cheeks. Then, her face muscles twist into a sour grimace, as she can't contain her resentment any longer. "I knew it all the time. There was something odd about her. I never trusted her, never. But you, my dear, you were totally under her spell."

# CHAPTER 19

# THE SUMMONING

*The time has come to face our past, change our present, and build a different future.*

As night falls, Shaillah hears the helicopters hovering around the farmhouse barrier once again. Through one of the front windows, she watches the rows of police cars and soldiers that have now set themselves up close to the surrounding fence. She can't contain the derisory smile flashing through her face.

The knowledge that she is entirely unreachable, the fact that she can set the terms of engagement and decide how future events will unfold, makes her feel invincible.

She has taken her time inside the farm, reminiscing on her past life, saying her final goodbyes, and relinquishing her few old possessions, now worthless to her. In fact, it all makes perfect sense now. *At last, all wrongs have finally been righted*, Shaillah says to herself.

As she paces slowly over the backyard's lawn, she stares at the dark horizon. The threatening thick clouds beginning to form in the distance bring her the impending signal she has been waiting for, the go-ahead order from Kuzhma-Or himself.

The blinding lightning bolts fork their way through the towering cumulous clouds, while the crackling booms of the almighty thunder soon transform the blackened landscape into a doomsday setting.

The panicked crowd attempt to flee in all directions, but they find themselves unable to move—as if metal screws were bolting their feet to the ground. Shaillah has them under her total control; they can only move if she allows them to. They cover their heads with their hands and crouch on the ground, praying for a miracle to stop the encircling storm. Even all vehicles still trying to approach the farm have come to a halt, but the howling wind and billowing clouds are relentlessly advancing.

Suddenly, the ground starts rumbling and shaking violently. Its shifting surface ruptures and cracks wide open all around the gathering crowd. As an encircling chain of collapsing sinkholes relentlessly shoves forward, Shaillah allows the petrified people to move again. Everyone flees in panic from the crumbling ground. They jump over the fence or drive through it, until they all end up congregating close to the farmhouse, the newly formed wide moat surrounding them all.

*They must understand our power. There cannot be any doubt about our superior force.* Kuzhma-Or sends his message to her.

The black swirling clouds finally burst into thick torrents of heavy rain as hurricane-force winds form broad menacing tornados, violently rotating all around the farm field. Everyone runs to find a safer place, drenched by the constant deluge, encircled by the relentless wind, and deafened by the incessant cracks of thunder. They cram into or underneath the parked vehicles, but many of them cannot find shelter, ending up in a tight group of mud-covered bodies relentlessly battered by the fierce storm. The collective fear soon turns into a helpless wait for certain imminent death.

Sam and his family have found refuge under one of the police vans. They can see Captain Walker and Professor Khan also hiding under one of the scattered trucks nearby. Sam feels powerless as he watches his mother and sister scream in panic, lying under his father's arms. He drags himself as far out as he can from under the vehicle, and while surveying the chaotic scenes in front of him, he starts to suspect that this mighty terrifying turmoil may not be completely natural. Despite the fierce wind, the drenching rain, the shuddering tremors, and the ear-splitting thunderbolts, it all seems entirely controlled to cause extreme fear but not actual damage to the people.

The ominously growing twisters seem to keep spinning around the farm perimeter. The collapsing sinkholes have stopped at the very edge of where everyone has desperately congregated. Even the pelting rain has turned into a warm pouring stream.

*This is weird—tornados, tremors, sinkholes; yet we seem to be in one piece,* he thinks, trying in vain to move out from underneath the vehicle against the strong wind.

"Erin, Shaillah, will you stop it? Stop this for God's sake," he shouts as loudly as he can.

By now, the ARA's large Navy fleet is approaching the island's west coast. As the surveillance planes fly as close as possible to the Lobarts' farm site, the officers watch in awe at the multiple tornados rotating around the farmhouse, encircling a confined area of torrential rain and strong downdrafts holding everything down to the ground.

The bright flashes of lightning occasionally illuminate the darkened scene, allowing a better view. At least they can report that a large number of people, crowding in a packed gathering, all seem to be still alive.

At times, Sam keeps calling Shaillah's name. But as time passes, his hopes of some respite are fading fast.

"Oh Sam, what's she doing? When will it stop?" Martha cries, fearing the worst is yet to come. She hugs her son tightly while straining her eyes and looking into the distance. She can hardly see through her sore eyes, but suddenly, a light manages to pierce through her swollen eyelids.

"What's that bright light?" She points at the flickering light floating over the farmhouse porch.

Instinctively, Sam crawls forwards from beneath the van, and as he stands up outside, he can hardly believe he has made it out in the open. He looks up and stretches out his arms as if he has won a mighty battle, feeling relieved that the howling wind is not pushing him back any longer and there is no sign of the frightening tornados. Soon his father, mother, and sister crawl out from under the vehicle and stand beside him.

They stroll forward, focusing on the point of light quivering and spreading over the concave invisible barrier. All over the glimmering surface, fast-moving multicolour light waves suddenly appear, intertwining and vibrating in synchrony. As the shifting light patterns keep swirling and throbbing, casting an eerie glow all around, Sam scans his surroundings with an uneasy gaze.

The dazed crowd slowly approaches, walking like hypnotised zombies lost in a foggy night, leaving behind their muddy, parked vehicles. As they keep moving forwards, never taking their eyes off the enticing display, they welcome the radiant warmth bathing their shivering bodies.

Behind them, the collapsed ground and trenches are flooded to the brim, its surface glimmering like a sleek river of flowing mercury as it reflects the fluorescent light show.

As Sam looks towards the farmhouse, a heavy hand lands on his left shoulder. He knows it is Professor Khan before he turns his head to look up. He notices his once white beard, entirely caked in dark soil and his restless pupils, reflecting the wild dancing flashes in front of him.

"What's next, eh?" Khan ponders with a flabbergasted expression.

Before Sam can respond, a pulsating drumming sound rumbles across the site. He turns to watch the striking display in front of him as the growing light streaks, all vibrating at the same rhythm, seem to be creating the distinctive pounding tune.

Even the disembarking soldiers can hear the overpowering sound thumping through the air. It's like a summoning call, a solemn invitation to a pre-announced gathering. They send more helicopters and more combat vehicles to surround the still inaccessible site.

Shaillah's silhouette is barely distinguishable behind the vivid translucent barrier. She looks up and around, counting the number of heavy weapons and spotlights pointing directly at her.

"Don't shoot!" She hears multiple voices from the loudspeakers.

"As if that would make any difference," she smiles triumphantly, walking with her head held high into the open air. Immediately, the light show behind her turns into a barely visible shade of ghostly swirls, making her figure stand out like a brightly burning candle.

Time seems to stand still. Her radiant body appears to have robbed the midnight moon of the limelight as her floodlit silky white hair and silver bodysuit contrast sharply against the hazy background. Her eyes sparkle in the deepest purple glow, commanding undivided attention.

She smiles back at the gathering as if acknowledging their bafflement; then, as the booming sound stops, she opens her arms while looking directly at the sky.

"Suan enjie Rom-Ghenshar!" she exclaims.

Everyone is in a daze as she slowly scans the front row of people until she finds Professor Khan's startled face. "By now, Professor Khan, you must have realised this is not a hoax."

Khan feels a hardened lump in his throat as he tries to answer. He manages to open his mouth, but he can't utter a word as his muscles freeze in absolute shock.

"Very well." She continues as if she had heard an affirmative answer. "Let me introduce myself. My name is Shaillah. And I bring you a message from my ancestors, the Rom-Ghenshars. The time has come to face our past, change our present, and build a different future."

Shaillah intently stares at the crowd as she speaks in a loud, firm voice, pausing from time to time to focus her defiant eyes on the armed soldiers pointing at her.

"The Rom-Ghenshars have returned to their ancient frontiers to make it right this time, as it should have always been, from the beginning—ten thousand years ago.

"And our message to you is this: We come in peace. Let hatred, treason, and war be bygones."

She pauses for a brief moment as everyone is standing still, all eyes on her, in complete awe and astonishment.

"Right! I see you understand very well. So, my friends, we must hold our first meeting. We are sure you will accept our invitation. We want to meet you tomorrow at midday, at the ARA headquarters. We want to tell you more about us and reveal our plans for the future."

Shaillah broadly smiles at the startled crowd. "I see you accept our invitation … perfect!" She concludes before running back into the farmhouse as the barrier's light show changes into a wispy wall of smoke.

No sooner than she reappears, holding her dog close to her chest, all the aerial and ground spotlights converge once again on her as she runs towards Sam.

"Please look after him," Shaillah softly asks while putting Blazer into his hands.

"Don't go," he pleads with her while holding the unusually quiet terrier.

Shaillah slowly backs away, her eyes begging him to forgive and forget her, before turning around and disappearing into the farmhouse.

Everyone is in total disarray as they struggle to understand what has happened, but no one tries to move even an inch forward.

A few minutes later, a radiant parabolic path burns brightly into the night sky as the scouting-craft jets off from the farm's backyard, veering off in the direction of Diablo's cave.

## CHAPTER 20

# THE SPACE WARRIOR

*Anything that takes me closer to you, I will do.*

The scouting-craft darts through the rolling waves like a sharp needle through a silky shawl. Its sensitive antennae rapidly pinpoint the darkened entrance of Diablo's cave before retracting its side wings and jetting in. As it makes its way through the rocky maze in rapidly anticipated twists and turns, Shaillah instinctively ducks and then laughs at herself as she realises she has nothing to fear.

The last time she passed here with Sam, she was so worried she couldn't appreciate the striking cave interior. But now, she has time to explore the intricate rock formations at her will. She can slow down and stop the craft in mid-flight, hovering around her favourite areas. She's completely fascinated by the spectacular basalt columns and jigsaw-like ledges patiently summoned up by nature through millennia.

As the scouting-craft flies through the waterfall's passage, the dark wall where the fast-flowing stream irredeemably plunges comes into full view. The craft gradually slows down and then starts hovering over the swirling torrent.

The transparent cockpit gives Shaillah a clear all-around view of the rugged enclosure. As the craft goes down, she admires the rapid downward currents cascading all around her while the waterfall's mighty roar stirs all her memories. *The end of an old world and the start of a new one begins here, and my whole life goes with it,* she thinks.

She checks the flickering light sensors on the cockpit's automated sequence as the engines faultlessly keep a steady balance on the unstoppable descend. *Seya en Shaillah, yei kejah* (Welcome back, my brave Shaillah). As she hears Rothwen's welcoming words inside her mind, her heart impatiently beats faster.

The scouting-craft touches down in the brightly lit hangar while the ion engines hiss and charge the surrounding air, building up a dense mist of floating water droplets. The top cover slides open, and as she breathes in the moist air, she sees Rothwen waiting for her, his head tilted forward, his scowling stare burning through his frowned eyebrows, exuding a troubled mood.

"Rothwen, Rothwen, Rothwen!" she excitedly calls him as she jumps into the air and flies towards him.

Rothwen's hardened expression briefly softens into a smile as her body clashes against his. He holds her by her waist as she wraps her arms around his neck. Completely ignoring his glaring eyes and clenched jaws, Shaillah covers his face with avid kisses. He clutches her long hair into his hands while rubbing her face against his and letting go of an exasperated groan.

"What's wrong?" she asks him, trying to soothe his temper with an appeasing gaze.

"They obviously have no idea what they're up against—pointing their puny guns at you, trying to catch you. It is pitiful!" he sneers.

"Well, they don't know, do they?"

Rothwen proudly smiles at her and then turns her around, her back against his chest while his powerful arms encircle her shoulders. He kisses her on top of her head while taking out the Quark-Star diamond from inside her bodysuit's collar.

"I followed your every move from here. You were fearless, my brave Shaillah," he whispers. "Your heart beats with the boundless energy of this diamond. Do you know? Kuzhma-Or gave it to Zula while she recovered from her injuries. She would've never given it to you had she not seen something truly extraordinary. I'd go as far as saying that she sees herself in you."

"I feel so honoured. I'll never disappoint her!" she pledges, tilting her head back and intensely gazing at him.

"I do not doubt it," he says, stressing every word.

Shaillah's eyes sparkle, and her face beams with a graceful smile as she feels Rothwen's vibrant energy stirring every pore on her skin.

"I bet it wasn't so difficult—saying goodbye to everything, to your past." he declares, his burning gaze drifting all over her body.

"In the end, it all fell into place—as it was meant to be."

"So much to look forward to, now that you are ready for the final transition to become a space traveller."

"Is that next?" She turns around within his arms to face him, her eyes stuck to his alluring gaze.

The last traces of anger in his face blend with a desperate, smouldering desire. Still, he manages to contain himself, biting his tongue. "The final transition … will—"

Rothwen starts explaining, but his words end up drowning under her lingering kisses, as she tells him with her thoughts. *Rothwen, anything that takes me closer to you, I will do.*

Her passion sends him into a frenzy. He hugs her so tightly that she starts gasping for air, so she forcibly pulls away from him. In a fully apologetic gesture, he opens his arms and raises his hands, giving her a forgive-me look that she promptly accepts with an I-forgive-you smile.

"What about a space warrior? What does it take to become one?" she asks him after getting her breath back.

"You have to lead an army," he boasts with a self-satisfied grin, "and win a war."

"Oh! A war, a war," she says in despair. Her face turns sombre, and she looks away as in deep thought.

Rothwen lifts her chin and makes her look back at him. "Sometimes," he says in a stern tone, his eyebrows snapping together, "sometimes war is the only option."

"I understand your powers," she says while stroking his forehead and cheeks, trying to soften up his tense muscles. "I know about your past battles and victories, but if we can avoid a bloody conflict here, then I must try."

"The invasion has to happen. It's all been decided. Can't change it now," Rothwen firmly states, staring coldly into the distance.

"They will defend themselves if you invade them. They will fight!"

"Of course, I could simply eliminate them first. Problem solved." Rothwen smirks.

"You wouldn't do that, Rothwen, would you? Would you?" She holds his face within her hands, looking at him with a lingering pleading gaze.

"You do care about the humans, don't you?" Rothwen takes her hands off his face, casting a wry glare at her imploring eyes. "It all depends on them, how they react."

"We have shown them our power. I will try to explain even more—"

"They will never understand. This is not going to end well. I foresee war, destruction … again," he seethes.

"No, Rothwen, not war, not again." She pleads with him.

Rothwen folds his arms on his chest, keeping an impassive gaze on her. "Right! You have the answer then."

"I'll never give up, never stop trying," she firmly replies.

"And I'm prepared to let you try. But there will be a limit," he warns.

"You say it as if I have no chance at succeeding."

"You will give it all. I know that. It's not you I'm worried about failing, but them."

"I still have faith in the human race," she counters.

"I hope you're right because nothing"—his eyes glint with a dauntless spark—"can defeat our army!"

"I'd like to see a Rom-Ghenshar army in front of me—"

"Now that you mention it … we don't have to go far."

Shaillah is utterly stunned. She wasn't expecting to see any army right here, right now.

He takes her by the hand, slowly walking out of the hangar and into the vast white-walled workroom she remembers so well. But the scene of devastation in front of her leaves her speechless. The large ebony table is tossed upside down against a corner, every single leg splintered and trashed into dangling twisting shreds, its glossy top lying scattered in smithereens all over the place. All the worktops dangle in pieces, their jagged fragments seemingly held together by some invisible wires.

She looks up at Rothwen, waiting for his explanation, although she already has an idea.

"I got carried away … while the humans were aiming at you," he starkly says, hurrying up his pace while leading Shaillah away from the shard-covered area.

"It's fine. Everything is replaceable, discardable. The robots will fix it soon. Nothing to worry about," he adds in a dismissive tone. But he doesn't tell her how close he came to sending his army into Tinian this very night.

Rothwen stops at the long corridor's entrance and makes Shaillah stand in front of him while asking her, "Are you ready, my brave soldier?"

She excitedly nods. "Soyelani!"

Rothwen takes her hand, and as they are about to enter the steep downhill aisle, Shaillah suddenly stops in amazement. She gasps as she surveys the impressive sleek army of robots glistening against the high arching walls. In a perfectly aligned formation at each side of the path, the rows of android robots stand face to face at attention, their line-up extending right up to the corridor's end. She closely studies the robots' sinuous features, trying to take in every detail of their slimline, seamlessly assembled metallic bodies. The robots look similar to those she saw in the UniverseScope arena, but these are taller, with wider eyes and even longer limbs.

Rothwen leads her down the middle of the aisle, and as they pass by each pair, the robots lift and join their arms above them, forming an arch salute.

"These are soldier robots—not guarding robots," he explains.

"How many are there?" she asks in complete awe.

"How many?" Rothwen wryly grins. And then staring into the stalwart robots' tracking eyes, he boasts, "As many as necessary. They replicate, integrate, or separate, depending on what I set them up to do. And they do not stop until the mission is complete."

Rothwen and Shaillah continue walking down the aisle as Shaillah keeps admiring the robots' faultless alignment. The robots instantly react to Rothwen's scrutinising glare, blinking and straightening up their bodies if he makes the slightest gesture at them.

As they reach the exit chamber, Rothwen sends a command for one of the robots to unlock the ground gate. The soldier robot immediately moves forwards and slides its long arm around the floor, dislodging the tunnel's entry. Then the robot takes Shaillah by her hand and, looking straight into her eyes, bows in deep reverence. Amused, Shaillah looks back at Rothwen. *This last command was not necessary*, she chides him. He responds with a smug smile.

"Suan enjie!" Rothwen cheers while casting a last look at the robots, his voice reverberating across the vaulted walls before they both slide into the scouting-craft waiting inside the tunnel.

## CHAPTER 21

# THE TRANSITION

*I haven't seen that look on your face for thousands of years!*

In the laboratory room's cold atmosphere, Shaillah's body lies carefully wrapped in crisscrossed wide silver bands, resting on a free-floating thin bed, while Rothwen, Athguer, and Zula-Or wait for her to make the first move.

Shaillah listens out for her heartbeat, and she can feel it pounding under her tightened chest. *At least I must still be breathing*, she reassures herself. But no matter how hard she tries, she still cannot open her eyes or move her limbs. To her dismay, it seems that the harder she tries, the weaker she gets.

A rush of anxiety surges through her body as she starts hearing hushed distant voices, progressively getting clearer and louder. *I can hear!* She cheers herself up. *Soon I will be free of these shackles.*

"She has been like that for too long." She hears Rothwen's impatient voice.

"She'll soon wake up," Athguer assures him. "The process will take longer for a replica."

"Athguer is right." Shaillah immediately recognises the voice of Zula-Or.

She tries even harder to open her eyes and speak, but not one part of her body reacts to her command.

"We must remember, the cells go in shutdown mode during molecular transfer. If they start resetting themselves too quickly, we risk losing the subject," Athguer explains in his deep self-confident voice. "Or we could end up with an incomplete transfer, and she'll never be a true space traveller."

"You know I trust you, Athguer. But check it out," Rothwen demands. "I must leave now. Kuzhma-Or is calling me from the central processor."

"Immediately!" Athguer obliges as Rothwen walks away, not even acknowledging him.

As the voices around her recede into vanishing echoes, Shaillah nervously waits for her fate. *I hope Rothwen comes back soon. I feel like I am disappearing into a dark infinite void.* Her last thoughts dwindle into a spiralling nothingness as she feels all her senses ebbing away.

Athguer inspects the molecular-mapping images on the holograms behind Shaillah's bed as Zula-Or attentively watches by his side.

"Only a few areas have not fully transitioned," Athguer explains, pointing at the black circles, "especially the most delicate neurons in her brain, which we know take the longest time."

"Yes, I know Athguer. Even after they're all converted, the conscious mind is the last to adapt as the new brain cells slowly assemble themselves into new pathways," Zula-Or poignantly adds in a reminiscent tone.

"A few more steps and the double transfer process will be complete," Athguer asserts, fully absorbed in his analysis. "Shaillah did go successfully through the first stage, from human to Rom-Ghenshar. There shouldn't be any problems for her whole body to convert to advanced Rom-Ghenshar supercells in this second and final stage."

"Yes, yes, Athguer, we all admire and appreciate your abilities. No need to remind us," Zula-Or grumbles as she walks towards Shaillah's motionless body.

"Rest for now, my dear child. You'll be returning to us soon, Shaillah!" Zula-Or exclaims in anticipation as she leans forwards and wishfully tries to discern any slight move coming from Shaillah's inert body.

"She may be half-awake from time to time during these last stages. She may be able to hear us now, but that does not mean that she can move freely," Athguer explains, standing at the other side of the bed and facing Zula-Or.

The wise lady lifts her head and proudly stares at Athguer, arching her eyebrows and spreading her red lips into a satisfied grin. "It must be a moment of glory for you, Athguer. When she wakes up, we'll have irrefutable proof that this *naenshi,* this double transition process, is successful. Think about what we can do to other civilisations—other worlds."

"I don't need the proof, Zula. I know it works," Athguer replies starkly, crossing his arms over his chest, his deep black pupils gloating in her admiring gaze.

"Very well. I am pleased you are so confident," Zula-Or says while in deep thought. She turns her attention to the symbol-packed images where the black markers keep disappearing, one by one.

"By the way, I haven't erased her human memories or feelings. Her brain can form new neural pathways that we cannot predict. What the final Shaillah will be, only time will tell," Athguer announces.

"That is typical you, Athguer, halfway experiments, halfway results," Zula-Or protests, sneering at Athguer in glaring displeasure. "That will make her more confused, more unsure of herself. She must be relieved of her human spirit."

"One step at a time, Zula, one step at a time." Athguer tilts back his head, looking down on Zula-Or while stressing his words as he starts walking away. "Besides, Rothwen explicitly asked me. And I agreed."

"What are Rothwen's plans? He keeps playing with her mind for his own selfish game. He is playing with her life, her destiny."

Athguer stops and turns around to gaze undauntedly at Zula-Or. "You know Rothwen. He is unpredictable. You know he never tells us what he'll do. All we can do is guess."

"I've never seen him like this. I'll guess that he'll do anything to keep Shaillah by his side, even if it means not finishing our plans."

"Then, my dear Zula, we must start thinking about that possibility … seriously," Athguer warns as he starts walking away.

Zula-Or grudgingly swallows her frustration as she glowers at the back of Athguer until his figure disappears through the arched doorway. But soon, she has to forget her misgivings, as the ruffle coming from Shaillah's tightly wrapped body suddenly attracts her attention.

The tight mesh loosens up and falls away while Shaillah sits up, instinctively opening her eyes and mouth as if emerging from under a deep ocean dive. As she draws in a deep gulp of air, she rapidly blinks to clear her clouded eyes and inspects her surroundings.

She slides out of bed and cautiously stands on the cold polished floor. She is entirely focused on finding the exit from the blueish dimly illuminated room, never noticing that Zula-Or is standing behind her, fully attentive to her actions.

"At last, my dear child, you are returning to us, Shaillah."

Shaillah rejoices at the vaguely familiar honeyed voice welcoming her, even though, as she turns around to face Zula-Or, she struggles to recognise her.

But Shaillah's lost distant expression does not perturb the wise lady in the least. "It has been a long journey, my child. But finally, you've made it."

As Zula-Or congratulates her, Shaillah's memories come rushing through her mind as a sudden unstoppable avalanche. She holds her hands firmly on her temples as her hurting head feels as if spinning out of control.

Zula-Or patiently waits as Shaillah goes through her trance, whispering and reassuring her that the writhing turmoil will soon be over.

Shaillah slowly slides her hands down from her tightly closed eyelids, over her cheeks, and through her neck as she feels her turbulent thoughts gradually settling into a peaceful, soothing stillness.

"That's right, my girl, all your memories are back." Zula-Or cheers.

As Shaillah slowly opens her eyes, Zula-Or's radiant smile calms her even further. She smiles back at Zula-Or, but soon her gaze wanders around the room, looking for Rothwen.

"Oh, I see. Your very first thought is for him."

"Zula, thanks so much for coming to see me," Shaillah mumbles with a nervous smile.

"And how could I not?" Zula-Or opens her arms wide and beckons Shaillah towards her.

"My dear child, you are back. The naenshi has finished successfully." The wise lady holds Shaillah's arms while looking at her proudly. "Some minor adjustments to your cells were necessary to transfer you to our race fully. It was, as I call it, an upgrade."

Shaillah inspects herself, twisting her body around, thinking that, for some reason, she feels lighter than ever before. Thick elastic white-and-blue straps tightly wrap around her skin, and as she inspects her fingers and toes, she notices they sparkle if she rubs them against each other.

"You have advanced immortal supercells now, Shaillah. They can fully regenerate themselves even faster. They can absorb higher energies and withstand any sudden space distortions. A fully fledged space-time traveller, as our great Rom-Ghenshar race."

As Shaillah excitedly smiles back at Zula, the thoughts of how she will use her newly acquired abilities overwhelm her.

"And you can harness your mind beyond your own body. That means you can transmit your mind into a copy of yourself and traverse entangled space-time frames," Zula-Or exultantly adds.

Shaillah admires Zula-Or's radiant, self-confident presence, her gem-studded headpiece and elegant pearl-embroidered tunic. It all gives the lady such an air of distinction.

*Zula looks so majestic. One day, I will be like her*, she thinks, as she keeps looking at Zula-Or in expectant silence.

"Here, put on your favourite gown," Zula-Or says, holding the gold-trimmed silver silk tunic and sliding it through Shaillah's arms.

Then, Zula-Or brings her a tall goblet. As Shaillah thirstily drinks the energising liquid, Zula-Or arranges her hair over her shoulders.

"You look beautiful," Zula-Or praises her while taking the goblet from her hands and looking straight into her gleaming purple pupils.

"I can see it in your eyes. I know what you are going to ask me next, dear Shaillah. Rothwen is coming to see you soon."

Shaillah can't hide her eagerness; an anxious sigh breaks through her lips while she half-closes her eyelids, her cheeks blushing as she looks away from Zula-Or's prying gaze.

"I haven't seen that look on your face for thousands of years!" Zula-Or marvels.

"How come?"

"Dear child, I was also *in love* . . . once," Zula-Or confesses half-heartedly.

"Oh, Zula! How was it? Please tell me," Shaillah enthuses.

"I'm afraid it did not end well," Zula-Or replies sullenly, briefly looking down. "He never loved me—choosing to be with his army in endless space adventures. And I never saw him again. For a while, I cried and desperately longed for his return. For a while, I fooled myself, thinking he'd still be remembering me. But he never returned. That's why I was so relieved when I could rip that feeling out of my ravaged heart, never to suffer again."

Shaillah's vision blurs behind her sudden tears as she hears Zula-Or's recount her story, but the wise lady's stern expression hardly shifts. Her poignant words are more of despite rather than anguish.

"You're treading a fine line, Shaillah—between despair and passion. And he, Rothwen, can be the breeze that dries all your tears or the mighty storm that drowns you in a sweeping flood," Zula-Or cautions.

Shaillah nods as she keeps mulling over Zula-Or's warning.

"But at least, you have the choice now, my dear Shaillah. If you ever want to cut him out of your mind"—Zula-Or glides the edge of her hand over her forehead—"just ask Athguer."

Suddenly, a shaft of white light rushes in through the massive arched door opening up at the back of the room. Shaillah's heart misses a beat when she sees Rothwen leaning on one of his arms against the towering side column while intensely staring at her.

Every sign from Rothwen's body is telling her that he is waiting for her. She runs towards him so quickly that, before she even realises it, she has fallen right into his arms, her nervous tears briefly tainting his black glossy uniform.

"Seya, Shaillah, yei shen Rom-Ghenshar" (Welcome, Shaillah, my Rom-Ghenshar soldier), Rothwen holds her chin, drawing her face close to his, his intense gaze bursting with admiration.

Zula-Or observes them as she slowly steps back. Rothwen and Shaillah have entirely forgotten she is here while they embrace and kiss. There is no doubt in her mind now. Something stronger than any reasoning and stranger than any miracle is happening. But she knows she is powerless to interfere. Before her body copy disappears in a puff of particles, she sends a goodbye message to Shaillah, but she gets no reply.

The lovers bask in their magical moment; all they can think about now is themselves.

"I missed you." She fakes a giddy glare. "I feel dizzy. Please take me back to my smartroom." Then she laughs and starts running away from him through the long corridors.

Rothwen smiles in amusement as he follows her, purposely letting her take the advantage. When she gets to her smartroom door, she waits for him, her back against the door, breathing heavily.

Rothwen's hungry eyes pierce through Shaillah's vulnerable soul as he slams the door with both hands, trapping her between his arms.

"Will you open the door?" he asks her in an inviting tone.

They slump on the floor as the door slowly opens, their lips locked in a desperate breathless kiss. As they rub against each other, the searing heat burns the skin under their garments.

"You're sweating," Rothwen whispers in her ear as he pulls off her tunic and the straps wrapped around her body.

He caresses her wet naked skin with his bare hands, his fingertips drawing glowing lines as they slide up and down in swirls while his eyes follow her soft curves in an ecstatic gaze. Then he pushes her into the deep pool.

She plunges through the swathes of bursting bubbles, relishing in their airy fizzle refreshing her skin, but she can't wait to reach out for the surface. As she swims up, a fast-moving jet of whirling foam thunders past her and then lifts her out of the water. Rothwen is holding her tightly against his muscled chest while smiling at her mischievously. She reprimands him with a sultry look.

"Do you feel dizzy now?" he asks teasingly.

"More than dizzy. I feel … lost …" She sighs, melting her lips into his while opening up his vest and sliding it down his broad shoulders.

They disconnect entirely from the brain network to be with each other, alone, together. As they succumb to their enthralling passion, feeling every cell in their bodies intertwine, their thoughts about future obstacles fade into nothing. Now they know, this final transition was the inevitable step to bring them closer than ever before.

# PART IV

## CHAPTER 22

# THE DAY BEFORE THE FIRST MEETING

*Oh yes, sir, I must be present at this meeting!*

As dawn breaks, the last onlookers have finally started to move away from the farm fields after repeated calls by the police to clear the area. A murmur of protest and confusion spreads throughout the crowd as they gather and cross the surrounding waterlogged moat in the amphibious rescue boats.

An ARA search team, led by Air Marshal John Sanders, has flown in on helicopters and has set up its survey equipment in front of the farmhouse. They have sent in three remote-controlled rescue robots, equipped with high-definition cameras and contamination detection instruments. The robots advance, their tank-like wheels rolling onto every corner, photographing all areas and checking for booby traps, harmful chemicals, or radiation. Their telescopic arms pick up any item, however small, and insert them into the leakproof leaden boxes fitted on their tops.

As one robot reaches Erin's room, its cameras transmit the image of a broad light beam coming from the top of her bed. Sanders instinctively sends the command to halt the robot and to sweep the entire room with its cameras. Like packed collimated torches, a bright multi-shafted light column emanates from a slimline one-metre-high glass pyramid standing on the bed. The brilliant light shafts hit a central point on the ceiling and then spreads from there in concentric waves, shining in all the rainbow colours. The expanding waves spread from the top centre point, down the walls, and over the floor and then crawl back up over themselves, dazzling with their pulsating interference patterns.

Professor Khan carefully inspects the fast-changing light display in his handheld pad. He had been standing outside the farm gates with Sanders, Walker, and Sam, who has sternly refused to go back home with his family, insisting he could be of help.

Sam tries to get his head in front of Khan's, and as he glimpses the images, he yells in excitement, "The bright light column!" Sam points at the collimated shafts of lights.

"Have you seen it before?" Khan asks in a dismissive tone.

"It is not harmful, by the way," Sam quips.

"How do you know?" Walker asks sarcastically.

"I touched it. I went into it—the night she came into my cell."

"Go on," Walker orders Sam with an even deeper cynical tone.

"The night she came into my cell—before the hearing—images came out of thin air from within the light field, above the ground. They looked so real, like live holograms."

"Images of what?"

"Their cities, their world, their planet."

"What about this glass pyramid that seems to be creating the light column?" Khan asks.

Sam thinks hard, trying to remember if he ever saw any pyramid at that time.

"She didn't have anything like that when she showed me the light column." He ponders.

"Oh, this is nuts!" Walker sneers.

"I think … I think it must be another one of her gadgets," Sam suggests.

Finally, as the bright reflections start to subside, Professor Khan can carefully inspect the glistening surface of the mysterious pyramid-shaped object coming into focus in his handheld pad. But he has no idea what it could be made of.

"We need to bring special equipment to retrieve this thing," Khan concludes. "I'll send a request to the ARA Navy for a specially shielded larger container."

"I can go into the farmhouse and take a closer look. I'm sure I'll be all right." Sam eagerly jumps in, realising in the middle of his sentence that he will never be allowed.

"I'm sorry, boy, but we need to follow the security procedures," Khan scolds him, still glued to the images of the pyramid, zooming in and out.

"It could be dangerous … radioactive," Walker warns.

"We've found no traces of radiation or dangerous chemicals," Sanders intercedes, refuting the captain's idea.

"See? Nothing to worry about," Sam insists.

Captain Walker shakes his head, unconvinced, as he watches the line of remote-controlled robots carrying the steel boxes into the back of the shielded truck parked outside the farmhouse. "Yes, you would say that," he grumbles, thinking hard on what to make of the obvious but implausible reality.

The captain's troubled thoughts are interrupted by a wheezing ear-piercing sound as if a giant drill has been suddenly turned on.

They instinctively duck their heads when they see the swiftly gyrating pyramid shooting out of the farmhouse roof. It surges up into the sky, and as it rotates, a dense haze gushes from its edges, forming a swirling trail around its body. As it reaches a high altitude, its sharp nose veers towards the east and then disappears into the distance through an iridescent parabolic path.

"Well, I've never seen anything like it." An astounded Sam breaks the glaring silence as everyone's eyes are stuck on the dissipating trails in the sky.

"It could be going towards LA, towards the ARA headquarters," Khan suggests.

"The ARA?" Sanders ponders.

"Well, she mentioned the ARA meeting tomorrow, remember?" Khan notes.

Khan's words suddenly shake Sam up. The thought of meeting the culprits that had taken Erin makes him shiver in fear. But if that would mean seeing Erin again, he is utterly determined to be at the meeting. "Of course! So, we are clearly in the wrong place here! We must take the first plane to LA—like … right now." Sam demands.

"We? What do you mean *we*? Khan scolds him.

"Oh yes, sir, I must be present at this meeting!" Sam replies in a resolute tone. "I can be of help. I'm very close to Erin. She will listen to me."

"Sam!" Walker intervenes. "You should respect Professor Khan's judgement."

But Sam keeps looking at Khan with an intense pleading gaze, sensing that the professor is on the verge of giving in.

"I'm going to this damned meeting! Who else knows Erin better than me?" Sam impatiently shouts, trying to push his luck.

Sam waits for a barrage of rejections, but Khan's silence tells him he has won this fight.

"Come on, Sanders. Call the airport. Order that flight!" Professor Khan finally relents, looking at Sam with a searing gaze first that ultimately softens up as he can't help but acknowledge Sam's steadfast resolve.

"Oh, what nonsense. That weird object has probably fallen into the sea by now, and this stupid meeting is a complete washout," Walker grumbles, but he is suddenly interrupted by the loud ringing of Sanders's phone.

As Sanders answers, he turns on the loudspeaker and reaches out the handset into the middle of the group.

"Good morning, sir, Sergeant Gawk here from the ARA headquarters. An unidentified flying object has just dashed into the building through the skylight. It is very sleek, pyramid-shaped and glowing all the time. It went through all the doors, ripping them apart, vaporizing the flying debris and avoiding everyone on its path. We have evacuated the building with no casualties. We have located the object."

"Where is it?" Sanders frowns, while Walker looks, with embarrassment, at the group's stunned faces.

"It's standing in the second floor's planning room, sir, on one of the tables at the back … and it's constantly buzzing."

"Okay, Sergeant. Keep everyone away. Build a security ring around the building. We'll be arriving in a few hours," Sanders orders in a quick-firing outburst.

"Yes, sir!"

As the call terminates, they find themselves staring at one another, saying nothing but united in the realisation that there's no point in continuing to deny that something beyond their control is taking over their lives—something unpredictable, incomprehensible, yet very real.

John Sanders hands over the search of the farm and calls the airport. The flight to take him, Professor Khan, and Sam Sheppard to the ARA headquarters will be ready in minutes.

All over the news channels, the numerous headlines cover the stories of Sam and Erin, the farmhouse's terrifying events and mysterious findings. The world is holding its breath in daunted anticipation of what the future may bring, and soon all sorts of conspiracy theories and end-of-the-world predictions abound.

# CHAPTER 23

# THE DAY OF THE FIRST MEETING

*And here we are, asking for your gracious welcome.*

The police-escorted car carrying Sam Sheppard, Professor Khan, and John Sanders, makes its way through the high-security fence's opening gates. They pull over by the row of heavily armed officers guarding the building entrance as Sam eagerly stares at the large, glossy doors, his heart rapidly pounding.

It's 11 a.m. in LA on a breezy September morning, and the serene blue sky portrays a deceptive image of tranquillity. The events of the past two days on Tinian Island are fresh on everyone's mind. They are all feeling nervous but, at the same time, curious.

The ARA live stream channels broadcast the images from its headquarters to the world. Everywhere, there is a heightened sense of anticipation as the composed experienced men, accompanied by the keen youngster, step out from the black vehicle. Flanked by the highly eccentric but revered Professor Khan and the worldwide admired John Sanders, Sam looks like a rooky intruder eager for the limelight.

Before entering the high-rise building, they turn around to wave at the row of closed-circuit cameras focusing on their every move. Their resolute faces reveal an iron determination, like fearless rescuers on the verge of entering an unknown dangerous place from where, perhaps, they would never return. They put on and seal their see-through helmets on their protective suits.

In preparation for the first meeting, the highest security measures are in place. The whole compound and its surroundings had been evacuated in a hundred-metre radius. Heavily armed guards patrol the fortified wire security fence. Rows of wide-field cameras, radar detection systems, and telescopes constantly survey the sky while fighter jet squadrons fly over the area. Inside, closed-circuit cameras, speakers, microphones, air contamination sensors and motion detectors line up all the corridors and rooms, transmitting their signals to the central operations office, their command centre. Located outside the main building but behind the security fences, the buzzing command centre is where the ARA generals from the North and South Regions have gathered to oversee the event. All their systems are now on high alert.

Only the chosen interlocutors will be allowed to enter the main building and walk into the planning room, where the pyramidal object has landed. The order is for everyone to stay at home and close all windows and doors or retreat to their underground shelters. The city is in complete lockdown.

The men cautiously go up the stairs towards the second floor and turn into the broad aisle. As they walk towards the big empty room where ARA rescue teams usually plan their long-term missions, Sanders looks at Sam to his left. It strikes him that, one month ago, he was preparing to rescue Sam from Diablo's cave. Now, the spirited teenager, whom he helped to pluck from the perilous side alley, is decisively walking next to him, as determined as he is to face the unknown unpredictable power of the mysterious visitors.

They stop at the smashed entrance doors, inspecting the iridescent outline of the alien object as it stands upright on top of the long table at the back of the room, glowing in tenuous rays of multicoloured hues.

"We are ready, sir," Sanders announces to the command centre, speaking firmly into his microphone.

"We hear you. Go ahead." General Stewart's stern voice comes through their earphones and the wall speakers.

Holding their breath, they cautiously make their way inside. Standing at a prudent distance in front of the glassy pyramid, Sanders, Sam, and

Khan impatiently wait, transfixed by the colour changing light shafts glowing on them and their surroundings.

They keep glancing at the rows of time zone wall clocks, as the minute hands seem not to be moving fast enough. But soon, the long thin pointers strike midday in LA.

Suddenly, they hear a rumbling buzz ringing in their ears. The persistent sound whizzes around their heads, ebbing high and low until they can start to discern some spoken, albeit unintelligible words. It's not any language they know, although they can distinguish distinct syllables.

"Sheban lai. Sheban lai. Seya" (It is high time. It is high time. Welcome)!

The speaking voice keeps repeating the sentence as a spinning hazy flat disc begins to form off the floor, floating in between them and the pyramid.

Startled, they watch the unravelling images, their tense faces and wide-open eyes fixed on the expanding revolving disc.

Swirls of sparkling bands thicken and brighten inside the rotating structure, eventually coalescing into the shape of a beautiful spiral galaxy while its centre glistens in a golden ball of light. The men are so focused on the captivating display that they do not notice someone else standing at the glowing disc's edge.

"Look to your right!" The alerting voice from the command centre makes them jump.

They all look to the right simultaneously. Even though they can clearly see her, it takes them a few seconds to realise that it is no other than Shaillah standing in front of them.

Immediately, she sends a thought-command, making the floating galaxy tilt and rotate until it stops and zooms in on the Orion spiral arm.

"Welcome, my friends! Let's fly to your local zone through our beautiful galaxy, shall we?" She readily greets them.

The men can't take their eyes off the breathtaking images; swathes of billowing star-forming nebulas, crisscrossed by dark, dusty gas clouds are constantly flying in one after another in front of their eyes. The spectacle is so realistic they have the sensation of actually flying through the Milky Way.

Miraculously, they feel as though they are gliding over the orbits of familiar planets and moons until the frame stops at a close-up of the serene white-blue image of planet Earth.

"Yes, we have come from very far to visit the humans," she adds in a vibrant voice.

"Where … do they … come from?" Khan opens his eyes wide, his voice faltering and breaking up at every word.

Shaillah looks back at the galaxy as its free-floating image slants backwards, revealing the bulge below the galactic plane. It keeps zooming in until a glistening double star system appears as its centre.

"The Rom-Ghenshar system, in the direction of the Eridani constellation from your location—seventy thousand light-years away, below the galactic plane, on the other side." She amplifies the image even further, revealing the majestic binary system of an immense yellow star and its smaller red companion, bound in an oblique orbital path. The extended line-up of multi-sized planets poised around the glowing double stars soon appears in the unfolding view. Zooming in further, the image veers off and focuses on a colourful globe, accompanied by four golden-red moons locked into a close embrace through a thin, dusty ring.

"And this is our mother planet!" she proudly announces.

"May I remind you, Erin Lobart, you were born here on this planet. How can you claim you're one of them?" A rattled Professor Khan erupts in a challenging tone, as if he has regained his confidence.

"Ha! Correction, Professor Khan. My name is Shaillah. I may have been born here, but my genes and my cells are not human anymore—"

"Not again, Erin! Tell us the truth. He kidnapped you against your will," Sam yells as he runs towards her.

Shaillah does not make the slightest move to avoid him. Instead, she waks towards him. And Sam finds himself running through a puff of sparkling particles that reform themselves back into her image behind him.

The men's gasps blend in with the clatter from the room's speakers as everyone watching cries out in utter confusion and amazement.

"She's only an image, a hologram!" a stunned Sanders shouts.

"Right. At the moment, I am, but I can get even stronger, unreachable and impassable," Shaillah replies while Sam runs back to the side of John Sanders, straining his eyes while staring at her in disbelief.

"What do you want from us?" Khan says in a tone of utter resignation.

"Collaboration, understanding, trust. That's not much to ask," she responds, slowly pacing in front of the startled men.

Shaillah shows more details of the majestic multicoloured planet. In front of them, there is a crimson watery world peppered with long rocky islands beneath pearly and gold city skylines, each island surrounded by a thick green canopy.

"We call our mother planet Rom-Enjie, the largest of the watery worlds in the Rom-Ghenshar system. This is our ancestral home. More than ten thousand years ago, our ancestors travelled to planet Earth from Rom-Enjie. They came, they stayed, but it ended in tragedy. It was a shame that they had to leave in a hurry, but that is another long story. The important thing is that we have now returned, with a new plan, a new beginning. And here we are, asking for your gracious welcome, but above all … your understanding."

"Erin or Shaillah," Professor Khan starts, hesitantly, "tell the Rom … uh—"

"The Rom-Ghenshars, sir."

"That we're ready to collaborate … but we need to know their plans first and foremost!"

"And where are they?" Sam daringly asks in a sarcastic tone while looking around him.

Shaillah arches her eyebrows, warmly smiling at Sam. "Our Supreme Commander Kuzhma-Or says he feels privileged to visit the humans but apologises for his absence today. He has urgent matters to attend in another star system. And I'm bringing you his message."

Shaillah pauses and looks at each man in the eye one by one. Then she broadly smiles, trying to reassure them. "We can help you recover the planet, restore the weather, rebuild everything, and restock food supplies. Our Supreme Commander Kuzhma-Or says that he appreciates the human race. You work together to achieve your goals. That is how intelligent beings can prosper—through widespread, increasing collaboration. That is why the Rom-Ghenshars have come back, hoping that we can work together for the full benefit of our beautiful galaxy."

As she finishes speaking, she walks towards Sanders, Sam, and Khan, stopping a few steps from them while focusing on their blank startled faces, as if measuring their degree of fear. They stare at her with trepidation, waiting for her next move. Only the constant hum emanating from the luminous pyramid breaks the tense silence.

"Anything you say now, Kuzhma-Or will hear. You can speak to him through me. What do you have to say?" Shaillah says in an uplifting tone, encouraging the men to talk.

"Well, welcome, Mr Kuzhma-Or. Thank you for the offer to help. We look forward to meeting you soon," Professor Khan replies in a resigned tone.

"Our Supreme Commander Kuzhma-Or says that he is grateful for your welcome. His guardians will soon come up on shore, and the humans should not feel threatened or frightened. Everyone must follow the robots' instructions. We will rebuild this planet. We mean no harm." She opens her arms and slightly bows her head. "It will be the start of a new era for us all!"

"It's rather difficult to trust strangers, especially when they have not come here in person, and he is not talking to us directly," a cautious John Sanders objects.

"Our Supreme Commander Kuzhma-Or apologises again for not attending the meeting today, but he is sure that it will happen in a not-too-distant future," Shaillah affirms.

"Why did you not come here in person either?" Sam says in suspicion. "Are you leading us into a trap?"

"If I wanted that, I'd have done it already, Sam. This visit is a brief introduction. Soon, you'll be hearing and seeing more from us."

She looks back at the cameras in a stern focused gaze before continuing. "And this is a special message for the ARA generals, General Stewart and General Ming. I know you are listening attentively from your command centre. When you walk out of here today, you can be sure to remove all the security, armed forces, and police units. No Rom-Ghenshar will attempt to harm a human. That's not in our plans. In exchange, we ask for your cooperation.

"Be sure of this. Any resistance will be futile. We, Rom-Ghenshars, can listen and control every one of your thoughts. We can watch any point on this planet at any time. We have invisible impenetrable shields fully protecting us. You can never reach us. You will see us if we let you see us.

We are now waiting at the bottom of the ocean—with a limitless army of robots standing by. We could paralyse you, instantly or, even worse, destroy you—if you try to attack us."

"Did you get that, General?" Sanders mutters into his microphone.

"Stand firm, Sanders. Keep your bearing." Sanders hears General Stewart's through his earpiece, but the general's tense voice makes him feel even more uneasy.

"A limitless army of robots. What do you mean?" Professor Khan asks while looking at Shaillah in disconcert as she turns to face him.

"Professor, look!" Sam interrupts and points towards the wall-high windows at the back of the room.

Sanders, Sam, and Khan rush towards the windows, leaning against the glass panes, their jaws dropping, as they can hardly digest the spectacle developing in front of them.

As far as they can see, thousands of identical android robots are rising from the sea, marching on the sandy beach and heading towards the city. The androids' sleek bodies glow in shiny, metallic skin, their shoulders adorned with silver and golden badges. They walk in a tight formation, their flaming row of forward-facing eyes focused ahead, on their relentless advance.

"Who the heck are they?" a stunned Sam shouts, turning his head towards Shaillah.

"They're Rom-Ghenshar guardian robots, and they mean no harm. They are starting the reconstructions," Shaillah responds impassively, walking towards the startled men.

"Reconstruction?" Sanders frowns.

"Yes, we are reconstructing. Building the new cities of the new world … and there is nothing that you can do about it—nothing!" Shaillah warns.

Bewildered, they slowly turn their heads to look through the glass windows, following the swarms of robots taking over the beaches and every path leading to the main streets. The ARA personnel run away in all directions trying to hide in any city buildings they can get into, sometimes stumbling against a robot, who ignores them as if they were not even there.

"Don't shoot. Don't shoot at the robots!" Sanders shouts on his microphone as he watches in dismay at some police units aiming their weapons and firing at the unstoppable invaders. But all the ammunition instantly stops against their shiny bodies and falls to the ground.

The robots' relentless advance and the guards' inability to stop them are all plain to see. Eventually, everyone realises that they have no other alternative but to retreat—to run and hide as quickly as possible while the invading army occupies each and every street.

"Professor Khan, we must get together with the rest of the ARA command. There's nothing we can do here," Sanders suggests, peering at Shaillah through the corner of his eye.

"That is … if they let us go," Khan sneers, glaring back at Shaillah.

"Of course!" Shaillah says while pointing at the way out.

Sam runs towards her in an impulsive move, but he stops dead before reaching her. He has remembered she is nothing more than a hologram.

"Erin, what have you done? Can you stop this invasion?" he pleads with her.

"Sam, there's nothing I can do. It's all been decided a long time ago," she impassively says.

"What will happen next?" Sam's worried expression deepens as he stares questioningly at her.

"Everything will be all right. We are only reconstructing. Making this planet a better place. And by the way, you can take off your protective gear. It's perfectly safe for you here." Shaillah explains in a reassuring tone, raising her voice to make sure everyone can hear her.

"What will happen to your parents? They're still in a coma," Sam poignantly says, as if letting her know that he would not feel safe in her presence.

"I'm so sorry," she replies, looking away and avoiding Sam's reproving stare.

"You and your *new* friends have caused enough destruction, Erin—"

"It's time to go," she announces as she brusquely walks away from him.

She stops dead in front of the revolving galaxy and turns around, looking at them with her strongest warning glare yet. "Remember, don't attack the robots. You must follow their orders!" Shaillah restates.

Immediately, she and all the floating images disappear in a puff of bright sparkles in front of their stunned faces. Only the glass pyramid remains, faintly glowing while hauntingly standing on the planning table.

Sanders, Sam, and Khan dash out of the room, running as quickly as they can through the nearest fire exit.

"We are all okay. Everybody, please stay inside. Don't attack the robots." Sanders keeps saying into his microphone.

As they run out of the building, they see some security guards still trying to stop the army of robots from making their way into the city. But the robots push through the steel barriers as if the fences were made out of paper, throwing away the guards' protective gear like hollow plastic junk. The unrelenting robots walk through the blocking army tanks, overturning them like small toys and sweeping away the heavily armed men like rag dolls.

There is no doubt by now; the invasion of Rom-Ghenshar robots is unstoppable.

## CHAPTER 24

# THE DAY AFTER THE FIRST MEETING

*These are untested times. These aliens might be our friends, or they might be our terminators.*

Professor Khan is pacing in front of the stack of monitors covering the side walls of the ARA's central operations room. North Region General Ed Stewart and South Region General Xiao Ming are standing in front of him, listening attentively to his latest report.

"This is what we know so far." Khan pauses, looking sternly at the ARA generals while trying to control his profound concern. He points at one of the screens behind him, showing the glossy pyramid standing at the back of the planning room, its softly glowing emissions still pulsating at a steady rate. "Any attempt to reach this object has failed. We cannot get closer than one metre from it. We don't even know what type of energy is powering it. But we strongly suspect it is of electromagnetic origin."

"In other words, we are none the wiser, while these robots are invading our cities!" General Stewart's impatient voice crackles as his face contorts in boiling anger and sheer dissatisfaction.

"Sir, you have to understand, these aliens have technology far superior to ours, beyond what we can understand. You read Sam Sheppard's debriefing report … and you heard what she said to us yesterday." Khan's assuaging tone does nothing to appease the generals as they all helplessly watch the images coming into the monitors.

As far as their cameras can reach, they show the swarms of unstoppable robots roaming around every deserted street and desolated park. The paralysed cities seem to have been abandoned in a flash; there is no sign of life anywhere. Cars are left stranded with doors wide open in the middle of the roads, mugs are tilted on café tables, all kinds of mangled rubble are scattered everywhere. Myriads of deserted objects roll aimlessly, pushed by the reeling wind.

"Any attempt to stop or at least divert these robots has failed," General Ming adds glumly in a defeatist tone. "As you all know by now, we cannot even reach them."

General Stewart's cheeks swell and blush as he holds his breath to contain his rattled nerves. He presses his thin lips as he puffs out air noisily through his nose. The sturdy general, dressed in his usual military fatigues, looks impatiently at Professor Khan with a scolding gaze.

"How have they passed through our NEO" (Near Earth Objects) "satellite network undetected? How can they raid our cities in a matter of minutes? How can they—"

"Undetected is their modus operandi. As for the raids, you can see the unrelenting robots are their chosen strategy ... so far," Professor Khan interrupts impassively.

"We must be able to disrupt their shields. We have to try," a furious General Stewart yells, his deep-set, fiery eyes following the unsettling fast-changing scenes on the wall-mounted displays. He looks around the room, full of desks and wide monitors, where the ARA team leaders are busy tracking every new event along the coast.

"Generals, we have something here!" The excited voice of John Sanders makes everyone stop what they're doing and gather around his desk.

They all watch in amazement as the computer screens fill with the lines of robots, appearing from a long winding trench that seemed to have cracked open at the bottom of the ocean, forty-five kilometres west from Long Beach.

"Wait a minute. So that's where they all come from," General Stewart seethes, rubbing his chin and narrowing his eyes before shouting in a vengeful tone. "We've got them! We've got them!"

General Stewart feels triumphant. Discovering the robots' exit point has given him renewed confidence that they may be vulnerable after all. He brashly continues. "So, hiding in the deep, eh? So much for their invisible shields. We are promptly sending our most powerful war submarines to this place. There is no time to waste!"

General Ming is nodding firmly, joining in Stewart's resolve and growing confidence.

But Khan is shaking his head; his hesitant reaction frustrates the generals. A raging gaze from General Stewart prompts him to explain his thoughts.

"These are untested times," Khan cautions. "These aliens might be our friends, or they might be our terminators. We must tread carefully. We must keep our dialogue with their leader—"

"I believe that talking to them will be of no help whatsoever. We must act while we have time," General Stewart interrupts sharply, looking dismissively at Khan as the ARA teams erupt in his support.

Everyone in the ARA commanding room stands up and cheers, mobilised by the general's resolute stance.

"Yeah! Let's destroy them," they shout out in explosive fervour. "Let's destroy them!"

Professor Khan frowns his thick eyebrows, his forehead wrinkling in disapproval, but he realises there is no point in contradicting the general any further.

General Stewart stares in annoyance at the door as he hears a loud knock. "Come in!" he shouts.

A grim-looking dishevelled Captain Walker appears at the room entrance, accompanied by a startled tired-looking Sam. They hesitantly stop, observing the commotion in the room.

"Silence, silence. Let's hear it from Captain Walker," General Stewart orders, reckoning that the captain has come with grave news.

"On my way here, I heard about what's happening on our d-dear island," Walker stammers. Then his face muscles contract in a grimace. "It's being destroyed. The robots have completely torn down the tuna farm … there is nothing left there."

"The tuna farm?" John Sanders jolts in disbelief.

"Yes, unfortunately, yes." Walker bows his head, raising his arms in a helpless gesture.

"How's everyone?" Sanders asks in utter shock. He fumbles with his phone while trying to contact Tinian's port authorities. But he gets no response.

"The robots are pushing our people to move underground. Many families in Tinian have made it into our cave systems. We need to make sure they get the help they need."

Sam nods nervously. "Yes, my family has gone into Diablo's cave … let's hope everybody has made it okay."

"Let's not get too emotional or defeatist," General Stewart interrupts, pacing up and down the room. "Now, we have to keep our focus and our resolve, for our ultimate goal is to succeed!"

The Generals grab their fists and hold their arms up into the air as they shout their slogans.

"We will prevail. We will succeed."

"How are we are going to stop the robots, General Stewart?" A doubtful Walker dares to interrupt the impromptu victory clamour.

A sudden, expectant silence sets in as everyone in the room waits for the General's response.

"We can surround them in their boltholes—stop the robots before more of them can get out and deploy their shields, then we sweep them back into their trenches … or wherever they come from."

"With respect, General Stewart," Khan intercedes, "we don't know how their shields work, but we do know that nothing, not even any of our laser-guided weapons, can get close to any of the robots."

"Well, what else do we know about them? There must be something we can do before they finish with the entire planet as they've done with Tinian," Stewart blurts out.

No one dares to speak a word. In their troubled, confused minds, the sheer recognition of an unfathomable menace beyond anything they have ever encountered finally begins to sink in.

"We should observe them for a while longer—without provoking them. We should be able to find their weak point." General Ming tentatively proposes.

"Yeah," General Stewart hesitantly replies, pressing his lips and closing his eyes as in deep thought. "We can certainly do that."

"Our main tasks now should be to get food and supplies for all our people in their shelters." General Ming continues talking in a more confident tone, encouraged by General Stewart's somewhat reluctant support.

"We should keep the lockdown in place in all the areas. Allow the rescue teams to walk through the cities to reach those in need. We have to keep the global help services going. We must keep open the main supplies of electricity, water, gas—"

"Agreed!" General Stewart states, this time sounding more convinced. "General Ming, we will need you to direct the central surveillance network. Professor Khan and his team will keep a close eye on those robots. We must be able to figure out how to disable their shields."

"Agreed!" General Ming affirms. *At least we have a plan we can execute*, he thinks.

General Stewart walks towards Sanders' desk and checks on the recent images from the ARA's suboceanic cameras. The long fractured trench looks eerily quiet, its dark crevices showing no sign of the robots.

"I'll instruct our fleet of submarines to set off towards our target at maximum speed," Stewart boasts. "Once we take up the robots' exit point, we'll hit them with everything we have—all at once. We won't let them come out of their holes. Shock and destroy!"

"May I remind you, General, they have 'all-seeing, all-hearing' powers. Right now, they may be laughing at us while we plan our helpless attack." Professor Khan tries one more time to discourage him. But his comments have the opposite effect, making the general even more reckless.

"Do you think I'm going to believe every word the aliens say?" Stewart snaps.

The exasperated general promptly orders all the ARA's submarines to assemble in full attacking mode at the newly discovered target.

All the while, it is impossible for him or anyone in the room to detect the sensory-sphere hovering under the ceiling, cloaked in its invisible shield, and transmitting everything to the Rom-Ghenshars' central processor.

"The sooner we stop these robots, the sooner we can free our cities before the whole planet gets destroyed. I'll be the first to order the attack," Stewart staunchly declares, moving towards the command panels and reviewing all the instruments' readings. He places his hand on a bulky red button and stops short of pushing it, sliding his fingers over it instead. Then, looking directly at John Sanders, he orders him, "Air Marshal Sanders, you need to go back to Tinian with Captain Walker, check on your people, then join the ARA Navy for the follow-up attack once we've destroyed their exit point. General Ming and I will closely supervise the operations from here."

"What about me?" The hesitant voice of Sam annoys General Stewart. He is not used to being reminded that he has forgotten about something.

"Oh yes," General Stewart says, looking at Sam dismissively. "We shouldn't forget we have someone here that may help us—"

"I'm sure I can help! Erin was one of us once; she can still be one of us!" Sam firmly replies, ignoring the general's scorn.

"Very well. You can stay. We need to keep all our options open, just in case," General Stewart concludes, walking away without acknowledging Sam's enthusiasm.

The generals gather around the tracking screens as they check every submarine leaving their bases. Unchallenged, the submarines' long metallic bodies pierce through the dense, deep waters, assembling into an ever-growing formation while approaching their target from all directions on their inexorable advance.

# CHAPTER 25

# THE CENTRAL PROCESSOR

*Now I'm sending my duplicate to the ARA headquarters.*

Rothwen takes Shaillah towards the back of the UniverseScope viewing platform, through the dimly lit corridor, leading them to the central processor, the very heart of their entire array of high-powered machinery.

They walk up to the dense grey mist of the antechamber, its bubbling surface dazzling with the steady pulses of rainbowlike light streaks, constantly merging into one another and then breaking up, scrambling into a radiant multicoloured framework.

*The antechamber … never ceases to amaze me!* Shaillah thinks as they enter the hazy fog, their bodies distorting the iridescent wispy lines as they advance. Then they begin gently falling through the ever-thinning cloud.

As they land in front of the crystalline medium of the inner chamber, she gasps in admiration. "Ah! It is so orderly—so perfect!" She contemplates the infinite lattice of kaleidoscopic trails of virtual particles, perfectly aligned in a three-dimensional matrix and vibrating through the all-pervading plasma condensate.

The sprawling inner chamber medium surrounds and insulates the antimatter core and its widespread web of interconnected filaments, powering the entire Rom-Ghenshar compound. The swarming matrix of entangled virtual particles processes all the data and executes all quantum calculations for their UniverseScope platform, brain network, and laboratory units.

"I wanted to show you something." Rothwen's pressing voice breaks up her contemplation as the rotating sphere of planet Earth appears right by her side. The bulky globe expands until matching her height, its surface teeming in a web of flashing orange dots.

"The orange markers are invasion zones—happening now," Rothwen points out.

"First, I want to see my home town. What is happening there?"

"We have started rebuilding the island and others around it. We have kept the humans from leaving their safe shelters," Rothwen starts explaining in a reassuring tone.

"Is everybody okay?" Her eyes dart from place to place as the barren landscape starts to unfold before her.

"Here, zoom in by yourself. Focus your thoughts on your island," Rothwen tells her while the globe rotates and tilts onto her chosen coordinates.

Astonished, she stares at the different sites appearing on the expanding island view. One by one, she dismays at the desolate images as they come into focus in increasing detail. Even the sturdy steel bridge from the tuna farm has disappeared, and there is no sign of the high steel control tower either. And to her utter shock, she finds a pile of rubbish where her family farmhouse used to stand.

*It is all in the past, and I should feel nothing for it,* she thinks, trying in vain to disregard her distress. But she can't help reaching out and touching the glimmering surface, even if her fiddling fingers only get to distort the harsh landscape.

"We're rebuilding the island and the whole archipelago, Shaillah. It'll be one of our main land bases on this planet," Rothwen explains, trying to take Shaillah out of her sombre mood.

But she keeps watching the grim scenes in silence as she struggles with her mixed confounded feelings. All the while, as she sees the islanders hiding in the relative safety of their shelters, she can't stop thinking about how she can help them.

Even though she knew about the invasion, the reconstruction, even if she thought she was ready to withstand the upheaval, she finds herself feeling this immense distress that she can't shake off.

"Now, we have much to do. The humans are still trying to fight a losing battle," Rothwen warns, attempting to get her attention. "They have sent these little toys they call submarines to one of our undersea exits, planning to stop our robots. My patience has a limit. But I'm prepared to consider avoiding a catastrophe."

"What are they planning?" Shaillah finally responds as if she has suddenly started to listen to him.

"Let me show you."

He shifts the image towards LA, showing the bottom of the ocean by the Pacific West Coast; the striking display of a large fleet of submarines comes into sharp focus. She surveys the submarine's slim metallic bodies waiting in ambush along the serpentine trench, the blue and red colours of the ARA's starry flag gleaming through the translucent waters.

"It is not a staged illusion. It's real—happening now." Rothwen speaks over her shoulders, "I let them see one of the trenches from where we deploy our robots, and the first thing they do is to prepare an attack.

"They are waiting for something to show up to fire their weapons," Rothwen continues in a derisive tone. "Unfortunately for them, it's the turn of our soldier robots to come out. If the humans were to fire their weapons, they would annihilate their entire fleet, as their useless arsenal would recoil off the robots' lethal bouncing shields.

"But that would be the least of the damage. The sudden release of energy from our shields will provoke a colossal explosion, ripping off through the mantle; melting the rocks; and causing major tsunamis, earthquakes, and volcanic eruptions. The disturbed shield's outer layers will continue expanding and contracting, causing more explosions and thick clouds of vaporized material and debris that will rise from under the water and into the atmosphere."

Shaillah looks up at Rothwen, speechless, her distress showing she fully understands the consequences of his dire warning but also that, deep inside, she feels the urge to do something about it. She nods her head in a reflective mood for a second. Then she asks him, "We can stop them, Rothwen. We can control and change their minds."

"And when do we stop? Shall we continue changing their minds until we finish the reconstruction?" Rothwen replies dismissively. "Frankly, it doesn't matter to me what they do. Besides, if they decide to attack, it will be far easier for us. And they will have learned their lesson. Or shall I obliterate their minds right now so they can't even reason?"

Shaillah's utter frustration rattles her mind, but she manages to stay calm and composed. "There is no need for any more destruction!" she says in an unyielding tone. "We will prevail in the end, we know that. But let me go and convince them to stop. I'm sure they'll want to hear what I have to say."

Rothwen's stern expression eases. He is so impressed by Shaillah's impulse that he even lets an approving look flash through his face. "That's precisely what I thought you would say. You don't give up, do you?"

"I am sure I'll convince them," she replies firmly.

"Well, let's do this. If you can convince the humans to retreat by talking to them, not by manipulating their weak brains, I will show mercy. Can we get the humans to listen and cooperate? Let's see."

"Show me the ARA headquarters," she prompts him as she inspects the underwater scenes in more detail.

"Here it is. We constantly monitor it," Rothwen says as the ARA's central operations room in LA immediately comes into view.

Her heartbeat momentarily jolts as she recognises Sam talking to General Stewart, pleading with him.

"Your friend Sam is obviously worried, quite rightly," Rothwen notes.

"I'll take one of our scouting-crafts and fly to talk to the ARA generals," she declares.

"You won't get there in time that way. Our soldier robots are programmed to step out very soon, in fact, T-300" (seconds).

"Can't you stop the robots?" she pleads with him.

"I could … but I'd only consider it if they withdraw first." Rothwen smirks.

"I'll go there with my body copy. No need for time-consuming travel," Shaillah replies, undaunted.

"I thought you would say that. And that's why I brought you here."

She closes her eyes and takes a deep breath as she turns around, pressing her back against the fuzzy edge of the inner chamber's until her body merges into the medium. In her mind, she goes through the chain of commands to activate a swift discharge of entangled virtual particles. Like a rising wind, the particles revolve around her body in increasing numbers until they completely cover her.

Soon, she feels as if her entire skin is slowly detaching and flowing away, and a mirror image of herself emerges a short distance in front of her. Through the hazy cloud encircling her, she examines her body copy as it replicates every move she makes.

Shaillah closes her eyes as she focuses her mind inward, on her deepest thoughts and fleeting sensations. At first, it's all a confusing mangled ball of chaotic signals. But soon, every thought and feeling separate into two distinct compositions, two independent realities of herself. She thinks of it as if two distinct bodies are waiting for her command.

When she reopens her eyes, Rothwen is smiling at her in anticipation.

*Now, I'm sending my duplicate to the ARA headquarters,* Shaillah thinks while watching her body copy vanishing in a flash and re-emerging at her chosen destination.

As she focuses her mind on a particular version of herself at will, she either hears the voices of the ARA generals arguing in their headquarters or feels the presence of Rothwen standing by her side. Soon, she can sense and react to both realities simultaneously with each side of her brain.

She revels in her ability to control her body in such a way, thinking in two distinct thought-spaces and having the power of precise distant control. It's as if she's playing a virtual reality game but with the difference that every move is very real.

## CHAPTER 26

# THE FATAL DECISION

*The last thing they will burn is my dignity.*

At the ARA's central operation room, the generals and high command officers double-check the readiness of their action plan. At the same time, they watch in horror as the robots demolish everything in their paths. Professor Khan and his team sit around Sam at the opposite table, reviewing and analysing every detail of what they know about the aliens' abilities. Yet the more questions they ask, the less they understand.

"Stop everything. Stop!" Shaillah's voice resonates across the room, drawing everyone's attention as she suddenly appears in front of them.

"Erin!" Sam shouts, startled.

But Shaillah seems not to be listening to him. She stares at the generals and starts shouting even louder. "Stop everything now or there'll be a catastrophe!"

General Stewart manages to overcome his bewilderment and walks towards Shaillah while dismissively staring at her.

"What do you mean, stop everything?" he fumes.

Shaillah defiantly holds General Stewart's belligerent gaze. "You must not fire at the robots … they are lethal soldier robots! You must not give that order," she insists, her tone more pleading than demanding.

"Our people are suffering. These relentless robots are invading our cities. Reports of even more invasions are coming fast from this continent and across the Atlantic. We must act!" General Ming stands up, his face twisted in a deep frown.

"There is no time to discuss now. Stop the order and let's talk later." Shaillah runs towards General Ming, shouting at the top of her throat, "Stop everything now!"

But she finds everyone's faces blankly looking at her, utterly unmoved by her pleas.

"You saw how we can disrupt the weather in an instant. You saw our unstoppable robots. You saw our powerful energy fields and impassable shields. You do not want to see what will happen next … if your missiles hit the robots' bouncing shields—"

"We've made the decision. *We're not* going to stand by, idly watching while our cities are destroyed. We will fight!" As she hears General Stewart's stern voice, she knows, this time, she has failed.

At first, no one moves, trying to figure out the source of the deafening noises and deep rumble shaking the entire room. But as the increasing tremors coming from below turn frighteningly violent, everyone starts running for his or her lives out of the crumbling walls.

As the whole building begins to collapse and the lights flicker rapidly before going out altogether, in the chaos, Sam finds himself pushed towards the exit. The masonry crumbles and falls and the thick choking dust cloud swiftly revolves around him, but neither touches him.

While his body is being thrust forward, he closes his eyes and presses his hands tightly against his ears. Surrounded by darkness and thundering noises, he is so confused and disorientated that he abandons himself to whatever is taking him. He lets his body go as he is relentlessly shoved and thrown outside the crumbling building, wondering how he's managing to stay upright over the shaking ground.

Suddenly an intense glow compels him to open his eyes. To his horror, he watches a giant mushroom cloud rapidly growing on the horizon, while a torrential downpour of thick mud buries the piles of mangled rubble scattered all over the desolate streets.

As the dusty air clogs up his throat and the pungent burning stench stuffs his airways, he tries to bury his face among his elbows. Even though Sam is firmly pressing his hands on his ears, he can still hear the loud noises of crumbling concrete, glass, and metal—as loud as the thunder and lightning across the darkened sky.

Amid the total devastation, he looks around in despair, wondering if he is the only one left on planet Earth. He checks his body for any sign of blood or injury and finds none. By now, he is sure that Erin has protected him and kept him alive.

"Erin, Shaillah, Erin!" He desperately shouts her name, even though he can hardly hear himself.

There's no answer to his screams, but he is sure she must be close to him as he watches the hurtling rubble flying past his body, never touching him, as if he was inside a protective shelter, saving him from any harm.

Encouraged by this seemingly unbreakable armour, he tentatively makes a few steps forwards. *At least I'm still alive*, he thinks. *And if I'm still alive, there is hope.*

But his relief is short-lived, as his skin feels sore under the intense heat and his eyes water in the dense smoke. Blazing flames suddenly burst out of the mangled ruins, devouring what little is left. He watches in awe as the ferocious fire spreads and multiplies out of control, twisting and swaying in a wild chaotic dance, merging into a massive, unstoppable fireball and heading towards him from all directions.

Sam knows he cannot run anywhere, so he spares his last precious minutes to think about his family; his beloved island; and his dear Erin, who was cruelly taken away from him. *She was never the enemy; they transformed her, changed her—those aliens, those evil beings.*

Nervously blinking and covering his cheeks with his sore reddened hands, he decides to confront the inferno with all the bravery he can grasp. "The last thing they will burn is my dignity," he whispers to himself, his body shaking as the searing heat and smoke start to suffocate him.

He watches the lapping flames as they get brighter and brighter, spluttering while conjuring weird, vibrant colours he has never seen before. They will soon turn him into ashes, yet he thinks it all looks beautiful.

He feels dazed and disorientated, starting to cough violently while desperately gasping for air. He thinks he is hallucinating when he spots a bright metallic object appearing in front of the firewall and flying towards him. He falls flat onto the ground as a cloud of dust and ashes completely buries him. But before it can settle, the fast-moving object briefly lands next to him, and he is pulled inside. The furtive aircraft jets off vertically into the sky, seconds before the devastating flames consume the whole area, soon followed by an all-engulfing tsunami flood.

All that is left of the ARA's compound is scattered heaps of concrete and steel. Only the glistening pyramidal object is rising intact from the scattered debris. It bathes the devastated surroundings with a brightening fulgour as if some revival energy is resurging from the ruins, ready to stop the fast-spreading disaster. But the pyramid soon jets off towards the Pacific Ocean, disappearing into the smothering sky.

Sam opens his sore eyes; they're still hurting from the smoke and soot, but he can make out Shaillah's welcoming smile as she softly wipes away the dark slime and muck covering his face.

"Where are we, Erin?" he asks, looking around and trying to focus his stinging eyes.

"We're safe. I rescued you from the entrance of the ARA headquarters." She comforts him.

"The ARA headquarters. Let's go back there—to LA. We must rescue Professor Khan and the others."

The sombre look on Shaillah's face makes Sam shudder. As she gazes downheartedly at him, he fears what she is about to say.

"Sam," she says in a shaky voice, "LA isn't there. The city is gone. Everybody is gone."

He stands up and stumbles and then tries to run away from her, ending up crashing against a solid glass wall. He tries to hit it with his hands, but then he spots a billowing dark cloud expanding down below, reminding him from where he has escaped. The engulfing black clouds are packed with floating debris, soot, and dust, throwing a dark blanket over everything.

He turns around, looking desperately at Shaillah, pleading for answers. He moves his mouth in an attempt to speak, but his muscles are stiffened, his mind blocked.

Shaillah walks towards him, looking at him sympathetically as if trying to calm him down.

He reaches out to her with his trembling hands and tries to touch her face, but his hands soon grind to a halt.

"At least you are not that spooky hologram now," he remarks. "You are actually here—although I can't touch you."

"Yes, I had to come to get you out." Shaillah tries to sound positive, but her gloomy voice can't disguise her sadness. "I saved you from the disaster the humans have created. I tried to stop it, but all my attempts failed. I protected you by creating a shield around you from our pyramid station. At least I managed to save you, my dear friend."

"What's that pyramid station anyway? Everyone was baffled. Professor Khan didn't know what to make of it."

"It's an energy exchanger. It takes in vacuum energy and converts it into any type of energy field, *any*—"

Sam tries to talk, but he starts coughing as his sore throat dries up.

"Here, I brought water for you." She fetches a glass bottle and puts it against his lips.

He swallows in big gulps as if he hasn't had a drink for days. He doesn't stop until he's absorbed the last refreshing drop. Then, looking resignedly at Shaillah, he plunges back onto his seat.

"You'll be all right. Only superficial burns I can heal. I managed to reach you before the shield from our departing pyramid station disintegrated," she says as she keeps wiping his reddened skin with a moist smooth fabric.

"Thanks a lot, Erin. But all I want now is … to touch your beautiful face." Sam's saddened dejected expression makes her feel guilty, even remorseful.

"Maybe … one day," she whispers in a vague hesitant tone.

"How does it work anyway?"

"What? My biomagnetic shield? It keeps me safe in my own atmosphere and protects me from the outside. It allows the used-up air to escape while filtering and recharging it on its way in."

"Weird! And all that while being invisible if you want," Sam raises his eyebrows in complete awe.

"And that's not all. Try touching me now." She says, trying to deviate his attention from the scenes of destruction down below.

Sam extends his hand towards her face, stopping hesitantly at times. Then the sudden discharge of electricity makes him jump back while stroking his numbed hand.

"Oh, that was too strong!" he chides her.

"Don't worry … I always keep it at the lowest setting when I'm near you!" she says with a reassuring smile.

Sam throws himself back onto his seat as he exhales with a long sigh of sheer distress.

"What happened, Erin? What have they done?"

"They who?" Shaillah asks sarcastically.

"Those aliens," He despondently replies, half-opening his reddened eyes as he looks back at her.

"You mean the humans? Everything that has happened has been self-inflicted. Humans caused the chaos, the confrontation, even though I warned them numerous times. The submarines fired at one of our posts. And their missiles bounced back off our powerful shields. The massive explosion that followed has caused billowing fireballs and ash clouds, all rising into the atmosphere. Not to mention the ensuing earthquakes and tsunamis … now that most of the cities are being destroyed in the entire Pacific west coast, the robots are busy rescuing whoever has survived."

"What about the radioactive fallout?" Are there any survivors?" Sam's face tenses up in an uneasy glare.

Shaillah smugly smiles. "Of course, the soldier robots would not let any of that linger in the atmosphere. The shields rapidly disintegrate any radioactive or toxic debris. Only the impacting energy and its subsequent shockwaves are released. And yes, there are survivors—because the guardian robots protected the people in their shelters in the first place."

"Oh, did they?" an incredulous Sam asks.

"Yes, I'm taking you to Tinian now to see your family. You can see them from here."

Shaillah looks at the dashboard and turns on the displays with a thought-command, revealing the scenes from Diablo's cave's interior. Sam breathes a sigh of relief as he sees his parents and sister sitting within a group of people, all listening to John Sanders.

"The Rom-Ghenshars, yes, that is what the aliens call themselves. They are pure evil," Sanders shouts impulsively, trying to fire up the crowd. "We must prepare for anything. But we must stick together no matter what. United we stand; divided we fall."

Everyone stands up and forms a close group around him, lifting their arms, holding bright torches and shouting all together, "United we stand; divided we fall!"

"What will happen to them? How will they survive?" Standing up, Sam looks out the cockpit window at the billowing clouds below. A wave of distressing thoughts quickly overwhelms him as he starts imagining the worst. "The ash cloud will get into the caves … the earthquakes will knock down the caves … the tsunami will flood the caves—"

Sam cannot stop shaking, fear and despair piling up and blurring his disordered mind. Shaillah runs to him.

"Calm down! Calm down!" She orders him while gazing intensely at him and gradually defusing his panic attack.

"Do you think we are going to let the catastrophe alter our current reconstruction tasks on the islands?" She calmly says once Sam settles down and his breathing eases. "We are not going to let any of that reach Tinian—"

"So …. No earthquakes, no tsunamis—"

"None of that!"

Sam resignedly nods, feeling relieved from Sahillah's reassurance, but he can't stop worrying about the extent of the devastation. "How many people have survived? What's happening down there now?"

Shaillah sets up the coordinates to display a bird's-eye view along the Pacific Ocean coastline. Sam can barely believe the desolate scenes unravelling in front of his eyes. He can't discern the sea from the land, as the whole landscape is a vast expanse of billowing smoke pillars. It's an ongoing fallout of sweltering crackling boulders and burning rubble, hurtling through the sky and into the distance as the devouring ash clouds spread relentlessly in all directions.

*I thought I knew what it's like to be on a battlefield. I watched war documentaries and movies. I never imagined it smelt so bad or the noise was so loud, or the fact that the blinding fireballs make you feel so powerless. Is this the end of our world? Is this it?* Sam thinks glumly to himself.

"The end of the world as you know it, yes, but there will be renewal," Shaillah reassures him.

"Ah, I see," Sam snaps. "You and your alien friends are so ... so ... I can't find the words. You're preying on our minds, controlling us. But you're also quick to blame the humans for everything." As Sam speaks, his tone increases with anger at every word.

He keeps staring intensely at Shaillah as a deep frown spreads across his face. "Answer me this, Erin—I mean, Shaillah, because you are a Rom-Ghenshar, right? You are a Rom-Ghenshar. Why could you not change General Stewart's mind? You knew what was going to happen. Why could you not change it? Eh?"

Shaillah presses her lips tightly, her expression riddled with reproach. "And what do you know about mind changing? It takes much energy—"

"Well, I think that energy could have been worthwhile. It certainly wouldn't have been wasted."

"And for how long would we be changing their minds? When will they give the next reckless order? The soldier robots are lethal—and unstoppable. Their bouncing shields are the least powerful of their weapons. They are all programmed to reconstruct the planet. Any other attempt to stop them would lead to further upheaval and destruction. The only other option was to stop the humans from thinking or making their own decisions. Do you want that?"

He shakes his head while sombrely watching the engulfing smoke and dust plumes rising even higher.

"Is there anything you can do?" he pleads with her.

"I am trying to help the humans. I am trying to help you. But my power and my influence are limited. If I can't convince the humans to listen to me, how can I convince the Rom-Ghenshars to change their plans?"

"I see it all clearly now. It is the end—the final moments of Earth as we know it."

Sam's doomful words are met with an air of heavy-heartedness by Shaillah's blank expression. Her cold, indifferent demeanour only confirms his worst fears. All that's left, he reckons, is trying to survive.

"You said there would be renewal," he mutters in a sarcastic tone. "What renewal?"

"The Rom-Ghenshars will rebuild the Earth and will help the surviving humans. And let this be a wake-up call. Fighting is futile, reckless and counterproductive. We have abilities far beyond your imagination, far beyond your reach. But we have come in peace. We have no desire to exterminate your race … as, indeed, the humans tried to do to our race in the past."

Sam dismays while listening to Shaillah's dire warning. He can only infer revenge and domination rather than hope and peace. His mind spirals into a wave of distressing thoughts. What will become of him and his family? What will be their future and that of their invaded island?

As the rugged coast of his beloved Tinian appears on the dashboard screens, they take their seats. At last, he can see the billowing black clouds receding in the distance. He shivers inside, recalling his implausible escape from the crumbling concrete and engulfing fireballs. He throws his head back, covering his eyes with his hands, as his body presses against the backrest while the aircraft descends for landing.

# CHAPTER 27

# THE HAUNTING PAST

*Remember this. I'll always be here for you—always!*

The vast army of guardian and soldier robots has taken over every single island in the Mariana archipelago. Their full-scale advance is relentless but they slow down as they allow the residents to take their essential possessions, move into their underground shelters, or go inside the coastal caves. On Tinian, a large group of people have made their refuge into Diablo's cave. They walked doggedly through the narrow passages trying to get as far from the entrance as possible.

Now that they have claimed their space in the scattered open areas, in between the winding tunnels, they gather in close-knit groups and comfort each other. They are tired and hungry, albeit relieved that they have finally reached a safe place. Some cry, and some shout words of encouragement. Mothers cuddle their children close to their bosoms. The families lay down their makeshift beds and share their food rations, preparing for a well-earned rest.

There's enough room to make their encampment, even though they have to share it with a multitude of animals that relentlessly fight for their patch, their ear-piercing squeaks and obstinate howls adding to the chattering of the human commotion.

Most birds have found shelter high within the wall ledges, but the farm animals and pets have taken their place right among their owners as if that was quite their entitlement.

As they settle down in their hard-fought quarters, tiredness finally prevails, and the tumultuous noise starts to gradually subside while the torchlights flicker until they all eventually go out. As if shrouded by a ghostly cloud, the whole place succumbs to an eerily quiet darkness.

John Sanders and Captain Walker take this chance to make their way cautiously back towards the entrance. They tread carefully among the slumbering mass, guided by the tenuous light of their dimmed torches, their path perilously narrowing as they advance. Once they reach the rock-strewn ledges surrounding the wide internal sea lake, they hasten their pace into the narrow side-corridor. At the opening edge of the rugged walls, they get on their knees and stretch their necks so they can get an unobstructed view of the outside.

The thick dust cloud, blowing in the warm wind, hurts their eyes and sticks on their sweaty skin. But they soon forget their discomfort as they watch in utter bewilderment the unrecognizable landscape.

They use their binoculars to scour the coastline, following the endless lines of flying machinery and constantly moving robots, their glowing lights making it look as if a giant swarm of fireflies have come to invade their island. Far away, on the horizon, even the ocean surface is awash with light, the dividing line looking like a freshly open wound, bleeding into a turbulent black river.

"We'd better return to the back aisles," Walker suggests.

Sanders nods as he starts slowly retreating while insistently looking back, trying not to miss any details up to the last minute.

As the curved, jagged walls start blocking his field of view, Sanders notices a bright glow breaking through the darkened sky. Judging from the way it's getting brighter and brighter, he reckons it must be flying very swiftly directly towards them. His next thought is soon confirmed as he focuses the image with his binoculars. Walker joins him, his arms trembling as he tries in vain to stay in focus.

"Friend or foe?" the captain asks hesitantly.

"It looks like that same kind of alien aircraft," John Sanders reckons, still holding his binoculars tightly against his face.

Walker starts walking backwards on the narrow ledges, dislodging some loose rocks into the water as he briskly speeds up. Sanders soon turns his attention behind his back, thinking his friend has fallen into the water, but he is relieved to see Walker clumsily running away.

"There's no point in fleeing, Walker. Let's wait for them here. Whatever it is, it'll be better for us to handle them upfront, far away from our people," Sanders shouts, trying to sound as convincing as possible.

"You're right. You're right. Whatever it is," Walker replies in an embarrassed tone as he stops dead in his tracks. He turns around, starting to walk in an overconfident stride as he retraces his steps, trying to hide any signs of nervousness.

Sanders nods as Walker slowly approaches him, showing his approval of his friend's newly found bravery. But as Walker's demeanour becomes even more boastful, pulling up his belt and inspecting his gun, John has to try hard to stop himself from laughing. At least for a moment, his old friend has managed to make him forget about their predicaments with his overtly confident act.

Both men put their arms on each other's shoulders as Walker says with added impetus, "Let's do it, John! Let's show them! I'll be damned if … oh God!"

Walker crouches abruptly, taking John Sanders down with him, and both men find themselves under a thick white mist spreading everywhere over their heads. As they hear a sudden splashing thump, they realise that the flying object has landed at the back of the lake.

As the mist dissipates, they recognise the arrowhead-like features of the alien aircraft, bobbing over the rippling waters.

They stay motionless, warily on guard as they watch the sleek craft moving towards the side, barely touching the rugged edge with its pointed nose.

But their sweeping fear turns into unexpected joy as the top half of the alien craft gradually rises.

"Mr Walker, Sanders!" Sam excitedly shouts as he jumps out onto the rocky path. "I'm okay. I'm back."

As they run into one another and embrace in a long enthusiastic hug, Sam swallows hard to contain himself from breaking the news about the catastrophe.

"So pleased to see you, boy!" Sanders cheers but soon frowns when he sees the burn marks on Sam's face. "What happened to you?"

"I'm okay, Sanders!" Sam tries to look unconcerned while quickly changing the subject. "How's everything here? How is my family?"

"Your family is okay, Sam!" Mr Walker butts in. "Even the Lobarts are okay. They were moved into the hospital's basement."

"But I'm afraid the robots are still destroying everything ..." John Sanders adds in a sullen voice.

"I need to see my family now. We need to talk ... and soon," Sam says as he stares intently at Walker.

"Then I'll go and get them for you. They're far inside, but I know exactly where," Walker replies, pointing out in the distance.

Suddenly, Walker realises that Shaillah is quietly watching them by the lake's shore.

"Hey, why is she still here? Is she causing more trouble? We've had enough!" Walker yells nervously.

"She saved my life, Walker." Sam tries to calm down an impatient Walker.

"Well, I'm sure she brings a message from the evil visitors, doesn't she?" Walker snaps, his voice quivering as he tries to contain his anxiety.

Shaillah starts walking towards them; her firm but graceful pace makes it look like she's hardly touching the ground.

"I think ... I think ... I'd better go and get Martha and Bill. I'll be quick!" Walker drawls as he starts running towards the side passages, managing to avoid Shaillah's path altogether.

Sanders nervously awaits her approach, trying to anticipate her next move. But her blank expression and hypnotic gaze are impossible to read. Sanders feels the building tension on his skin; his heart's beating faster, sweat running down his cold forehead. As he fears, she makes a beeline towards him. And as he keeps looking at her, despite her piercing, focused stare, he's surprised and then proud of his inner strength.

"John Sanders! Good that you stayed put inside the caves. Good that you followed my orders," she says with a satisfied grin, standing short of two metres in front of him. But then her stare turns sombre as she adds, "Others didn't. And they weren't so lucky."

"Ah, those were the voices endlessly repeating inside my head. I felt compelled to obey. Wait! What do you mean they weren't s-so lucky?" Sanders stutters, attempting in vain to remain calm. He looks back at Sam, but Sam looks away, purposely avoiding Sanders's uneasy gaze.

Sanders looks back at Shaillah as she speaks in a regretful but cautionary tone. "The explosion happened because the ARA submarines fired at the soldier robots—the completely wrong thing to do! The impact energy bounced back, instantly obliterating the submarines, liquifying metal and ripping giant rocks out of the seafloor. The ensuing fireballs, ash and dust clouds are now spreading, engulfing the cities. Unfortunately, nothing remains of the ARA headquarters … or LA."

"The ARA headquarters … the city … gone," Sanders gasps. His eyes nearly pop out of their sockets while his jaw drops in a sudden spasm as he struggles to believe what he's hearing.

"The super-heated cloud of rubble and ashes soon will engulf the entire continent. The high temperatures are causing fires everywhere. The only safe place for humans and any living creature is underground," she coldly continues.

"What have you done? Why? Are we all going to die when it gets here?" Sanders yells in anger and despair.

He snaps, trying to grab her shoulders in his blind irate state, but his arms are hit by a sudden bolt of electricity, violently pushing him backwards.

As Sanders clings to the rugged walls, Sam puts his body against Sanders' back to help him keep his balance. Shaken, Sanders manages to stand upright while nervously looking back at Shaillah.

"Several times, I warned not to attack us. Know this. Resistance is futile." She keeps talking, unperturbed, her intense gaze focusing on Sanders.

Suddenly, her hardened expression softens when she hears the distant echo of a familiar sound. She turns around, looking for the source of the insistent, high-pitched barks until she sees the shape of her beloved Blazer coming into view out of one of the cavities.

"Blazer, Blazer, my dear boy," she shouts as she runs towards the dog.

But her cherished pet freezes, baring his teeth and growling at her.

"Blazer, it's me. Come here." She crouches and waves her hands in a friendly, welcoming gesture. But the dog digs his back legs harder on the rocky ground, barking at her even more furiously.

As she is about to calm her dog down, a pair of dirty boots partly covered by ripped trousers suddenly stand between her and Blazer.

Sam rushes towards Stella and hugs her tightly. "So good to see you, brother!" Stella says while keeping a wary gaze on Shaillah.

Then, Stella picks Blazer up and squeezing him firmly against her chest, she blurts out: "He doesn't know you anymore, you weird creature!"

Shaillah stands up slowly, not taking her eyes off Stella.

"Don't do anything to my sister, please," Sam pleads, standing in front of Stella.

Shaillah looks directly at Sam, but her gaze seems to have gone right through him. All the while, she isn't thinking about Stella or Blazer either. She's trying to confront and dispel her unwelcome haunting thoughts. A sudden sadness disrupts her mind, and she cannot fully understand why. She thought she had transited totally into a new body, a new identity, but here she is, pining for an embrace with her adored pet dog. *The past stays in the past*, she repeatedly says to herself, trying to erase the irritating pining feeling.

Building up her inner strength, she manages to discard *those useless thoughts* and return to her cold calculating self.

Feeling more confident and revitalised, she comes out of her brief impasse and focuses her attention back on an imploring Sam. She doesn't even feel sorry for her best friend now.

"Time is running out. I have to go," she finally says as she walks briskly past Sam and Stella. She doesn't even turn her head when Blazer starts whining.

Then she stops and looks back at John Sanders, hurrying her words as she watches Sam's parents approaching in the distance. "The devastation will never get here. We're making sure of that. The guardian robots will bring all provisions you'll need to survive until we finish the reconstruction. Don't do anything stupid, okay? They'll be here to help."

Sanders nods his head as if fully hypnotised while Shaillah resumes her march towards her awaiting scouting aircraft.

"Erin! Erin! Please wait!"

She hears Sam running behind her, shouting her name louder and louder, but she doesn't slow down. As she puts one foot on her aircraft, she bluntly turns around to face him. Still, her blank expression doesn't deter him from running towards her.

"Now what?" she snaps as if she is reluctant to even talk to him.

He stops in front of her, staring at her with a grateful smile. "You came back. You saved me. You care about me!"

"Don't be melodramatic, Sam. I had to do it—no big deal. But now I must go." Shaillah looks at him impassively, as if she couldn't care less about how he felt. "Your parents are here. Please send my regards to them."

"Okay, I hear you … I suppose you have a new life, and our childhood dreams are over—"

"You know nothing about my dreams."

"That much is clear," Sam replies sullenly, bowing his head as if completely giving up. But then, he boldly looks back at her. "Remember this: I'll always be here for you—always!" he firmly declares.

Shaillah jumps into the craft's shiny hull and never looks back. Still, as she takes off, Sam's emotional, heartfelt vow keeps ringing in her ears.

# CHAPTER 28

# INVASION

*I want to get rid of whatever it is that's invading my mind.*

"Reijen" (Perfect)! All is proceeding as expected. Almost too easy," Kuzhma-Or boasts as he glances at the UniverseScope's bustling scenes with a furtive smile of satisfaction.

As they planned from the very beginning, magnificent sleek cities rise from under the rubble, transforming planet Earth into one of their permanent bases on this galactic zone.

New buildings, interconnected by wide roads and high bridges, sprout under the soldier robots' never-ending toil, effortlessly lifting giant pieces of granite, marble, and precious metals and fitting them like a pre-planned giant 3D puzzle. The robot's pace is unrelenting, like a finely tuned unstoppable machine. Awe-inspiring, capriciously shaped structures keep mounting on under their persistent advance. In some buildings, the robots waste no time setting up more machinery production lines and robotic workshops.

The robots wander busily in and out of the rising constructions like rows of leafcutter ants. Every building site is buzzing with giant flying cranes, laying and securing every block in the precise position as heaps of material arrive in never-stopping conveyor belts running from the bottom of the ocean and open-air quarries.

The heavy rain and flash floods wash away what remains of the dust and the rubble, leaving behind immaculate marble and gold skyscrapers rising amid beautifully crafted green parks. They build a magnificent gleaming pyramid at the centre of each city, its edges lined in gold. On each of its smooth sides, a message in bold, bright letters can be read along the bottom—"Welcome to the New World"—in both the local and the Rom-Ghenshar language.

"I must say I have somehow enjoyed controlling this planet's weather and its inhabitants. Let the atmosphere recover first. Let the remaining animals thrive. Then we can bring out the humans," Kuzhma-Or sneers, basking in his majestic throne while keeping an eye on the never-ending constructions.

"By the way, Athguer, how are the humans doing?" Kuzhma-Or asks in a dismissive tone.

Immediately, the bustling construction scenes change to the underground passages where people have managed to take refuge before the devastating, earth-shattering explosion.

They sing their prayers out loud, huddling together and begging for a way out of their dark, filthy shelters. Soon they are surrounded by soldier robots, digging underground to make ample rooms for families to gather. Helpless crowds anxiously watch as their surrounding are made roomier, healthier, and more liveable and as provisions are brought and equally distributed by the guardian robots. All the while, humans give thanks to the robots.

"How are the people from our island base doing?" Rothwen asks.

Athguer complies with Rothwen's request by zooming inside Tinian's cave system, where the soldier robots have already finished their reconstruction. Here, life seems to be thriving.

"It appears that they are doing quite well," Athguer notes in an indifferent tone.

"Yes, I see Shaillah even saved her friend's life. Pretty impressive, eh?" Kuzhma-Or remarks.

"She wanted to. I let her go," Rothwen mutters, letting them know with a scathing look that his volatile temper is simmering at the edge.

"She seems to be taking much of your attention." Kuzhma-Or keeps riling Rothwen nevertheless. "We've got to keep her under tighter control until we finish the reconstruction everywhere. She will cause nothing but trouble up there."

Anticipating a flare-up, Athguer intervenes with an appeasing gaze at Rothwen. "Yes, Shaillah has gone through a dramatic transformation, and she is still unsure of herself. We must keep her out of this."

Rothwen bottles up his anger while nodding reluctantly at Kuzhma-Or.

"You're right, Yei Boishen. We must keep her out of this," Rothwen relents; he knows he cannot do anything other than obey now.

"Shewe!" Kuzhma-Or stands up while sternly looking at his master navigator. "Come with me, Rothwen. We must start setting up the hyperspace coordinates—ready for our destroyer-crafts," Kuzhma-Or orders as he regally walks down the glistening steps. He strides along the side corridor, his tall, dark figure disappearing through the vaulted walls. Rothwen watches in silence as he senses from the mounting tension in the air that his supreme commander's temper is near breaking point.

"I'll be right there, My Commander," Rothwen finally says before turning to look at Athguer, his face set in a riled but resolute expression.

"I'll be absent for a while, Athguer. I need to focus all my energy on the tasks ahead. Make sure you look after her."

"Absolutely!" Athguer solicitously replies. "What shall I tell her about you?"

"Nothing." He bluntly says. Then, looking intensely into Athguer's eyes, he asks him, "What are my options?"

"Options for what?" Athguer feigns his response, trying to gain time to gather his thoughts.

"Don't be acting out, Athguer. What are my options?" Rothwen seethes, his tight muscles twitching on his reddened neck.

"If you allow me, Rothwen, I can fix whatever is troubling your mind."

The dejected silence tells Athguer that he started with the wrong suggestion. He looks down, trying to avoid Rothwen's infuriated gaze as he continues. "You could keep her here, in suspended animation, in case you would ever want to return to this planet. Or we could erase all her earthling memories and emotions, making her automatically respond to your every single whim. Or"—Athguer hesitantly clears his throat—"in the unlikely event that … I mean, it's very unlikely, but I must mention it." Athguer folds his hands, tapping his fingers on his elbows. He's now saying completely the opposite of what he's thinking, and he knows Rothwen knows it. "In the unlikely event that you would have to take her with you by force, there's still a small chance that she would not survive intact her first departure flight … if her cells are damaged."

"How small?"

"Do you want the exact number?" Athguer briefly looks up to find Rothwen's exasperated stare, waiting for his answer.

"It's a minimal risk, one in thirty trillion," Athguer states nonchalantly.

"Oh, that's too big a risk. Is there anything you can do about it?" Rothwen counters, looking incisively at Athguer.

"I'm afraid not."

Rothwen scowls, holding up Athguer's chin with his writhing fingers. "Athguer, I may ask you this question again. But next time, I expect a different answer," he rumbles as he lets go of Athguer and pulls at the lapels of his black jacket, his nostrils flaring.

"I'll see what I can do." Athguer's startled face breaks into a reassuring smile, trying to ease Rothwen's ill-temper. Much to his relief, Rothwen's tightened face muscles finally relax, nodding in reluctant acceptance.

Still, as Rothwen steps back, he keeps a warning stare on Athguer until eventually he turns and disappears into the back aisle.

Athguer raises his thick eyebrows in sheer astonishment as he watches Rothwen walk away. In all their aeons of space ventures together, he has never seen the headstrong space warrior showing that edgy state before, constantly flipping between anger and anxiety, impatience and concern. This must be something far more serious than any obsession, far more enduring than a simple pastime. This must bring nothing less than an unfathomable upheaval. Then he congratulates himself. He must have done the naenshi transition to perfection if Shaillah is affecting Rothwen so profoundly. He sends a thought-message to Zula-Or: *I have no doubts about Shaillah. She is the one to bring far-reaching changes to ourselves.*

At the central processor's inner chamber, Rothwen joins Kuzhma-Or. The supreme commander closely inspects the large three-dimensional images of each planet of the solar system, their striking surfaces slowly rotating and displaying their distinct landscapes in exquisite detail.

"Interesting and diverse, even though it's a small planetary system compared to ours," Kuzhma-Or notes.

"Compared to most," Rothwen adds.

"Yes … yes. It will be a quick but exhaustive invasion. I've already started selecting the takeover grid coordinates in the Oort Cloud."

"I will do my part on-site—on every planet. I need to take a trip out … to clear my head."

"You have much to do, Rothwen. But this is your speciality. You're so good at it. You are the undisputed expert of the destroyer-crafts." Kuzhma-Or stares at his master navigator with a satisfied grin.

"After I finish, I may go to meet our approaching Grand Fleet. I want to go away for a long while, to get rid of whatever it is … that's invading my mind."

"I think you worry about her too much, Rothwen. It is not like you at all. You may not be functioning at full capacity, I believe," Kuzhma-Or grumbles, a warning glare flashing through his dark pupils as his tone turns sullen.

"She's one of us now, My Commander, like me, like Athguer. What's wrong with caring about her?" Rothwen contends, trying to play down Kuzhma-Or's mounting anger.

But Kuzhma-Or lashes out, grabbing Rothwen by the neck, his curled fingers menacingly opening and closing. "She is blurring your mind. That's what's wrong!" Kuzhma-Or snarls, his lips almost touching Rothwen's tightened cheek.

Rothwen keeps still, looking sideways into Kuzhma-Or threatening eyes with an equally fierce gaze. "What's upsetting you?" Rothwen challenges him.

"You know it well. Our mission here is at an end. I won't allow any more changes, no more deceptions, no more delays. You must comply with my orders!" Kuzhma-Or rages, tightening his grasp around Rothwen's neck.

"I always do." Rothwen stands his ground, hardening his neck muscles and stopping Kuzhma-Or from closing his fists any further.

"Shaillah is in the way! She still has human feelings. She's weak, and she is weakening you!"

"And?" Rothwen tests Kuzhma-Or's patience by turning his body rock solid until the supreme commander's grasp starts to slip.

"Do I have to spell it out for you?" Kuzhma-Or seethes, waving his arm through the air and discharging a bolt of electricity in front of Rothwen's face, making him jump back.

"Are you fighting me?" Rothwen frowns at Kuzhma-Or, warning him to back off.

But Kuzhma-Or's response is to throw a barrage of even more powerful bolts at him in quick succession. In no time, Rothwen swiftly jumps out of the way, avoiding every single one of them while Kuzhma-Or laughs out loud in contempt.

"You think you're fast. Think again! I'm missing you on purpose," Kuzhma-Or growls as he runs towards Rothwen and grabs him by his uniform's collar, scrunching up its golden badges. "If I don't paralyse you completely now and send you and her"—Kuzhma-Or twists Rothwen's uniform even further around his neck—"to the bottom of Rom-Enjie's doldrums until I happen to remember it, it's because of who you are!"

He pushes Rothwen away dismissively, surrounding him with a ringed column of discharging lightning bolts and trapping him inside. All the while, Rothwen keeps glaring back at Kuzhma-Or in defiance through the burning wall of crackling flames and incandescent arcs.

"Tell me, Rothwen, what is your plan on the last day of our departure when we finish our mission here?" Kuzhma-Or dares him, walking around Rothwen, pursing his lips in disdain.

"I haven't thought that far ahead yet, My Commander," Rothwen states, confronting Kuzhma-Or with an even more rebellious glare.

"Well, think about it now!" Kuzhma-Or roars. "Tell me now before I lose my reasoning beyond repair!"

Rothwen straightens his body and holds his head high, feeling his skin scorching as Kuzhma-Or makes the ring of discharging bolts thicker and even more intense.

"I will forget her. That's always been my plan anyway," Rothwen sneers.

"Will you?" Kuzhma-Or glowers sceptically at Rothwen.

"I'll leave now and don't intend to come back. After the takeover, you can deal with the humans, send Shaillah straight to Rom-Enjie, and then join me with Athguer in the Grand Fleet."

"Who do you think you're fooling?" Kuzhma-Or snaps, walking inside the incandescent wall and threatening Rothwen with his raised fist. "You and I know perfectly well that you'll be back! Willpower alone won't work. You have to delete it!"

Rothwen crosses his arm in front of his face in time to stop Kuzhma-Or's heavy blow, resisting the commander's thrust and holding his ground steadfastly.

"Deleting is for the weak, isn't it?" Rothwen grumbles through his clenched jaws while staying put with all his might until Kuzhma-Or relents and steps aside, making the ringed wall of discharging bolts so thick that Rothwen cannot even move.

"I'll do it on willpower alone!" Rothwen defiantly stares at Kuzhma-Or, placing half of his body inside the powerful discharge, letting his uniform melt on his skin, blue sparks flying off everywhere.

The supreme commander has no choice but to stop the discharges instantly, lest he disable his master navigator for a long while. He knows Rothwen is so stubborn he won't get out of harm's way. He also knows his implacable threat has gone as far as it can.

Kuzhma-Or keeps staring at Rothwen, his eyes menacingly flaring, but he can't stop a glint of admiration flashing underneath his raging glare.

"I'll do it on willpower alone," Rothwen single-mindedly repeats. "But if I fail … and if she fails, then all I can say to you, My Commander, is this: If you want to take our Invincible Grand Fleet, the most powerful mothership fleet in Rom-Ghenshar history, to Ankjeshur" (Omega Centauri), "then you will have to let Shaillah and I be together … whatever happens." Rothwen keeps his defiant gaze at Kuzhma-Or for a few more tense seconds so as to leave no doubt that he is dead serious.

"Sheban lai" (It's high time) "I'll be setting off. I'll go right now!" Rothwen soars through the antechamber cloud on his way out, leaving Kuzhma-Or seething with no option but to let him go. The veteran supreme commander knows full well that no one can navigate the Grand Fleet as skilfully as Rothwen does.

As Rothwen walks towards the rocky ocean shore, the departure spaceship slides nose first out of the water. Its bullet-shaped smooth metallic body reflects all the sunset's hues. The long, sleek fuselage splashes down onto the swirling waters, drenching Rothwen's body as he flies into the cockpit.

"I need a big shake-up," he mutters, staring at the dashboards as he sends his thought-commands to set up his route on the automatic flight sequence.

The spaceship jets off at an angle, breaking through the thick expandable walls of the central high dome and the insulating pressure-levelling shield, accelerating like a darting spear through the outer ocean and in between the rows of encircling towers. As it reaches one of the exit portals, the craft gets into a vertical position right under the opening interlocking gate. It shoots up through the dark tunnel as if sucked in by a powerful force, suddenly decelerating as it meets the rushing currents of an underground river, a river of boiling magma.

The aircraft pushes through the churning fast-moving mass, fully shielded by the magnetic halo of its all-surround armour, hurling the molten rocks away and against the crumbling inner walls. As it reaches the sucking edge of the volcano's vent, Rothwen turns off the positron jet engines, allowing the violent eruption to fully take hold.

The pure force of the unstoppable up-currents churns up the thick and sticky magma, twisting and turning the aircraft inside the incandescent mushy pulp. Rothwen lets his body take all the hits while ripping off the melted uniform from his skin. His back and head crack open in gushing wounds that his quick regenerating cells promptly heal, while all the craft's indestructible assembly withstands the relentless battering unscathed.

At the edge of the billowing volcano's throat, Rothwen turns back on the engines. The sleek aircraft shoots upwards, breaking through the spewing ash cloud and jetting into space in a blinding incandescent plume. Rothwen leans back into his seat, a wry smile flaring up on his simmering face. Through the transparent cabin, he stares at the whirl of turbulent trails, his mind blank. Still, sooner than he could have ever predicted, he finds himself wishing that Shaillah is there with him, sitting by his side.

# CHAPTER 29

# GUILT

*It's your memories that make you who you are!*

Shaillah is restlessly pacing in front of the twin golden columns leading into the space-tunnel. She looks up and around in despair. No matter how hard she thinks about going to the UniverseScope, she's still in the same place.

"What's going on? Rothwen!" she shouts, kicking the immovable columns' bases as if she were fighting an imaginary giant.

In the middle of her outburst, she realises that Athguer has appeared in front of her. Standing under the high arch, he is patiently looking at her, waiting for her to calm down.

"Ah, Shaillah, it's good to release your inner anger," he says as she suddenly stops kicking and dejectedly stares at him. Her ashen complexion, from her lack of sleep, is plain for him to see.

"Where is Rothwen?" she moans.

"He is preparing our departure," Athguer gently says.

"Why didn't he mention anything to me? Not even Zula-Or knows where he is."

"Oh, Shaillah. Never expect to know where Rothwen is all the time. That's how he is—"

"Why am I not allowed into the UniverseScope? Why can't I summon the scouting-crafts?" she snaps.

"Kuzhma-Or's orders. You should stay down here during the reconstruction."

"I suppose I'd better go back into my room. Or shall I call it my prison?"

"I was on my way to the lab towers. Do you want to come with me? It'll do you good to think about something else."

Shaillah can hear the muffled rumble of the transport-craft as it rises alongside the railings behind her. She turns around and walks towards the waiting craft without answering, biting her lips as she swallows the spurting bouts of bitterness and sadness.

She keeps looking towards the brightening horizon as they jump in and take their seats, avoiding eye contact with Athguer. As they slowly glide over the ocean into the pink-orange morning sky, he doesn't interrupt her thoughts, letting her come to terms with her predicament.

"If it makes you feel any better, he asked me to look after you before he left," Athguer says after a while, trying to break the lingering silence.

As the aircraft pushes through the dome walls and breaks out into the outer ocean, the capsule's smooth body slides seamlessly through the densest concentration of jellyfish and wandering sea creatures that cannot disperse fast enough, provoking a subtle smile on Shaillah's stony face.

"Kuzhma-Or is right. I shouldn't be witnessing all the devastation. It would be too hard to bear," she mumbles.

"Shaillah, it was going to happen anyway—one way or the other. Things are going to go the Rom-Ghenshar way," Athguer replies in a matter-of-fact tone.

"Killing, exterminating, obliterating?" she mutters in distress, covering her face with her hands.

"No, no. Recreating, transforming, expanding, creating a better world," he ripostes with a reassuring tone.

"A better world?" she asks dismissively.

"Yes! When we finish rebuilding the cities of the new world—"

"A new world," she says in a poignant tone, "ruled by the Rom-Ghenshars."

"That's the law of the universe, isn't it? The superior mind will, in the end, prevail," Athguer boasts, firmly staring at Shaillah.

The transport-craft reaches one of the towers. Steadily, it swerves around the enclosing iridescent rings as it rises higher and higher. Shaillah looks away from Athguer's piercing eyes as she keeps gazing at the tapering silvery walls right up to the very top.

"I should not feel for the humans anymore, Athguer. But most terrible of all is the guilt … the guilt!"

"Don't be so hard on yourself, Shaillah. You tried to convince them, they did not listen. It's their fault."

"Maybe it isn't such a good idea to keep my memories. I feel so vulnerable, so tied to my past. It's hard to bear. I can't take it any longer."

"Yes, you can, you can. You are a Rom-Ghenshar, remember?" he rebuts. "But with that very special ancestry I'm reluctant to destroy. It's your memories that make you who you are!"

Shaillah is taken aback by Athguer's deep-felt response. With a long drawn-out sigh, she tries to cast out her wrenching insecurities and jitters. "I thought you were wary of my memories, my state of mind."

"Let's say I was concerned … but not anymore," Athguer reveals as Shaillah inquisitively stares at him. "As it turned out, it's been fascinating to see how you've flowered into this amazingly fierce but sensitive creature, able to conquer even the coldest, bleakest of hearts. I'd hate changing you any further."

Shaillah's face beams up with a widening grateful smile, but it soon turns sombre. "I haven't conquered anything," she glumly replies.

"You don't know it yet, but you have. Remember my words, Shaillah. I'm seldom wrong. No. Correction. I'm never wrong," Athguer asserts.

"It's hard to be a Rom-Ghenshar with human feelings. You have to fix it, Athguer," she pleads.

"You'll find it will get easier. Accept your past and then embrace the future. But remembering where you come from will make you even stronger." Athguer stresses his words while briefly patting her shoulder.

As they reach the very top of the tower, the spiky cap opens up like a thorny flower, swallowing the hovering craft into its haul. They descend slowly, swerving around a thick luminous central column, its shiny edges flickering like a candle's flame.

"It's a photonic mast," Athguer explains. "There's one in every tower powering the labs. It comes from our central processor's antimatter core."

Spellbound, Shaillah looks down, following the swirling edge of the light-producing column. As she looks back up, she inspects the transparent overhanging decks, lining up the inner walls and forming an infinite winding helix. Inside the spiralling wide aisles, the busy android robots and automated machinery bristle with activity. She tries to focus on a single action, but her eyes cannot adapt soon enough to the fast-changing goings-on flashing through her startled pupils.

"Machines making robots, which make machines, which make robots, which make machines." Athguer gloats while Shaillah keeps utterly engrossed in the never-ending movements.

"Ad infinitum." She marvels.

The transport-craft keeps descending, swerving around the dense photonic mast. As it approaches the lowest level, it softly comes to a complete halt while the side doors slide open.

Shaillah follows Athguer into a vast chamber awash with white light from every angle. In the distance, she can see rapid flashes of lightning crashing against each other and bursting into multiple afterglows. Soon she finds herself standing under a mesh of interconnected fibres, tendrils, and globules, all brightening and bursting randomly around her with a subtle all-pervading crackling sound.

"Welcome to one of our brain network hubs!" Athguer announces.

"Fascinating!" Shaillah exclaims. "It looks like an everlasting lightning storm."

"Ah, it is the brain energy field, communicating, relaying information."

Shaillah opens her arms and starts spinning around, tipping her head back while taking in the mesmerising spectacle all to herself.

"Here, I can load any particular brain field and closely inspect it, even edit it in detail. Do you want to see yours?" Athguer prompts her.

She suddenly stops her whirling dance, staring at Athguer with a mixture of doubt and suspicion.

"It will last as long as you want. Relax, think of nothing, and I will load it here. As soon as you start thinking about stopping the transfer, it will unload automatically," Athguer reassures her.

"Okay." Shaillah nods as she stays perfectly still and folds her arms tightly around her body.

Suddenly, myriads of fluorescent light streaks brighten the whole place up, frantically bursting and merging into each other while noisily crackling all across the rapidly warming air.

"Oh, who are you thinking of, Shaillah?" Athguer chuckles.

She immediately stops the transfer while sheepishly looking at Athguer. She knows he knows who she's thinking of.

"Let's go back now." Athguer starts walking away while beckoning her to follow him. "You need to rest. And after that, you have so many things to occupy your mind. I can show you more of my labs. You can visit Zula-Or and the beautiful Rom-Enjie cities, swim in our beautiful ocean, play with the tame marine lyshars. There's so much to do."

As they reach the transport capsule, Shaillah never says a word, deeply absorbed in her thoughts.

Athguer puts his hand over her shoulder, stopping her before she boards. "And another thing, Shaillah. Do not feel guilty, my dear. You've achieved something amazing already," he proudly tells her.

"What's that?"

"You have changed Rothwen. He's never been the same since he set his eyes on you. He's changed all our plans, been very lenient—and I mean very lenient with the humans—because of you."

"Oh!" she exclaims while staringly dumbfoundedly at Athguer.

"He could have finished here long ago. He could have sent the destroyer-crafts in advance, eliminating every single living thing, making our takeover far easier. But instead, he chooses to keep this planet alive, builds one of our command bases here so he can be close to you; waits until you're ready to fly with the Grand Fleet, and, in the meantime, reconstructs the whole planet while trying not to harm the humans. He even sends the guardian robots to protect them before the soldier robots—all because of you!"

Shaillah's bewildered face glows with the intensity of her reviving soul. Never in her wildest dreams could she have imagined the extent that Rothwen would go to be with her. Then her tumultuous thudding heart starts aching so badly that her chest feels as if it's collapsing, trying hard to understand why he has gone away without even an explanation.

"Will he ever come back?" she wonders.

"Wherever he is, I'm sure he is thinking of you!" Athguer tells her, without a shadow of a doubt in his deep-set sharp eyes.

# PART V

# CHAPTER 30

# TAKEOVER

*"What has to happen will happen."*

"I can feel the space-time waves vibrating through my body," Kuzhma-Or roars as he surveys the gleaming surface of the UniverseScope platform while Athguer is sitting by his side.

Like a perfectly choreographed squadron of giant incandescent rockets, the Rom-Ghenshars' Invincible Grand Fleet suddenly emerges at the outskirts of the extended ring of iced rocky objects surrounding the solar system, the Oort Cloud. In a seamlessly synchronised manoeuvre, the milliards-strong mothership fleet spreads out into a vast semicircular formation. Their fuselage rings blaze in an intense blue glow as they widen and swivel until they lock into position. Expanding over ten astronomical units wide and five units deep, the swarming mothership fleet seems bound to infiltrate the solar system's defenceless outer domains.

Kuzhma-Or tilts his head back and breathes in deeply in infinite self-satisfaction.

"Faultless!" he booms. "Can't wait to reach Ankjeshur. Our biggest, most challenging mission yet."

"Ah, the great giant globular cluster! Rothwen will conquer all of it in no time," Athguer proudly declares.

As Athguer mentions Rothwen's name, they get a message from him with his current coordinates. Immediately, Athguer zooms in onto the precise location with a thought-command.

The seemingly endless sleek hull of a glistening spaceship points right at them, its sharp nose poised at a steep upward angle. The rows of flickering orange spotlights along its smooth elongated body make it look like the giant lead mothership is softly breathing while the thick rim of its triple synchrotron rings, flashing in an incandescent blue glow, makes it look like it's about to jet off.

Like a stalking predator, the massive spaceship, five hundred kilometres from stem to stern and one hundred kilometres in diameter at its widest, is ominously hovering by the dark side of the moon, unseen and unsuspected by its potential victims.

"*Ei Reishojen*" (*The Prestige*). Athguer jumps from his seat. "He has brought in *The Prestige*!"

But Kuzhma-Or hardly reacts, stoically raising one of his thick eyebrows. "Hmm. As I expected," he rumbles. "Our master navigator never leaves anything incomplete. He never flees from anything—nothing!" Kuzhma-Or stands up, his face flaring up in an exultant gesture. "That is why he's so infuriatingly good."

"I guess he brought his commanding mothership to finish here even quicker," Athguer surmises.

"Yes, Athguer, in whatever way he is thinking of finishing it."

"We have agreed with Zula-Or. We know what is going to happen, don't we?"

"I'll reserve judgement until we leave for Omega Centauri. But in any case, he'll have to face the Great Ancestors Council for any of his misdeeds." Kuzhma-Or glowers while exhaling loudly.

They keep tracking Rothwen's movements as he sets off from *The Prestige* in one of the departure-crafts. The breathtaking speed he's flying at tells them they won't have to wait long before seeing him entering the UniverseScope. The glowing countdown swiftly rolls back from T-200 (seconds).

Rothwen's impetuous entrance electrifies the confined air of the arena. A muffled metallic crackle spreads throughout the dense atmosphere as the guardian robots rise in unison when he suddenly walks in and directly looks at them with his penetrating gauging gaze. With a brief thought-command, he orders them all to sit down.

Rothwen's eyes blaze in an unflinching glow as he stares expectantly at Kuzhma-Or.

"Seya" (Welcome)! Kuzhma-Or greets his master navigator with a tense, albeit forbearing glare.

"Ai yei seinekh, Yei Boishen" (All my respects to you, My Commander), Rothwen declares, bowing in deep reverence before walking towards Kuzhma-Or and Athguer in long fast strides.

As Kuzhma-Or and Rothwen greet each other, crossing their hands over their chests in their solemn army salute, their past quarrels and disagreements seem to be long-forgotten. The welcoming smile from Athguer as they embrace each other softens the mood even further.

"You are right on time, Rothwen. Most of the reconstruction has finished. We are ready to depart." Kuzhma-Or cheers.

"I was making sure everything is in place for our planned departure and our next mission," Rothwen announces, his smug glare of total confidence fully pleasing Kuzhma-Or.

"Not much of a challenge for you," Athguer quips while looking admiringly at Rothwen.

"I have set all the takeover-grid coordinates for every single planet, major or minor. I have set up every departure stage in *The Prestige* in minute detail and every hyperspace sequence in the Grand Fleet's motherships." As Rothwen speaks, Kuzhma-Or's face beams with the anticipated thoughts of victory.

But there is still an uncanny, unsettling question in the air as Rothwen recounts all his exploits and preparations. Finally, a brief haunting silence makes it clear. Rothwen is well aware that Kuzhma-Or and Athguer are keen to know about his plans for Shaillah as he stares at them defiantly, avoiding mentioning her name altogether.

Athguer is the first to break up the blatant expectation.

"I'm sure you know about Shaillah's current state of mind. She won't talk to anybody, not even Zula," Athguer mentions cautiously.

Rothwen presses his lips together while folding his arms and looking away as in deep thought. "I've come to the conclusion that this obsession of mine has to end now. Shaillah will have to decide for herself what she's going to do. But above all, she has to accept our actions. I will make sure of that," he impassively says.

"Shrena" (Exactly), Kuzhma-Or boastfully rumbles. Then he sends the entangled signal to all the motherships, activating the fleet of destroyer-crafts. "Kleehern" (Deploy)!

With their long, spiky bodies, the destroyer-crafts, fully armoured with plasma rays and antimatter cannons, suddenly eject from their holding vaults, deep in the bowels of *The Prestige* and every Grand Fleet's mothership. Aligning in multiple conical grids, rapidly extending as even more crafts join in, they twist and turn as if they were part of a single throbbing living system, destroying any obstacle that gets in their way, rocketing in and out of the raiding network's hyperspace. Their takeover is swift and overwhelming, surrounding every planet and its moons, sweeping and penetrating their defenceless domains.

"This was going to be the first stage of the plan—until we had to change it, at your request, Rothwen." Kuzhma-Or fumes with a seething gaze at Rothwen.

But as the supreme commander watches the destroyer-crafts' unstoppable advance, surrounding and then pulverising all the human spaceships and interplanetary bases, the writhing spirit of overdue revenge fills his indomitable soul with immense satisfaction.

"We've come to an end—in reverse order—but we've come to the long-awaited end," Kuzhma-Or's gloats in his booming voice.

"What has to happen will happen," Rothwen glowers, crinkling the corners of his eyes as they all haughtily watch the unrelenting takeover scenes unfold.

As the ever-expanding network of destroyer-crafts enmeshes the outer planetary region and its forefront convoy from *The Prestige* surrounds the inner planets, and within them, the Earth and its moon, Kuzhma-Or and Athguer closely follow the takeover manoeuvres, relishing in their might and invincibility. But soon, Rothwen takes his chance to leave the UniverseScope furtively. He can't wait to see Shaillah.

# CHAPTER 31

# FORGETTING

*Why is it that, of all the places in this universe where I could be right now, I'm here with you instead?*

"Go away!" Shaillah cries in dismay. She is sitting on the floor, her back firmly pressed against her locked door, shaking her head as if trying to dispel her writhing torment. "Go away!" she repeats over and over, her croaky voice and unyielding tone showing no sign of giving up.

She hears Rothwen's voice inside her head telling her, *there's no use in fighting it, Shaillah.* But she disconnects his frequency and shuts down her transmission. Her stone silence says it all.

"I know you are upset—very upset," Rothwen admits, sliding down on his back against the door and sitting down, only the thick door panels separating them. He sets himself up to wait for as long as it takes while checking the steady signals from his stalking lead mothership and lurking Grand Fleet. Then, he sets all the entangled hyperspace tracking networks on standby.

But he doesn't have to wait long before he hears her voice and her thoughts again, albeit her tone getting angrier and more despondent as she speaks. "First, Kuzhma-Or forbids me from the UniverseScope and then from getting into any scouting-craft. And on top of that, you disappear without a word. I've lost count of the days before I gave up waiting for you. I stopped counting after two hundred sunsets. No one would tell me your whereabouts. Yes, you left me in this room full of fancy gifts and gadgets and this beautiful domed paradise. But that is not what makes me happy."

"And what does?" he eagerly asks her.

He waits for her answer, but all he hears is a sullen whimper.

"What does?" he insists.

"Being with you!" she exclaims, but then she exhales a drawn-out sigh of regret.

"I had to go for a while to prepare the Grand Fleet's operations. It was Kuzhma-Or's order to keep you away so you wouldn't visit the humans in that turbulent period. But now I'm here to tell you everything is going well. Your island is all finished. You'll be happy with the changes."

"Why didn't you come to see me … before you left?" she asks in a reproaching tone.

"I thought it would be easier that way."

"Maybe easier for you ..."

"The important thing is that I'm back. Now that it's all done, you'll appreciate it better."

"I'm not so sure."

"Please open the door, Shaillah."

Rothwen's pleading voice makes Shaillah even angrier. "Make me," she dares him. "You can control me. You rule over me."

"Never! When this door opens, it will be by your own decision."

"What difference does it make?" she asks despondently.

"It makes a difference to me. I want to be with the real Shaillah—the one I wanted despite everyone and everything. If you want to be with me, on your own terms, please open the door!"

No sooner than he finishes his clamouring words, Rothwen feels the door moving behind him. He promptly jumps to his feet and readily smiles as the door slides open. But a disgruntled Shaillah is blocking his path, warning him to stay away from her, holding up the palms of her hands.

"Are you happy now?" she says in disdain. "Now you've seen me … you can go away. Go away!"

He frowns in disbelief, confronting her scolding gaze, trying to piece together the utter mess in front of him.

Her white tunic hangs in shreds, sticking onto her wet shoulders and legs; caked-up make-up is smeared all over her face; dirt trails cover her body, even tarnishing her diamond necklace. Her oily, tangled hair is all knotted on top of her head in dishevelled matted tresses.

"What have you done to yourself?" Rothwen gently waves his hands in a calming gesture.

But Shaillah scowls at him, pulling her belt strap from her waist and yielding it over her shoulder, threatening to throw it at him.

Rothwen surveys the disorderly room. Jumbled fabrics and jagged broken mirrors lay scattered throughout the aisles. On the central pool, all kinds of rubbish float along with slashed cushions and ripped pieces of furniture. Long trails of glowing gemstone shrubs spill from the overturned golden vases.

"Don't come any closer!" Shaillah warns him harshly.

He can see the wrath burning within her blazing eyes, like a runaway wildfire, ready to ignite anyone who would dare come near. But he walks towards her nevertheless. She backs away with a warning glare, kicking even more rubble into the pool with her bare feet.

"It's all right, Shaillah. I'm making my way to the balcony to breathe some fresh air," he calmly says.

As she realises they are reaching the end of the room, she hurls her belt at his face, letting all her anger explode in a howling scream. But he nimbly grabs the twisting straps and, extending them with both hands, wraps them around her waist, trapping her inside. In a flash, he is holding her against the wall, grasping both her hands behind her back, pinning her legs with his knees. She struggles to break free, desperately jolting and writhing as if caught in a tangled net. "Let me go!" she yells, banging her head against his chest.

Everything turns black, pitch-black inside her head. Her dizzy altered mind makes her sick to her stomach. As she starts coughing, Rothwen briefly loosens his grip, and she manages to free her hands. She hammers him hard on his face, neck, chest and shoulders, waves of fury rolling off her coiled fists. She rips his uniform apart, tearing open the golden clasps on his vest, renewing her pounding with even more force and rage, lacerating his skin with her split nails.

Rothwen bears it all without flinching. Like a stone wall, he takes everything she throws at him until, eventually, tiredness and frustration overcome her. Her limp pounding head ends up resting on his chest, her sore eyes and throat reminding her of every moment she has spent crying and shouting.

"I hate you. I can't be with you anymore," she sobs inconsolably.

Rothwen gently puts his hands on her shoulders, shaking her slightly until he manages to make her look directly at him. Their gazes clash in a sweltering flame, neither of them willing to stifle it.

"Tell me that again tomorrow. And I will leave," he says, kissing her on her tight-lipped mouth.

Shaillah tries to keep her unforgiving stance, but Rothwen's poignant words and imploring gaze are making her anger slowly fritter away. Her unyielding stare starts to soften up as she breathes more calmly.

"I see we both failed miserably trying to forget each other." He chortles.

"Why have you come back?" She asks, her face changing into a frosty expression.

"Why? Why is it that, of all the places in this universe where I could be right now, I'm here with you instead?"

Shaillah closes her eyes and slumps her head on Rothwen's shoulder while stroking his battered chest as if trying to make it heal even faster.

"Shaillah, look at me! Can't you see? I'm desperate to …" He holds up her face close to his, their pupils almost touching. "I want to feel you, one more time, many more times. I want to feel … that long-lost sensation, that long-lost *sheiren*."

"*Sheiren*, passion, love," she breathes in deeply. Her whole body shivers as he runs his kisses over her matted hair.

"Your scent will always be like an elixir to me," he tells her, drawing in the air from her sticky, sweaty neck.

"Do you love me, Rothwen? Do you love me?" She stares intensely at him, her eyes glazed with runaway passion.

"I … I don't know," he coldly says, all the while he is unable to conceal the feelings of deep longing for her, flashing through his piercing gaze.

"Right. You are so confused. But by the way you look at me, I can tell that you do. You do!" she whispers, caressing his face.

"I can't stop thinking about you. But it could be a phase I'm going through."

"While you were away, I found out … I can only be myself when I'm with you … Let me love you, Rothwen. I'll show you what love is. Let me love you."

"Something rattles my mind. Something crushes my heart when you are not with me," he confesses.

"Stop trying to be harsh. Stop denying it," she says, covering his face with kisses.

But Rothwen holds her head in his hands while looking sombrely at her. "I'm too mean for you. My soul hides behind dark clouds, the dark clouds of destruction. I'll make you suffer. It'll be easier for you to desist. Desist right now!"

"It's too late, Rothwen. We're right in the middle of this storm. We can't escape. We have to ride it, spin inside its mighty wind, swim around its vortex," she says, letting her body fall over his chest.

She feels like disintegrating from within his arms as he undresses her, tearing down the ragged pieces of her tattered tunic.

As she tries to unclip her diamond necklace, Rothwen holds her hands in place. "No, don't take it off. Leave it on," he says, caressing her shoulders. "I want to be reminded of something you once told me." He holds the diamond in his hands, scraping off the layer of dirt. "'Like this diamond, I am hard to ignore.'"

They hardly feel the shattered glass piercing their skin as they slide down the wall and onto the floor. They roll over and drag their bodies until they climb on the soft, cushioned covers of the corner bed. The silky sheets wrap all around them like a smooth, silvery cocoon while the blood and sweat stains trace the lines of their moving bodies.

"I missed you!" he whispers as he wraps his arms around her thin waist.

"I love you, Rothwen! I will love you … forever! Let me save you from your darkest demons."

She breathes out in ecstasy as her smooth skin glistens against his rippling muscles, their lips finding each other and melting into a long-awaited desperate kiss. Like a searing flame, their irresistible desire consumes all their senses. It's addictive, overpowering, and something they can never fight or escape from. As their bodies merge into one, the long days of separation, insomnia, and fruitless tribulations suddenly feel wasted, forgettable.

# CHAPTER 32

# CELEBRATION

*They should witness your almighty unrivalled presence.*
*And they will worship you like a God!*

As Shaillah leans over her balcony, she receives Rothwen's message to join him at the UniverseScope. She watches the tremulous sunset while checking on her emotions and thoughts. She must show no anxiety, no anger, no fear. She slows her breathing and closes all her thought transmissions. This is no time to break down.

As she walks through her smartroom's aisle, the pool waters sparkle with the purple spotlights, its wobbling crystalline surface casting its swirling reflections onto the white nacre walls. There's no trace of the shattered glass or the ripped furniture, no sign of anything out of place. Rothwen ordered the guardian robots to restore and polish everything while taking Shaillah to one of their hyperspace travel recovery rooms, where the high-energy deep-treatment capsule reinvigorated every cell in her body.

Walking into the UniverseScope arena, she advances confidently on the long straight aisle, holding her head high, her eyes glinting in a daring glare, no vestiges of tears or long sleepless nights. Her velvet-white tunic sways along her graceful body, and her shiny white hair bounces softly at her every step.

She keeps her eyes fixed in the three expectant figures sitting at the end of her path, hardly sparing any time to acknowledge the line of guardian robots intently watching her at either side.

Kuzhma-Or finds himself admiring Shaillah's poised self-assured pace. Still, his eagle eyes flash with rapid glints of reserved judgement.

Rothwen is struggling hard not to show any emotion. He holds his breath, keeping all the dense air in his inflated lungs for as long as he can, managing to appear unimpressed.

"Seya, Shaillah!" Kuzhma-Or greets her as she reaches the gleaming steps leading onto the platform. He gestures at the empty chair between him and Rothwen. "Please join us."

She raises her long tunic as she walks towards her chair and ceremoniously sits down, sliding her hands over the ebony armrests as she brazenly meets Kuzhma-Or's penetrating stare. Her purple pupils stand out through her long eyelashes and heavy dark eyeliner, shining as bright as the hanging pink diamond on her chest. Her deep red lips, in stark contrast with her pearly-white skin, slowly curve into an unwavering smile.

"Jeinesh, Yei Boishen" (It's an honour, My Commander)! she replies, her body language oozing a distinctive regal air.

Kuzhma-Or reclines on his intricately decorated backrest, stroking his glossy beard in a pondering mood. With his potent invasive brain field, he tries to get into Shaillah's mind, but all he can read is her resolute thoughts, her unbreakable spirit. He glances at Rothwen, who can't take his approving gaze off Shaillah. Athguer is subtly nodding while looking back at Kuzhma-Or through the corner of his eye. Reluctantly, the supreme commander acknowledges that Shaillah has turned into the indomitable Rom-Ghenshar soldier he once thought she could never be.

"Your confidence sparkles in the air, Shaillah. I hope you're feeling at home now." Kuzhma-Or probes her.

"Nothing feels more homely than my ancestral abode," she briefly tilts her head back in an exultant gesture.

"No doubt Rothwen has helped you come to terms with your new self. We are nearing the end of our mission here. Drastic changes are coming for you."

"Everything is perfect. I'm ready for the next stage in my life," she firmly replies, feeling the stirring presence of Rothwen by her side.

A few suspenseful seconds pass while she tries to control all her brain channels, keeping impeccably still and indifferent, hoping to hide her true feelings of anxiety, burning so deeply, so intensely inside her head.

"Shewe" (Very well), Kuzhma-Or nods in approval as his throne swivels while he gets up and starts walking over the glassy curved surface. "Unda ye."

Shaillah feels encouraged, noticing that the great Kuzhma-Or wasn't able to read her innermost thoughts, never mind detecting her innermost feelings. The endless hours she has spent practising how to control her brainwaves has paid off. She has managed to fine-tune her thoughts' frequency to create shifting interference bands, effectively blocking any external probing waves.

But all the steadfast control over her thoughts is soon put to an even harsher test. As she stands next to Kuzhma-Or, the images of the sieged planet Earth threaten to break down all her mental defences.

"It is time to visit the humans again, for the very last time. But now it will be simpler. By now, they all know and have accepted that the Rom-Ghenshars are here—here to stay—and that fighting is futile. The planet is ours. We will consider if we'll share it with the humans … at our leisure," Kuzhma-Or roars in a triumphant war-winning discourse as he zooms in on the rebuilt cities.

She watches impassively as the open-mouthed humans look up into the sky while the destroyer-crafts dash in and out of the atmosphere in ambush, long trails of space debris flaring up behind them. The morning sunlight concentrates on the crafts' spiky metallic bodies, reflecting across the sky and through the clouds in myriads of scattered flashes as if countless meteor showers were coming from all directions.

"It's a display of force, Shaillah, to remind the humans that *we* are in charge now," Kuzhma-Or gloats.

Shaillah reins in her emotional tidal wave, her expression barely shifting at the sight of petrified people and confused animals running away while the destroyer-crafts swoop down to the ground.

Kuzhma-Or stoically continues to sift through locations, revealing more of the reconstructed landscape. Soaringly high jagged-shape skyscrapers line up in circles around open green parks. At each park's centre, a massive golden obelisk rises even higher than the buildings.

Rothwen and Athguer join Kuzhma-Or as they continue zooming in and out, inspecting every detail, while Shaillah manages to stay calm.

"The humans never wasted any time to reorganise themselves and have moved their ARA headquarters to a city called London," Rothwen says as he centres the view on a small but elegant bridge, looking out of place with its surroundings. Decorated in blue, white and grey and flanked by gothic towers, the bridge is dwarfed by the two newly built arched golden bridges rising at each of its sides.

"Tower Bridge!" Shaillah exclaims. "I've always wanted to go there."

"Very intuitive name, isn't it?" Rothwen remarks in a sarcastic tone. "I ordered the robots to leave it in place. We sometimes leave a reminder of what the place looked like."

"Shrena" (Exactly). "We take what we like from them," Athguer adds as he walks down the steps and starts pacing in front of the robots.

"London, eh?" Kuzhma-Or arrogantly grins as he glimpses through the images, finally stopping south of the city river, close to Tower Bridge. He zooms in on one of the three sharply shaped pyramids with highly polished white walls and gold-encrusted edges. A twinkling sensory sphere revolves over their pointed golden tops, perfectly balanced by a levitating force.

"They're massive," Shaillah exclaims, looking in awe at the pyramids. "They must be four or five times as massive as the ones in Egypt."

"Oh, yes. Those. The humans used to build them, trying to imitate us. We destroyed every single one of our magnificent pyramids before we left. The humans did quite a good job but never managed to replicate ours," Kuzhma-Or brags.

"What happened to the ones in Egypt? Are they still in place?" Shaillah asks as if making a request.

"They're still there. Just as a reminder … of what humans can't do. But we will replace them soon …" Rothwen starkly replies as Shaillah holds her nerves and manages to keep her dismay well away from his prying gaze.

"And, of course, we're going to do what we couldn't finish thousands of years ago; only this time, it will be much better," Kuzhma-Or gloats.

"London is a beautiful city," Rothwen notes, as the images continuously reveal the newly built areas, "even more so that it is now a Rom-Ghenshar city."

"Precisely!" Athguer intervenes as he approaches them. He's followed by a guardian robot carrying a shiny tray with tall, frothy glasses, while at the platform's edge, other robots start serving colourful exotic food dishes on long polished tables.

As Shaillah savours the sweet, tingling beverage, she glances at the city's vivid sightings with a shade of melancholy. Still, she can't help feeling overwhelmed by the sheer beauty of the sumptuous sky-high constructions. *As it turns out, it's not so bad after all*" she cheers herself up, looking at Rothwen with a forgiving grateful smile.

"What are you thinking, Shaillah? I can't properly connect to your channels." The stern voice of Kuzhma-Or makes her jolt.

"I'm thinking that, for our next meeting with the humans, you should be there, My Commander," she says, bowing her head in reverence. "They should witness your almighty unrivalled presence. And they will worship you like a God!"

Kuzhma-Or stares at Shaillah, his eyes glinting in deep reflection, as he raises his chin. "Maybe," he rumbles.

She lets her brainwaves flow as she fills her mind with the memories of the Rom-Ghenshars' legendary conquests. Inside her mind, she sings the Rom-Ghenshar victory chants: *Invincible Space Conquerors, Rom-Ghenshars. Masters of our Galaxy! Masters of our Universe! Suan enjie.*

They hear her thoughts, and they shout them out loud. They keep celebrating for hours, eating, drinking, and laughing; reminiscing about their past adventures; and planning new ones.

"After Omega Centauri, we must have a victory conclave with all our vast fleets at the Andromeda galaxy," Kuzhma-Or announces. Then, standing over the images of the planet that they have been transforming to their ultimate wish, in two hundred and fifty fleeting Earth days, he roars, "Suan enjie. Rom-Ghenshar might and wisdom will always triumph. Yeiren Ojserahni. Unshe" (This is our universe. Forever)!

## CHAPTER 33

# THE LAST MEETING

*Earth is a precious planet. Let's celebrate its revival.*

As the first rays of sunshine bathe the pyramids' glinting edges, all the paths leading to the towering structures fill up with people coming from all directions. The crowd moves forwards in increasingly packed expanding swathes, reined in only by the meandering banks of the splendid River Thames.

Thousands of faces merge in an awestruck euphoric thrill. Eagerly the people wait, their voices rising. They chant and applaud as if clamouring for a long-awaited encore, their enthusiastic cheers filling up the air, echoing across the sprawling squares.

"Hurrah, hurrah. Hip hip hooray! Welcome, Rom-Ghenshars."

"Long live the Rom-Ghenshars! Long live planet Earth!" Large white banners display the words in big bold letters, waving in the wind alongside large flags with colourful designs. Some flags depict the Sun and Earth, others the twin suns Rom and Ghenshar, and Rom-Enjie. The guardian robots make their way through the crowd, dispensing drinks and boxes full of food, as well as colourful T-shirts and hats to the humans.

At each side of the ample avenues, rows of large screens atop high poles display images from the elevated stage assembled in front of the Central Grand Pyramid. The countdown in minutes and seconds flickers at the bottom of the screens. For the people waiting, the seconds are not moving fast enough.

Since they first came out of their shelters, the humans have been preparing to meet their alien visitors.

The broadcast helicopters transmit through all the ARA channels, ensuring no one can miss the most important event yet after their arduous long-suffering days.

The newly appointed ARA's North and South generals are pacing around the stage, checking the microphones, glimpsing at the giant screens, listening to the reports from their central command. The two men keep a firm, focused posture, altogether hiding their internal nervous disposition. They must make sure they don't repeat the mistakes of the past.

The Rom-Ghenshars have shown that they keep to their word. The robots have healed and fed the people. They have rebuilt their cities, industries, and hospitals; they've even brought the unstable climate under control. The Earth hasn't had an extreme weather episode for months now. If the former generals had listened to them in the first place, millions of lives would have been saved. The order "Don't attack our saviours" is now enshrined in all ARA's stations.

The message for the much-anticipated meeting had come suddenly but was nonetheless well-received. The ARA broadcasting channels had been interrupted by Shaillah's smiling face. "London, the Rom-Ghenshars want to invite the humans to our long-overdue meeting. Tomorrow, from six in the morning to late at night. A summit of friendship. A summit of celebration. A multi-world summit!"

The Rom-Ghenshars had set the time and place, but they'd never said how they would arrive. The live streaming stations and lookout telescopes frantically scour the hovering destroyer-crafts, failing to detect any giveaway signs. But all of their equipment, even to the last second, is pointing in the wrong direction.

The dazzling figures of Shaillah and Kuzhma-Or suddenly appear at the centre of the stage, making the generals jolt and momentarily lose their composure.

The large screens instantly show the striking stage images as the jubilant crowd cheers and waves in perfect lockstep, as if they had rehearsed every move for this very occasion.

"Good morning, London. Good morning, Earth," Shaillah announces, her crystal-clear voice chiming through the loudspeakers. She smiles and waves with both hands, enticing the crowd with her warm, gracious demeanour. Her face fills every screen. It's as if all the cameras are stuck on her rosy cheeks, glossy red lips, and expressive gaze.

"Ahhhhh!" the crowd exclaims as if everyone has been seduced all at once. Their clamour gradually turns into an expectant silence as everyone waits for the ARA generals to speak.

"Welcome, friends. Our planet is your home!" ARA's South Region General Ali Sheik greets them in his raspy, grovelling voice. The tall, sturdy officer tries to sound as firm as he can while swelling sweat droplets cover his bald head and forehead, and his glasses briefly slide down his wet nose.

"We look forward to working together for a brighter future," North Region General Jason S. Bowden adds in an overly enthusiastic voice. He is about to continue his speech when one of the stage assistants brings him a note. His face turns grey as he reads the grim message, but nobody is paying attention to him. Everyone's attention is firmly focused on Kuzhma-Or's and Shaillah's hypnotic appearance.

"People of this glorious planet, let me introduce you to our galaxy's supreme commander— our illustrious Kuzhma-Or!" Shaillah announces.

The imposing figure of Kuzhma-Or now takes centre stage on all the screens. His immaculate military uniform, bristling with gold decorations and badges, has all the hallmarks of a legendary invincible commander. His smooth white beard and piercing eyes, twinkling with a fearsome spark under his sleek helmet, summon the conjuring power of an all-victorious warlord.

"Sheban lai. Seya" (It is high time. Welcome)! Kuzhma-Or's booming voice resounds across the vast square. He extends his arms from under his long black cloak as a row of multicoloured lights sparkles across his belt. His welcome message, in both English and the Rom-Ghenshar symbols, appears on all the screens.

By now, at their central broadcasting hub, the ARA technicians realise they can't control the live transmissions. It seems that the Rom-Ghenshars has effectively taken over the worldwide broadcast.

Stunning images of alien star systems and detailed views of breathtaking landscapes of unknown planets suddenly appear on the pyramids' sleek walls and throughout colourful holograms floating above their heads.

"We have so much to show you," Shaillah announces, her face beaming with excitement. "We have so much to share with you. Our Supreme Commander Kuzhma-Or, illustrious veteran of countless planetary missions, blesses the Earth, this extraordinary planet, with his infinite kindness."

"Welcome, welcome! We love you," the people excitedly clamour over the cacophony of applause and cheers.

Shaillah's spirited voice raises over the rowdy crowd, instantly grabbing their attention.

"We, Rom-Ghenshars, can tell you that Earth is one of the most beautiful planets in this galaxy—so delicately blue and lushly green. It's worth our every effort to preserve it."

As they listened to her words, the crowd is spellbound by the beautiful images from alien cities—intricate structures rising high through the clouds or crisscrossing the bottom of immense oceans. The Rom-Ghenshars, it is plain to see, can build and live anywhere, on any planet, and in any environment.

In the background, the stirring fast-paced haunting music puts everyone into a feverish state of triumph and joy.

"Sheban lai!" Kuzhma-Or repeats, throwing both fists into the air and electrifying the crowd even further. Wherever he focuses his eyes, all faces align to that direction, followed by their awestruck applause and cheers. The supreme commander revels in his total supremacy over the humans as he casts his dominant glare across the ecstatic crowd.

The ARA's North and South Generals haven't moved from their positions throughout the whole spectacle. General Bowden has given up attracting General Sheik's attention, as the latter is utterly mesmerised with the show while occasionally reading the prepared welcome message and the questions he is hoping to ask.

The rousing beat of a bellowing drumming tune reverberates through the speakers and comes to a sudden stop as the images of Kuzhma-Or and Shaillah fill the screens once again. An exasperated murmur from the crowd reminds the ARA generals that this is their opportunity to speak.

South Region General Ali Sheik moves closer to his microphone to read his message. "Supreme Commander Kuzhma-Or, Lady Shaillah, we want to express our profound gratitude for all you have done after one of the most devastating disasters in our planet's history. Without you, humanity could have been extinct by now. We profoundly thank you, from every human that is still standing today, may you receive our warmest welcome and wholehearted gratefulness."

Kuzhma-Or and Shaillah nod at the same time, acknowledging the general's deep-felt proclamation.

"Earth is a precious planet. Let's celebrate its revival," Shaillah responds to the cheers and cries of "thank you" from the crowd.

"We would like to ask some questions, Great Kuzhma-Or," General Ali Sheik eagerly speaks into the microphone. "And our first question is: what is the meaning of life?"

A subtle smile ripples through Kuzhma-Or's long lips as his eyes sparkle in a bright green flash, his face beaming with an overpowering glare. "Life's purpose is to exist against all odds, to thrive, to adapt, and to conquer all environments," Kuzhma-Or booms. "That is the goal, that is its meaning—to reach a superior state of intelligence in order to prevail over non-sentient non-living matter. It is to develop a superior form of mind energy, able to transform our constantly evolving universe, and eventually being able to recreate it … at our will."

At the central processor, Rothwen is standing next to Kuzhma-Or as the supreme commander speaks to the humans while checking on the destruction of Earth's high-orbit satellites. But Rothwen is solely focused on setting the range and power of the destroyer-crafts' plasma rays.

As soon as Kuzhma-Or finishes speaking, Rothwen transmits the command to blast the rays onto the Earth's magnetic field, forming an intense tidal current of charged particles.

Suddenly, the city's sky is ablaze with bright, colourful flashes of fast-moving, wispy light pillars. They flow across the sky in irregular, fanciful shapes as if painted by thick fluorescent crayons.

The onset of the beautiful bright aurora covering the entire sky and outshining the morning sun surprises and astounds the spectators. At once, everyone takes his or her eyes off the stage, beholding the random fast-changing light dance, wholly overwhelmed by the hypnotic experience.

“Let the celebration begin,” Shaillah gleefully announces as hers and Kuzhma-Or’s images slowly start to dissipate until they disappear entirely.

“Don’t go away yet,” General Ali Sheik protests. He grudgingly looks at his long list of questions he never got the chance to ask. *Perhaps next time,* he thinks to himself.

As General Sheik looks back at the cheering carefree crowd, sharing their drinks and food, chanting in rapturous hordes, and enjoying a splendid sky spectacle, he feels comforted in the thought that the worst must surely be over.

“A new bright future awaits!” Sheik enthusiastically says.

But General Bowden twists his lips into a grimace while gloomily shaking his head. “Well, according to the latest report, which I happened to receive while you were all celebrating, after repeated attempts, we can’t contact any of our interplanetary missions, and none of our satellite communication systems responds to any of our commands. It seems the aliens’ takeover of our whole solar system is complete.”

## CHAPTER 34

# PREMONITION

*Once it gets hold of you, it never lets go.*

The fine wet sand sticks to Shaillah's face as she wakes up by her private lake's shore. She turns on her back beside a seemingly dormant Rothwen. As she attempts to wipe her mouth, Rothwen holds her hand and avidly licks on her lips. Her giggles mix with the splattering thud of their bodies hitting the slushy silt as they rustle and roll. They move further into the water, their half-submerged bodies, covered in frothy bubbles, sparkle under the evening's suns. As they gradually sink, the undulating surface fizzles and splatters all around them.

Under the water, they feel free. Inside their oxygenated orb, they can forget about everything and everyone. They surrender to their addictive passion, hardly noticing the playful lyshars and colourful luminescent creatures swimming nearby. As they make love, the entire submarine world disappears from their senses.

Time passes by, but for Shaillah, it feels like a fleeting moment. She runs her long tender kisses up and down Rothwen's naked chest as he lies motionless on her lap, his eyes closed. He wishes she would never stop. It's such an uplifting sensation, the kind he had never experienced. It makes him feel different, elated, desired. *This drug might not be a bad thing, after all*, he thinks.

"It's not a drug, Rothwen," she says as she continues kissing him up and down his gleaming chest.

"What is it then? It makes me want it, but at the same it makes me try to escape from it."

"It's called love, Rothwen, falling in love ..." she gently replies while he caresses her hair.

"Space travellers don't fall in love, Shaillah." Rothwen sits up and holds her cheeks with both hands. Looking deeply into her eyes, his lips part as if he is about to say something. But instead, he pulls her towards him and into a long, breathless kiss, as if this would be his very last one.

"Love ... How long does it last? Does it go away as quickly as it turns up?" he asks.

"Once it gets hold of you, it never lets go," she whispers, rubbing her face against his.

Their pupils clash in a fulgurant spark, full of unrestrained desire.

But then his face hardens. A chilling glare stifles the passion from his eyes. He swallows hard while gently pulling away from her.

"I must get things ready," he states. "Our departure is imminent. This is our last sunset here."

She sighs. "The last sunset ..."

"Don't be so gloomy, Shaillah. Wait until you discover our beautiful universe. You will never miss your Earth again."

"As long as I know the humans are doing all right, I'll be fine. Yesterday, everybody was so happy at the summit. They seemed to have accepted the robots, their new cities," Shaillah enthuses.

But Rothwen hardly reacts, gazing into the distance with a blank eerie expression.

"What's troubling you? Is there something you need to tell me?"

"Humans have to learn to live with the robots, without attacking them. Otherwise, an even bigger catastrophe awaits them. It's as simple as that," Rothwen bluntly warns.

"They have learned their lesson. I'm sure they have. They have come to recognize and respect our power," Shaillah replies in a heartening tone.

"Might as well," Rothwen sneers, maintaining a harsh unyielding gaze.

"So ... are the destroyer-crafts staying behind? For how long?" she prompts him.

"Shaillah … I can't tell you what I'm going to do. It all depends on how everything goes."

"But I see you are troubled—"

"You don't need to worry about anything. I'll take care of it, as usual," he cuts her off, his impassive face plainly showing he's not prepared to tell her anything about what he's thinking.

"I'm nervous about the departure". Shaillah changes the subject as she tries to soothe his mood. "First time for me, travelling at such high speeds."

"You'll be fine, Shaillah," Rothwen reassures her, his face softening at last with a subtle smile while stroking her shoulders. "I'll make sure your trip goes smoothly."

"So … nothing to worry about?"

"Nothing! I'll see you at sunrise tomorrow," he declares before swimming away.

She wraps her arms around his neck and rests her head on his shoulders as he carries her upwards, breaking through the thin membrane of their protective orb. With broad, swift strokes, he rushes towards the shore. Soon they're back at the rear entrance of her smartroom under her balcony.

They slip into their drying bathrobes, and before she can even say a word, he has disappeared up the spiralled staircase. All she can hear is his hurried fading steps.

As she stares at the darkening horizon, a web of doomful thoughts envelops her mind, warning her of an impending disaster, making her feel deeply distressed. A haunting chilling premonition she cannot yet see but can detect with her sixth sense takes hold of her.

Then she remembers that she has a few hours left to say her final goodbye to Sam.

# CHAPTER 35

# FAREWELL

*I grew up with you, learned with you, celebrated with you.*

At the very end of El Cuchillo peninsula, Sam sits quietly, his legs dangling over the jagged cliffs. He stares into the distance towards Diablo's Point, glancing at the rocky arched passages leading to Diablo's cave entrance, one of the few places in the island that the robots left untouched. In his mind, he retraces every twist and turn of his boat ride with Erin. *We were so happy then,* he thinks to himself. The sea is eerily calm, but its currents still splash and foam against the rugged shoreline. As he contemplates the dawn's brightening sky, painful memories keep coming back.

"You are wasting your time. Come on!"

The insistent reproachful cry from his sister Stella doesn't bother him anymore.

"You go home. Stop following me," he retorts without even turning his head to face her.

"She isn't coming back," Stella says, raising her voice in scorn.

She waits in vain for a slight acknowledgement, raking the gravel with the tip of her boot in a bid to attract his attention. But to her dismay, Sam hardly moves.

"Every day you come here is a day less in your life that you can be free of her. Such a waste." She moans, letting go of a long deep breath as if she is about to give up.

She eventually starts slowly walking away while talking to herself, loudly enough so Sam can hear her. "That weird girl, she isn't worth even one second of my brother's time. She didn't even mention him in that London meeting."

"Stella!" her brother's anxious call makes her suddenly stop and turn around, a gloating smile showing on her face, thinking that, at last, he has relented to her demands.

But her face soon turns pale in utter panic. Her jaw drops at the sight of the rapidly approaching orange light gliding over the ocean towards them, from Diablo's cave.

Stella runs to her brother, pulling his arm in an attempt to make him run away. But Sam jumps up onto his feet and digs his heels into the ground. She watches in horror as the glowing object gets closer by the second.

When it seems that the craft is about to crash against the rocks, it comes to a sudden halt as its top cover springs open. Right in front of their stunned faces, Shaillah jumps out onto the ground and runs towards them.

"Erin!" Sam excitedly waves at her.

"Thank you for saving our lives, by the way," Stella growls, pointing at the waiting scouting-craft hovering by the cliffside. "I thought we were going to die right here, crushed and burned by your silly space junk."

"I can't stay very long." Shaillah speaks directly to Sam while completely ignoring Stella.

"I am so pleased to see you, Erin. I thought you had forgotten about me."

"I'd better go—better leave the impossible lovebirds in peace." Stella rolls her eyes as she pushes her brother towards Shaillah.

As Stella reluctantly walks away, she keeps looking back. Watching her brother gleefully smiling at Shaillah, she decides to climb behind the rocky ledge and spy on them. Hidden behind the cliff wall, she can secretly listen in on their conversation.

As she precariously crawls alongside the ragged wall, holding on to the protruding rocks with her bare hands, she manages to stay undetected.

Shaillah and Sam focus on themselves, staring aimlessly into each other's eyes, struggling to find the right words for what they want and don't want to say.

He doesn't want to break down, admitting how much he misses her. She doesn't know how best to tell him that she is going away, and this time is forever.

"I saw you at the London meeting. You looked fantastic," he admiringly looks at her while trying to suppress a nervous smile.

"Things have gone quite well for me. Getting to know my ancestry—it's been incredible."

"But I worry about you."

"Worry about me?" She giggles.

Her dismissive response makes Sam feel uncomfortably dejected. "Yes, what will become of you? Where are they taking you?" he insists.

"Everything will be okay, both for you and for me." She affirms.

"Are you sure? These aliens—the Rom-Ghenshars—do you know their true intentions?"

"Their intentions are noble, for growth and prosperity, not only for this planet but also for the whole galaxy."

Shaillah's encouraging words fall on deaf ears; Sam continues to languish on his most desperate thoughts. "I saw your fearsome *commander*. He doesn't seem very noble to me," Sam says in a spiteful tone. "They seem to have so much power. They build huge marble and gold cities in a flash with their advanced machinery." He gloomily rambles on. "They have tireless, all providing robots, and scariest of all, they can control our weather, our way of life. They can—"

"I know all that. You're overthinking. It won't do you any good."

"Overthinking? What about all these spaceships glowing in our sky, even in the daytime? What are they planning? There are all sorts of rumours. The ARA is trying to hide the real extent of the danger."

"They are here to help in the reconstruction."

"Yes, and to track our every move—every single second," Sam objects.

"That's the way it has to be, Sam. After the catastrophe, humans have to be kept in check," Shaillah counters.

Sam seems to quiet down for a moment, but his deep-rooted suspicions don't take long to return once more. "I'm not happy with obeying the robot's every command."

"How do you find your new home?" she asks, trying to change the subject.

"Our island has changed so much," he says in a resigned tone, "huge bridges and underground tunnels, towers, skyscrapers rising from the sea. The entire archipelago is now a new city, but I prefer the old times," he grumbles.

"There's no point in getting upset, my dear Sam," Shaillah says calmly, gazing sullenly at him with a pitiful half-smile.

"I d-don't like the way you are looking at me … Erin," Sam stammers, fearing some unwelcome bad news.

"The best thing, Sam, is for you to forget me," she says coldly, keeping a piercing gaze into his eyes.

Her words hurt him the same as if she has hit him with a massive blow to his head. His eyes aimlessly veer away as his body stays limp and unresponsive. He repeats her words to himself over and over, trying to make sure that he heard correctly. Hopelessly, he looks back at her.

Then, his expression hardens as he firmly tells her, "Ask me anything, but don't ask me that."

Shaillah smiles back at him. The fond memories of them together cannot be wiped out so easily; she understands.

"You can still see me in the stars. If you look towards the southern horizon in the spring, follow the line from the star Spica down to the constellation of Centaurus. You'll see a fuzzy nebula—Omega Centauri. That's where I'm going."

Sam slowly shakes and lowers his head, trying hard to face up to his vanishing hopes and to rein in his despairing thoughts without crumbling like a coward in front of her.

"I have come to say goodbye," she continues impassively, "for good."

"Aren't you going to visit your parents? They want to see you," Sam suggests, eagerly looking at her.

"I know, but I don't have time. My dear Sam, I've come to hug you for the last time." She extends her arms and gestures him to come closer.

As they hug, she slowly disables her shield. He buries his head into her hair, breathing in all her scent. Their bodies shiver, and their hearts pound in their chest as she lets him kiss her cheeks, her nose and her lips, but just for a few seconds, before she steps back and reactivates her shield.

"Sam, you have been my best friend, like a brother to me. I grew up with you, learned with you, celebrated with you. We shared so many things in the past. But in the present, our lives must go separate ways." Every word she utters carves a deepening lethal wound in his broken desperate heart.

"No, no! You came here for me. You turned off your shield for me. You care about me, Erin. Please stay … stay." As he speaks, he looks into her unyielding eyes, fully realising this is the end.

She closes her wet eyelids, pressing her lips tightly as if not wanting to speak her final words. "I can't live in your world, and you can't live in mine. Now I must go."

"No, no, Erin," he pleads with her, trying to hug her.

But she pushes him off, and his arms are left aimlessly clutching the empty space.

She runs towards her waiting scouting-craft. Time seems to be standing still for Sam. He can't bear watching her slipping away. Instinctively, he covers his face with his hands.

But a sudden commotion makes him jolt out of his daze. As he tries to make sense of what is happening at the cliff's edge, he sees Shaillah turning around and hitting someone with a swift swing of her hand as a bright electric arc sparkles, leaving a black smudge on the charred ground.

A scream echoes from the other side of the rocky drop, followed by a sudden splashing noise as if something has fallen into the water. Meanwhile, Shaillah is holding a heavy sharp rock with one hand. She briefly inspects it and then smashes it onto the ground, shards flying in all directions.

Sam runs towards the edge and leans over, looking for the culprit. He stares at the girl struggling to stay afloat, her forehead bleeding. He gasps as he recognises the partly charred curly hair of his sister Stella. Bewildered, he looks back at Shaillah. "Why?" he yells.

"I'm so sorry, Sam. She attacked me. I flipped. It was an accident," Shaillah hurriedly tries to explain.

Sam climbs down the ragged wall and then swims towards Stella, getting her out of the water. As Sam sits with his sister on the gravelly shore, Shaillah is relieved to see that Stella starts coughing and spitting out water.

*I could've killed you, and I wouldn't have forgiven myself. Goodbye, Stella*, Shaillah thinks, jumping into her scouting-craft and flying over the scene, while a distraught Sam looks up.

Soaring over the west coast of her beloved island for the last time, in a farewell lap, she finally accelerates towards Diablo's cave. All the while, she imagines the brittle chain tying her to her past shattering into a million pieces.

# CHAPTER 36

# OBLIVION

*You are Rothwen's great dilemma, the kind he has never faced before.*

As Shaillah returns to her smartroom, she goes to her balcony to contemplate the beauty of the starry night sky, the stars and constellations as seen from Rom-Enjie. She looks towards Earth's location, but she can't discern even the sun. She zooms in on that particular patch of the sky with a thought-command, focusing on a yellow, ordinary star and then on the third of its orbiting planets.

She had thought she had freed herself from her past, but Earth's serene and captivating image confirms otherwise. "My world—so distant and yet so close, so humble and yet so beautiful," she murmurs, letting all her nostalgic feelings take over her mind.

But soon, the thoughts of impending doom and destruction come back like a black whirling cloud, whizzing around her head, taking hold of her reasoning.

*Why do I feel so uneasy?* she asks herself. *Something is troubling me—something way dark. I must go and talk to Zula, she will help me clear my thoughts.*

She knows she still has time before sunrise, but she hurries out of her room and into the space-tunnel, taking her into the quasi-reality chamber, the gateway to Zula-Or's realm.

She sets up the four-dimensional coordinates in her mind before jumping into the dark abyss as the swallowing mist of swirling particles revolves around her. Even before the city's images come into sharp focus, she is nearing her destination.

As she reaches the contour of Zula-Or's spiky tower, she touches the bright circle on the wall with her index finger. She launches herself forwards, disappearing into the undulating mirror and transcending into the virtual tunnel.

Zula-Or is already waiting in her ethereal gemstone garden by the shimmering lake. The wise lady holds her head high in an expectant pose, sat on her regal chair under an elaborate crystal chandelier.

As Zula-Or makes out Shaillah's silhouette getting sharper through the bubbling haze expanding in front of her, she leans forwards, her face beaming with a broad welcoming smile.

They blend into an emotional embrace, feeling the warmth and the uplifting energy of their presence, excited that they can share the same time and space again, albeit for a short time.

"Welcome, Shaillah, look at you!" Zula-Or cheers, holding Shaillah's hand and making her body spin around. "You look fantastic!"

"It's been such a long time since we last spoke, my dear lady. I'm sorry." Shaillah bows, holding her palms together as a sign of respect.

"Don't worry, my child. Time is not something that bothers me, as you know," Zula-Or replies in her usual soothing honeyed tone as she leads Shaillah towards the glittering lakeshore. "The most important thing is … the moment, the realisation. It's great having you here now."

Shaillah got to admire and respect Zula-Or as the wise lady patiently guided her through her journey into the Rom-Ghenshar world. Zula-Or was always there for her, to listen to her fears and self-doubt; to break the barriers of her self-imposed limits; and to help her learn to be bold, curious, and daring, the Rom-Ghenshar way.

"Today, I've had a dark premonition." Shaillah's quivering voice unveils her uneased disposition. "It made me feel—" She gazes upwards, her eyes fixated on the prickly branches hanging over her head. "It made me feel as if the whole world came crashing down on me."

"Is it because of your impending journey? Or is it because of something else?" Zula-Or asks with a sharp inquisitive tone.

But Shaillah doesn't respond, her eyes still fixated on the intricate branches over her head, deep in thought.

"Oh, how silly of me. Why am I asking this?" Zula-Or says in a self-reproaching tone. "Rothwen, he is so unpredictably harsh—"

"It is not about him!" Shaillah snaps as she starts walking impatiently by the lakeshore.

"You will learn the hard way, but you will learn," Zula-Or warns, walking alongside Shaillah while peering into her face. "He is taking advantage of your inexperience. But you must not fall, not even a slip. Be strong, and you will prevail. That's always been my dictum."

"It is not about him," Shaillah repeats dismissively.

All the while, Zula-Or can perceive a subtle, albeit repressed, cry for help.

"I went through the same distress, the same. And I don't want you to suffer as I did. That is why I gave you the Quark-Star diamond, the energy giver, our token of strength and courage ... because I knew it was not going to be easy."

"And I thank you so much, my dear lady!" Shaillah gratefully replies, firmly holding her diamond as Zula-Or cuts across her pace, making her suddenly stop.

"Don't take his mood swings seriously. Don't let it blur your mind," Zula-Or says while softly stroking Shaillah's forehead, trying to soothe her with a gentle reassuring gaze. "You'll soon grow out of it. You'll be stronger and wiser, like a true Rom-Ghenshar."

Shaillah nods with a broad smile as she acknowledges Zula-Or's words. "You are right, Zula. Why should I even consider worrying about Rothwen? It's not for me to be distracted by those weakening feelings."

"Ah, that's my girl!" Zula-Or gloats, lifting Shaillah's arms while stepping back, leading her around the elegantly drooping branches.

"The thing is, Zula, when I last saw Rothwen ... he seemed troubled—to the point that got me thinking the worst. Then I said my last goodbye to my best friend Sam but nearly killed his sister. It's all piling into my mind like a doomsday finale." She sighs, her darting eyes clashing with Zula's persistent gaze.

"Oh, I see. So it is about Rothwen," Zula-Or surmises. "As for your best friend and his sister, I can assure you … you won't have to worry about them for much longer."

"What do you mean?" A sharp pain slashes through Shaillah's chest. Zula-Or's ominous words make her restless.

"Well, Rothwen was going to tell you before departure. He is leaving it up to the last minute because he knows the consequences. But I might as well tell you now. It will be the end of the human race by the time you leave their planet," Zula-Or reveals in a spiteful tone.

"The end?" Shaillah quivers as her shock turns into despair. She rests her back against one of the glassy tree trunks, trying to digest Zula-Or's grim news.

"It is all about neutralising any potential danger, now or in the future," Zula-Or adds matter-of-factly.

Shaillah looks upwards again, trying to find some solace in the rainbow-like reflections of the overhanging branches as she starts thinking ahead, imagining all kinds of frightening endings.

Zula-Or grabs Shaillah's chin, making her look directly into her penetrating eyes while adding in a poignant tone, "Shaillah, we are like tireless nomads. We never settle, never stop advancing. Of course, it was different the first time. We had to flee for our lives, and we lost many of our people. But never again, never again!" Zula-Or tenses up her body in a triumphant posture. Still, a drawn-out self-satisfied grin slowly softens up her face as she gloats, "Since then, we have confronted many dangers and surpassed many obstacles. And we always come through, ever victorious. Suan enjie … you may ask how."

"How?" Shaillah straightens up her body and expectantly raises her eyebrows.

"We close all the paths that could outsmart or outmanoeuvre us, in any shape or form." Zula-Or boasts while swaying her arm into the air as if wielding a long sharp sword.

"How?" Shaillah asks again, her desperate gaze fixed on the impassive wise lady.

"We eliminate any other intelligent life we find." Zula-Or's unwavering voice sends a clear signal to Shaillah that there is no use in trying to rebel or even argue.

Now more than ever, Shaillah is determined to overcome her desperation with all her inner strength. She nods slowly, keeping steady eye contact, her unfazed expression showing that she is not troubled anymore.

"Eliminate them?" Shaillah mutters in a fake indifferent tone.

"If you want to know the details, we will break their neural connections and destroy their advanced consciousness. They will never know what happened. It will be total oblivion. They will die a swift and painless death. Then we will replace their entire biosystem with ours. And the robots will take care of the planet, as one of our bases, in case we happen to pass by that side of the galaxy."

"That's evil!" Shaillah can't help but gasp in dismay.

"Well, when you think about the alternative, not so much. We could obliterate their entire solar system with our antimatter guns. But long live the Rom-Ghenshars! We are a generous race."

Shaillah fights with all her willpower to regain her composure as Zula-Or keeps an intense glare on her.

"All these words about 'working together for our galaxy's brighter future', they were a pack of lies," Shaillah bitterly says.

"Ah, Shaillah. I know you wouldn't think about lying, would you?"

Shaillah shakes her head while looking bewilderingly at Zula-Or.

"Yet, you are the sole reason for all the lies—all the changes, all the delays," Zula-Or reveals half-heartedly. "You are Rothwen's great dilemma, the kind he has never faced before."

"Tell me everything, my dear lady. I'm ready to confront the truth—head-on."

"He wants you. Oh! I know how much he wants you. It's the thought of losing you after this mission ends that's driving him mad. For the one thing he wants is the very thing he has to destroy—the human mind."

"Why does he have to destroy it?" Shaillah's face tightens, trying to halt a nervous grimace.

"First, Rothwen changed and extended the invasion plans to be with you for as long as it took." Zula-Or imperturbably continues. "He went to great lengths to avoid using his immense destructive powers, and then he lied to you about the aim of our mission while demanding we never mention it to you. He knew from the start that you would hate him for it. Still, he could not even consider taking away your human feelings and emotions because then you would never love him. Like you do."

"There must be a way out of this," Shaillah firmly states as if talking to herself, "and I must find it."

"That is impossible, my dear child. When Rothwen requested the change of all our invasion plans for the sole purpose of bringing you in, Kuzhma-Or accepted on one condition: The humans must die!"

"So much hatred for something that happened so long ago."

"Humans are a belligerent race. That has not changed for aeons. They must be eliminated."

"Tell me, Zula, all those aeons ago, how did Kuzhma-Or survive the humans' attack?"

"He survived unscathed—but not before seeing his whole family wiped out," Zula-Or gloomily recounts.

"How did he escape?"

"A human saved him—a woman. She hid him deep down in her husband's tomb for days—until he was finally rescued and taken to our departure starships."

Shaillah bites her bottom lip and tightly closes her eyes while in deep thought.

"Now, Shaillah, don't even think you can convince Kuzhma-Or on the grounds of some random gesture of compassion that saved his life."

"Not Kuzhma-Or … but Rothwen. I must convince Rothwen. He will listen to me."

"And if he doesn't?"

"Then I must leave him!" Shaillah takes a deep breath, folding her arms tightly around her chest, trying to control her trembling body as all her raw pent-up emotions finally burst out of her anguished self.

Zula-Or can't take her eyes off Shaillah's struggle against her inner turmoil. The wise lady can feel Shaillah's despair in her own heart while realising she would have done the same in the same circumstances. Inexplicably to her, as she tenderly embraces Shaillah, Zula-Or finds herself wishing that Rothwen would give in.

# CHAPTER 37

# DESPERATION

*Then don't look at me with those lust-hungry eyes anymore.*

*I can't change what they have prepared for me. I can't unwind this carefully woven path. All my past wishes will soon vanish as if they have never existed. A new era is coming for me. It is already in my body, running through my blood and soon will take over my mind, usher me into a new world. But there's still a feeble voice inside of me urging me to challenge all that.*

As Shaillah lies down in deep thoughts on the abyssal edge of the quasi-world chamber, she waits until the swirling cloud of virtual particles dissipates around her.

When she enters the space-tunnel, she can't stop thinking about getting one final view of her planet. All her thoughts lead her into the central processor's antechamber.

Descending through the sparkling mist, she agonises, thinking this would be her last chance to see Earth and the humans as she now knows them. She listens out for anyone's presence. As soon as she lands at the edge of the scintillating inner chamber, she thinks of the coordinates she's looking for.

The thin edges of Earth's globe start to take shape against the ghostly medium, getting sharper as wispy shades of blue, white and green glimmer over the whole curved surface. The full view of the planet comes into focus in an instant. It looks peaceful and majestic, as if nothing out of the ordinary is happening down below. She finds herself thinking that such beauty should and must always be preserved.

Shaillah makes the three-dimensional image rotate slowly until the vastness of the Pacific Ocean fills the whole surface with an intense dark turquoise blue. Scattered rosy clouds glimmer over the serene ocean as the evening sun shines through.

Shaillah's eyes widen as she zooms in on the island of Tinian. She finds it hard to believe that her beloved island has changed so much as she gazes upon the gleaming constructions rising so high from their shiny metallic bases and sprawling over the once rustic landscape. The remnants of her island seem about to crack open and collapse under the massive structures.

The large areas newly rebuilt are unrecognisable under the maze of marble and gold buildings and long-spanning bridges. But through the wild patches left untouched, Shaillah can still perceive the innate nature of her beloved island. The same seabirds glide through the skies; the same playful dolphins jump out of the water.

She scours her favourite places where she used to horse ride by the seashore or swim through the high tide's strong currents. *I was there last year. But it feels like a century has passed.* As she looks everywhere, she promptly discards her anxious thoughts, trying to deny to herself what or who she wants to find. But she keeps inspecting every place. She cannot stop her thorough search, even though she knows by now that time is not on her side.

Then she notices two widening frothy trails on the sea surface near El Cuchillo, and she zooms in as fast as she can. She smiles joyfully when she recognises the dark green colours of Sam's speedboat, followed by a second one in fast pursuit. The boats bump harshly over the waves, with ever-increasing speed, their bows pointing so high it seems they are about to flip over.

Shaillah suddenly fears Sam is in danger, but soon she realises what's going on when she sees the pursuer is no other than Bill Sheppard. Sam's lively hand gestures prompt his father to catch up, while his carefree laugh shows how much he's enjoying the boat race.

"I'm pleased he's happy," She whispers, "doing what he loves."

She allows herself some more time to enjoy the view. It pains her to turn off the projection, but she has to. As she's about to set off, her attention goes back to Sam as he does a swift turn while she zooms in closer into the boat. There, carefully strapped-in, a windswept Blazer, tongue sticking out while excitedly panting, is riding by Sam's side.

"Blazer!" she calls out as if her dog could hear her.

Her eyes hurt as the tears break through her aching eyelids, but she lets them flow in abundance, at the same time thinking that she must soon stop. Her face sets in a stern determined expression; she remembers that she has more pressing matters to attend to. *It's time to move on.* She firmly says to herself.

"Bye, Blazer. Bye, Sam!" Her voice quivers, and she can't get herself to turn off the projection.

Instead, she zooms out slowly and starts to imagine how she'll see her beautiful planet on her departure flight. The receding images of Earth are so realistic she thinks she's flying through space. Soon, she's weaving through the encircling destroyer-crafts' deadly web as she focuses her attention on the crater covered surface of the upcoming moon.

But it's the stunning views of a dazzling starship, floating majestically over the moon's edge, that ultimately takes her breath away. She contemplates its massive gleaming fuselage, realising she's beholding the long-pointed ringed body of the Rom-Ghenshars' lead mothership. She has seen it in Kuzhma-Or's bulky talisman he wears on special occasions. She has seen it on their uniform badges and the backrest's engravings, and she has seen it in the numerous stereoscopic images all across their compound. But she could never have imagined it would fill her with so much awe and fear the moment she saw it lingering so close to planet Earth.

Shaillah feels numb and helpless as she ponders the forthcoming doom. In her desperation, all she can think of is to go and find Rothwen and plead for his mercy. She flies up through the antechamber, then dashes through the UniverseScope's arena, accelerating with all her vigour and sheer force of will—before remembering she can get into the space-tunnel.

She reaches the central hexagonal platform, leaning over the golden rails as they reflect the tenuous rays of the looming sunrise. The flickering orange lights on the hovering departure-craft make her stomach churn, reminding her that, as soon they all depart, the human race will come to a devastating end.

She turns around, but her body suddenly bumps against a solid barrier. She is so overwhelmed with anguish that it takes her a few seconds to realise it's Rothwen, who is holding her close against his chest.

"Shaillah, at last you're here. What's wrong with you?" He tries to keep her steady, but she keeps breathing heavily, still struggling to break free.

"I asked Zula for guidance. I saw the mothership," she snaps, glaring at him through the wet hair strands dangling over her forehead.

"I see," he says impassively.

Rothwen's frosty expression disheartens her, but she continues with her plea nevertheless.

"Then I ran, I ran looking for you. I ran to beg you. Please stop this monstrous plan. What you are about to destroy is very special … irretrievable. It is part of my history—our history."

"I can't … and I won't," Rothwen grabs her firmly by her shoulders as if trying to make her abandon her plight. But Shaillah keeps looking at him with imploring eyes.

"Shaillah, we have bigger things to worry about. Soon, we will be leaving on *Ei Reishojen* and meet the rest of our Grand Fleet, ready for our next mission."

As Rothwen speaks, his face hardens up, his steely piercing gaze exuding such immovable resolve that Shaillah knows by now she has lost her battle. Her body writhes in torment as if she is at the point of total breakdown.

"Do it for us. Oh, Rothwen, do it for our love!" she pleads as if this is her final chance. But all she gets for her most heartfelt clamour is an indifferent glacial stare.

"What do you mean 'our love'? I don't love you, Shaillah. I don't care … about you," he bluntly tells her, every word hitting on her soul like a heavy axe.

"Right," she gasps as her shattered heart jolts and flips inside her aching chest. But deep down in her soul, Shaillah feels the tiniest of hopes that, after all, he may be lying. And that remotest of possibilities fills her with renewed purpose.

She confronts him again, looking straight into his searing gaze, their pupils locked in a silent contest of willpower. "Then don't look at me with those lust-hungry eyes anymore," she says, her gaze and voice full of remorse.

"Fine! Everything is going to be all right. Athguer can blank out all these weak human feelings of yours, and you won't have to worry about it—ever," he snaps.

"You do not tell me what to do. I can take care of myself," she shouts and spits in his face.

Rothwen groans, grasping her wrists behind her back as he walks up to the guard rails, making her walk close beside him. She has no room to even attempt to break free.

"Our aircraft is ready to depart. We must go now." He orders in an unyielding tone.

Shaillah stops struggling, easing her heavy breathing and nodding in submission. Her gaze turns humble and obedient, so Rothwen lets go of his tight grasp.

"Are you feeling better?" he asks her, trying to look into her eyes.

But she abruptly turns her face away.

"As you wish. It's up to you how you feel, what you think." Rothwen seethes while she stays resignedly still.

He extends his hand to her impatiently. "Take my hand. Let's go!"

"I'm not going anywhere," Shaillah steps back, still avoiding looking at Rothwen.

"You can't stay here. I probably won't come back for another thousand years." Rothwen softens his voice as he tentatively walks towards her.

"Get away from me!" she cries in despair while running to the other side of the platform.

She climbs on the broad railings and looks down on the wavy ocean as if she is about to jump into the air. And then she looks back at him, squinting her eyes and pursing her lips in contempt.

"Don't touch me, or I will burn you," she threatens as he approaches, her exasperated glare making him stop in his tracks.

Rothwen has never seen her so incensed before, not even when he returned after his long absence. For a brief second, he doesn't even recognise her and starts blaming himself. An unexpected uncomfortable shiver runs through his entire body. But he promptly dismisses it, determined to finish off this *brief impasse.*

He tentatively steps forwards, but immediately baulks at the sight of a scouting-craft rising behind her.

"Are you crazy?" he shouts, pointing at the hovering aircraft.

"That's right, Rothwen. We are all crazy—starting with you," She bursts out. "I'm going back home, my real home. You can do to me what you are planning for them."

"Shaillah, you'll struggle to survive if you leave." He warns.

"Good then! I don't care." She smirks as she jumps into the aircraft and jets off.

Rothwen leans over the slippery railings, watching her fly away, clasping the metal bars with such force they curve under his thick fingers. He shakes his head while focusing his piercing gaze on the dome's vaulted walls.

At the edge of the gaping barrier, Shaillah suddenly stops to gather her thoughts. She doesn't know what will become of her, but her turmoil is such she cannot think straight. She takes a deep breath and holds it while thrusting the aircraft forward.

But no matter how hard she tries, the aircraft keeps bouncing back, unable to break through the impenetrable wall.

"Damn you, Rothwen," she shouts over and over, trying time after time to push through while bearing the brunt of the violent crashes, with utmost resolve but without success.

Then she hears the roaring engines close behind her. As she looks back, she sees Rothwen inside a second scouting-craft, starting to push hers towards the ground. Immediately, she counter-attacks. She speeds off and swiftly turns around, ramming her craft's sharp front against the rear of Rothwen's aircraft. But to her dismay, now both aircraft are stuck to each other, and she cannot move hers, as her craft stops responding to her thought-commands altogether.

Rothwen controls both aircraft, keeping them hovering above the shore, while he walks out from the top deck of his and into Shaillah's cockpit. Before she has time to react, Rothwen holds her firmly in his arms while she is struggling to breathe.

"Sorry. I'm very sorry, but I have to do this," he whispers while tightening his powerful arms around her until she isn't moving anymore.

As Rothwen releases his grasp, Shaillah's limp body slides between his arms and slumps on the floor. He kneels beside her, checking for any injuries. She has multiple bruises, and she has stopped breathing, but her skin glows subtly under his touch.

"At the end of it all, Shaillah, you are a Rom-Ghenshar. And Rom-Ghenshars never flee from one another, never retreat, never surrender. Suan enjie."

He loads her body onto his back, tightening her up with his belt and back straps. As he stands up, her limp head rests on his bare neck, her long straggly hair sprawling over his broad shoulders. He jumps into the air, heading towards the waiting departure-craft. As he flies off, he sends a command to the jammed scouting-crafts to self-destruct in a fireball implosion, lighting up the sky and the ocean with a yellow-green incandescent glow.

# CHAPTER 38

# DEPARTURE

*Oh, brothers! We are on our way. On to bigger things!*

Kuzhma-Or and Athguer wait patiently at the departure-craft's flight deck, watching the whole fighting spectacle unfold and come to an end.

But Kuzhma-Or is more focused on the precise alignment of *The Prestige* and the faultless formation of the destroyer-craft's raiding network.

"Oishe" (Magnificent). "Superb job, Rothwen!" Kuzhma-Or roars, pacing in front of the flight panels, checking every detail in the packed rows of images and data.

Rothwen sends his message to Kuzhma-Or and Athguer as he approaches. *I had to resolve a small problem, but all is fine now.* As soon as he flies in, however, carrying Shaillah over his shoulders, her flaccid body shows otherwise.

"Was the fierce dogfight and the almighty fireball implosion anything to do with you and your 'small problem', Rothwen?" Athguer wryly asks.

"It's a pity it had to end this way," Kuzhma-Or adds in a markedly fake sorrowful tone. "What are you going to do with her?"

"Let her decide ... when she wakes up," Rothwen replies nonchalantly.

"How bad is it?" Athguer asks while walking towards Shaillah's limp head and pressing his thumb against her pale neck.

"Nothing to worry about," Rothwen states, looking in puzzlement at Shaillah's angelic face. "But I had to squeeze the last bit of oxygen out of her lungs to make her stop."

"I see her cells are starting to breathe again. Just starting, though. She won't wake up until we get to *The Prestige*," Athguer concludes.

"Even better. I can concentrate on the important things then," Rothwen shrugs dismissively. "Must go and change into a new flying gear."

"*Ei Reishojen* is ready to blast off. All engines on standby," Kuzhma-Or grumbles while directing a pressing frown towards Rothwen, implying he should hurry up.

"I'll be ready soon," Rothwen nods as he veers into the side aisle while Kuzhma-Or keeps a piercing gaze on him, trying to probe what he's thinking.

Rothwen momentarily stops and turns around to face Kuzhma-Or's persistent glare. The relentless flames from Rothwen's pupils plainly show the unmistakable signal of his ultimate decision. There is no compromise, no backtracking either. *I'm going to walk away now, My Commander. Stop me now. Or let me deal with it myself.*

Kuzhma-Or grits his teeth but does nothing as Rothwen walks away in fast strides, unimpeded.

Inside the changing cubicle, he carefully lays Shaillah's body inside his own deep-sleep capsule. He gets into the shower enclosure, while keeping an eye on her through the soaked translucent screen. The icy oxygenated liquid jets pierce and reinvigorate his body, but as the scattering droplets blur his vision, it seems that the spray is raining on her rather than on him. He cannot stop imagining that, out of the blue, she will get up and join him.

The whole extent of what he had to do in order to have her here suddenly dawns on him. He seethes inside as every past moment they spent together keeps flashing through his mind, crushing his indomitable ego. He finally comes to grips with the fact that he would have never left her behind, and this *unwelcome weakness* infuriates him.

He slips into the glossy white-and-gold flying uniform, the sleek badges in the shape of *The Prestige* glowing on his vest. Then, he stands by Shaillah's side and caresses her face while sending a message to Zula-Or.

"You were right, Zula. It would never have worked."

"But it was worth trying. And you gave it your best shot," Zula-Or replies in a heartening tone.

"I did. I gave it my best shot," he repeats as if doubting every word.

"She will make a fine space-traveller. I'm looking forward to welcoming her into our beautiful Rom-Enjie," Zula-Or says enthusiastically.

"Yes. She'll possibly decide to go straight to see you—as soon as she wakes up."

"Or join other fleets, meet other space warriors. Who knows?" Zula-Or replies, purposely rubbing on Rothwen's wounded ego.

"Sure. She'll be free to choose her own destiny," Rothwen sneers as he starts walking towards the exit in a daze.

"What am I doing?" he frets while pacing around before returning to Shaillah's side and calling Athguer.

Rothwen senses Athguer entering the room and standing beside him, but he doesn't take his eyes off Shaillah.

"As you correctly predicted, Athguer, her cells are too weak to … fully withstand this flight," Rothwen states. Then, exhaling an impatient breath, he asks, "What can we do about it?"

"This will do it," Athguer proudly announces as he produces a small square pouch from inside his coat and holds it by its top edge in front of Rothwen's eyes, making him pay attention. "It's a chain-reaction supercell gel. It will latch onto her cells, protecting them against any break-up."

Athguer drops the pouch on Rothwen's extending palm as Rothwen continues to gaze at him intensely.

"It works! I tested it on myself … several times—even under full space-time frame distortion," Athguer says triumphantly.

"I thought so, Athguer."

"Whatever you do, don't let the gel touch your skin," Athguer warns. "It's highly reactive, and it will cover you instead. I only have this sample left."

"Anything else?" Rothwen asks impatiently, rewarding Athguer with an appreciative glare.

"It lasts a short time, so you need to program the flight to reach *The Prestige* before the gel breaks down."

"How long do I have?"

"T-600"

"Fine!" Rothwen thunders, abruptly closing his hand and making Athguer jolt in fear that the soft pouch would tear open. But ultimately, Rothwen keeps the pouch's thin layer safe within his hollowed fist. "Thanks, Athguer. That'll be all. I'll be there shortly."

As he watches Athguer leave and lock the door behind him, Rothwen casts the remnants of his tumultuous temper from his mind and concentrates solely on Shaillah.

With one hand, he slowly unclips her belt and takes off her boots and then unzips and pulls off her bodysuit. As he drops the mangled clothes on the floor, he hears the clink of her necklace and belt hitting the steely surface. He parts her hair away and straightens her arms alongside her gently breathing body.

As he speaks softly to her, he wonders if everything he ever wanted is right in front of him. "Shaillah … your graceful figure, your beautiful face, your enticing eyes—it's all there to deceive. You may seem delicate … fragile. But you're not fragile like a crumbling wandering comet. No. You're fragile like the runaway burst … of a deadly supernova!" he smugly smiles as his fingers roam all over her smooth skin, leaving a shiny trail in their wake.

He takes a deep breath and carefully holds the pouch over her chest with his fingertips. As he presses along the sides, a translucent syrup pours over her skin. The glimmering gel rapidly absorbs into her pores, coalescing over every contour of her body and sticking on every thread of her hair.

When he is satisfied that she's completely covered and the gel has settled into a jellylike thin layer, he tightly closes the capsule's translucent lid, securing her body in place.

"Sleep tight, Shaillah, for when you wake up, that'll be when our paths will diverge or intertwine—forever!" he professes while picking up her belt and necklace from the floor.

Rothwen hastily makes his way towards the front of the aircraft, stopping right in front of the cockpit screens.

"My Supreme Commander, the great Kuzhma-Or, give me the order!" he roars, leaning over the dashboard, his hands resting on the engines panel.

Kuzhma-Or nods with a flagrant arrogant grin while puffing up his mighty chest.

Rothwen proudly watches as the calculated exit course swiftly sprawls across the dashboard holograms. "Oh, soyen" (brothers). "We are on our way—on to bigger things," he boasts. Basking in their glory, they lean back into their body-shaped seats as he announces: "Time of arrival to The Prestige—T-130" (seconds). "Estimated maximum distortion—one degree of full space-time frame."

Rothwen unlocks the flying sequence, using the encrypted code from his unique brainwave frequency. Instantly, the departure-craft's aerodynamic body tilts to a vertical position, deftly pointing upwards while rapidly spinning on its axis over the displaced waters of the whirling ocean. Like a fired-up missile, it shoots up, seamlessly breaking through the zenith of the high dome ceiling.

The engines' buzzing sound changes into a high-pitched hiss as the aircraft pushes through the interlocked tunnels. In a flash, it breaks through the Pacific Ocean's deep waters and into the looming dark sky, amid the explosive rumble of successive sonic booms, swiftly disappearing from view behind its radiant fizzling trails.

# CHAPTER 39

# DESTINY

*Impossible things are just hard. You only need to find the tool strong enough to break them.*

The departure-craft pinpoints its entry slot at the giant mothership's flight deck port. Like a piercing arrow, it perfectly slides into its target. As it comes to a sudden stop, Rothwen runs towards the changing cubicle and opens up the deep-sleep capsule. Shaillah looks so comfortable and peaceful, as if she has suddenly fallen asleep. He pulls her out of the snug-fitting bed, her body bending halfway onto his back. He carefully dresses her, wrestling with her limp body while wrangling with his turbulent thoughts.

The multi-port bay folds into the mothership's fuselage, merging into its sleek outline. At the same time, the synchrotron rings swivel, extending and locking at the perfect launch angle; its rows of flashing rim lights revolve faster and faster, flaring up with ever-increasing power. As the hyperdrive needles stick out from its front and the antiproton engines fan out from its rear, the autonomous space-time tunnelling spaceship prepares for its planned exit from the solar system.

Shaillah opens her eyes, rubbing her eyelids and peering through the blinding white glow. She tries to sit up but helplessly falls back onto Rothwen's shoulders. She feels half-awake, half-asleep as Rothwen carries her through the swirling aisle. Rows of white, rectangular spotlights brightly illuminate the glossy corridor, running endlessly into the distance as far as she can see. She wriggles her body, trying to break free.

As Rothwen pulls her over and carefully stands her up in front of him, she keeps looking at her feet, hiding her face under her long cascading hair.

"Good! You are back to normal now." Rothwen cheers. "It was only a blip."

But she ignores him, turning around and inspecting her surroundings instead. She reckons she's standing on what she thought was the ceiling, but then she realises that the ceiling looks precisely the same as the floor. Everything inside the broad gaping aisle is perfectly symmetrical and reflects each other, making her lose the notion of which way is up.

Then, the white, gleaming spotlights start getting progressively transparent as the whole surface turns into a boundless, see-through viewport. The spaceship's pulsating light beacons flood the entire inner space with its warm, soothing orange and blue glow, revealing the sleek outline of *The Prestige*, glistening against the daunting blackness of space, flanked by the glowing sun and the barren moon.

"Sheban lai" (It's high time), "Shaillah. You've got to get ready."

"I remember everything now—the dogfight, your choking embrace. What have you done to me?" She frowns.

"I saved you from certain oblivion. That's what I did."

"Where are my pendant and belt?" she asks while fumbling over her chest and waist.

"I've put them away for now … security reasons."

"I'm done with fighting you, Rothwen. I'm going to go away as soon as I can."

"Where to?"

"As far away from you as possible—but not before I make sure every bit of my feelings for you gets deleted from my brain. Or better still, I will keep them … to hate you forever. My soul will not rest in your presence." She seethes.

"You insist on your rebellion. Well, you are a free space traveller now. Do what you want. But now, you need to follow me onto the flight deck. Once we reach the Grand Fleet, you can take the first departure-craft to Rom-Enjie." He looks at her with such stony indifference it makes her despair inside.

"You can go ahead, fulfil your duty. I prefer to stay behind. I don't want to be part of your wicked plan," Shaillah scowls at him, her narrowing eyes channelling all her resentment. "As for you, I'll make sure I never see you again."

Rothwen presses his lips tightly together as his patience entirely runs out, realising that Shaillah will not change her mind.

She runs away from him, throwing herself against the transparent walls as if trying to escape from it all. "I hate you already!" she yells while hitting the glassy surface with her clenched fist.

"Shaillah, you must join me at the end of this aisle soon. We are setting off in T-1200," he orders, briskly walking away, never looking back.

The powerful assembly of antiproton engines lifts the enormous spaceship out of its locked position and aligns it at the precise launch angle. As *The Prestige* slowly climbs up over the moon's bleak horizon, the serene image of Earth comes into full view. Shaillah can see her homeworld emerging in all its majestic appearance. Like an enchanting white and blue oil painting, drawn out against the vacuum of space, the radiantly azure image hangs seemingly undisturbed. The thin iridescent atmosphere shields the bustling life below, a life utterly unaware of its impending fate. She leans over the glass, pretending to hug the planet with her open arms, breaking down in resigned sobs. She asks herself what else she could have done to save the humans, but she feels powerless.

At the flight deck, Kuzhma-Or and Athguer systematically check the departure sequences, the bright shapes and symbols constantly flickering, floating on the massive front viewing deck. Kuzhma-Or sends a message to Zula-Or, who is following every detail of the departure from her gem-studded garden.

"Is this the ending you were thinking of, Zula?"

"We have not finished yet, Kuzhma."

"I have a pretty good idea of how all is going to go. I told you so as soon as he returned in *The Prestige*. Yet, I'm prepared to give him the benefit of the doubt—in case he changes his mind at the last minute."

Zula-Or sighs. "Oh, why should we doubt? We have all the evidence."

"Let's see," Kuzhma-Or mutters under his breath.

"I tried to warn Shaillah against him. I even gave her the Quark-Star diamond to guard her. But she used all that energy to love him even more.

And Rothwen—every time he talks about her, he can't hide his fixation. Does it sound familiar, Kuzhma?" Zula-Or tries to break into the fearsome commander's impenetrable heart.

"I never think about it. I keep it hidden, buried, locked ... inaccessible," Kuzhma-Or growls.

"But you won't delete it, as I did. You are so strong!" Zula-Or praises him to appease him.

"Let everything take its course. We can always change it the way we want it—anytime."

"There's one thing we cannot change. We cannot change Rothwen," Zula-Or markedly reminds him. "Only Shaillah can."

"Lock up your hyper-shields," Athguer quips as he sees Rothwen entering the flight deck.

"Everything is ready. I'll proceed with activating the departure sequences," Rothwen announces.

"Go on!" Kuzhma-Or urges him on as he brings up the swirling hologram of Earth, floating by his side.

"Stage One," Kuzhma-Or boasts, "*The Prestige*'s powerful plasma rays will create fast-flowing currents through the planet's magnetic field, causing an unrelenting self-amplifying effect. This will dismantle their neurons into a useless mesh. The disruption will be short, but the impact, devastating. Our destroyer-crafts are already taking their positions to disintegrate what's left of their useless bodies." He zooms into the heavily built robot-packed cities, its terrified inhabitants disorderly running away as the destroyer-crafts further descend, forming a glittering web under the thin new moon.

"We won't have to worry about the residents of this planet any longer," Kuzhma-Or raves as he watches Rothwen pacing in front of the glimmering holograms, activating the preprogrammed flight path sequences with his thought-commands.

"Stage Two, *Ei Reishojen's* protective antiboson cloud will expand. Once we reach our cruising speed, our antiproton flash-jets will erupt. And we'll dart into the connecting hyperspace tunnel," Kuzhma-Or continues with his booming voice.

"Stage Three, we'll take command of the Grand Fleet. Then we'll jet off towards Omega Centauri ... as planned."

Rothwen walks away from the dazzling multichromatic sequences, signalling that he has finished the activation. He glances at the sequences countdown charts, and then he looks out for Shaillah. But there is still no sign of her. He stifles his impatience, staring at the rapidly flashing holograms.

*The Prestige* rises even higher over the moon's barren surface. A muffled whooshing sound reverberates through the aisles and flight deck. It feels as if the entire fuselage is taking a last deep breath before take-off.

The humming pulses stir Shaillah's body as she slowly gets up from the floor. With her spirit crushed and her hopes in tatters, she knows she must run to the flight deck now.

*T-200. Take your seat. The Prestige*'s sequence broadcast starts the countdown, transmitting the message directly to their brains.

Kuzhma-Or does a final check on the sequence stages before he and Athguer head for the high recliner seats on the main viewing deck. As they sit down, the densely padded cushions snug around them as in a perfect cast. In front of them, the glimmering bodies of planet Earth and its moon seem doomed, in all their fragility and vulnerability. Kuzhma-Or's eyes narrow while his face muscles tighten, thinking hard on his imminent response to Rothwen's actions. Even if the departure sequences appear perfectly set, the veteran supreme commander knows that his master navigator will have in mind an unexpected move. But he cannot foretell what exactly Rothwen is about to do.

Rothwen is still looking out for Shaillah.

*T-60. Take your seat*, the sequence broadcast alerts.

As Rothwen plunges into his seat, he sees Shaillah running past him while looking the other way.

*Ai shewe* (*All is well*). He sends her a thought-message, but she doesn't respond as the protecting, hyper-shields slide shut over their bodies.

*Stage One*, the sequence broadcast announces.

Shaillah closes her eyes tightly as the robotic voice sounding in her brain signals that the end of her cherished world is about to begin.

But an unexpected pause breaks the transmission. It lasts one second, but it feels like a long-drawn-out hour.

With a series of entangled thought-commands, Rothwen interrupts *The Prestige's* central processor and completely replaces the Stage One sequence in real time.

Kuzhma-Or raises his eyebrows. A disgruntled groan escapes his curved mouth as he observes the zoomed-in holographic images, showing that the destroyer-crafts have moved away from their lower-altitude attack positions.

*The Prestige* shoots up into deep space, leaving planet Earth untouched.

"As I expected," he seethes in his message to Zula-Or.

"All I ask you now, my dearest friend of a lifetime, is to show leniency to our most distinguished one-of-a-kind master of master navigators," Zula-Or pleads.

"The more he challenges me, the more I will push him," Kuzhma-Or rages.

But he is powerless to do anything. The protective hyper-shields won't open until Stage Two finishes, after they traverse the warped space-time frames tunnel and reach the edge of the Grand Fleet, on the other side.

*Stage Two, T- 300, Activating all antiproton engines. Full propulsion. Blasting off.*

As it reaches its nominal speed, *The Prestige* swiftly penetrates the emerging hyperspace tunnel, disappearing into the swallowing black hole. At the same time, a colossal blast of ejected radiation shines as bright as a second sun, but only for a fraction of a nanosecond.

Even as the potent afterglow shines out of Earth's line of sight, the planet's upper atmosphere glows through the shower of energized cosmic rays. By then, the swarming web of destroyer-crafts, hovering between the Earth and its moon, has already deployed its wide-ranging magnetic field, stopping most of the onslaught.

*Stage Two, Complete.*

As the hyper-shields spring open, Rothwen is ready to face his supreme commander, standing up on the flight deck platform as a raging Kuzhma-Or and an expectant Athguer walk towards him. Shaillah slowly gets out of her seat, trying to figure out what has happened.

Kuzhma-Or walks right up to a defying Rothwen, their fuming faces nearly touching. The surrounding air crackles and sparks, charged with their brainwaves' intense vibrations as they weigh each other up.

*Stage Three, T-600, Joining the Grand Fleet.*

"There, I've done it. And it is irreversible!" Rothwen declares, immovably holding Kuzhma-Or's fierce gaze.

"You disobeyed my command. You are a traitor," Kuzhma-Or scolds in his booming voice.

"My Commander, the order was to disable the humans. They're as disabled now as they can be."

"The order was to destroy them!" Kuzhma-Or fumes.

Rothwen impatiently exhales, walking towards Shaillah as she runs towards him and hugs him, instinctively trying to protect him from Kuzhma-Or with her own body. Any moment now, she fears, the furious commander will unleash his mighty wrath on them.

Rothwen holds her by her elbows, pressing her body against his to reassure her while frowning steadfastly at Kuzhma-Or.

"A broken order is always a broken order," Kuzhma-Or blasts. Then pointing his finger at them, he threatens, "You both will be held accountable, and I'll demand severe sanction!"

"My Supreme Commander," Rothwen states impassionedly, "as the undisputable leader of our Invincible Grand Fleet, I respect you. As our fearless, greatest space conqueror, I salute you." Rothwen pauses, his pupils ablaze with utter resolve. "But as the ruler of mine and Shaillah's destiny, I must confront you."

Shaillah suddenly realises the transcendence of Rothwen's actions. Rothwen is standing up for her values and their destiny together. She pleads for Kuzhma-Or's mercy. "My Glorious Commander, conqueror of a thousand worlds, we humbly ask for your mercy. The *human mind and spirit* should live on. We have so much to learn from them." Shaillah imploringly looks at him, trying to open up the slightest breach of compassion in Kuzhma-Or's unyielding expression.

But Kuzhma-Or's exasperation is getting even worse as he starts pondering what punishment he must deliver.

Still, Shaillah keeps vehemently imploring him. "My Commander, I beg you. Free your great spirit from its tomb's darkest shadows." Shaillah quivers, her eyes expectantly claiming forgiveness. She can tell that her words have rattled the supreme commander to his very core as he momentarily furrows his forehead in a hesitant grimace.

"A broken order is a broken order," Kuzhma-Or repeats in a thundering voice, hardening his face and quickly dispelling any glimmer of peacemaking.

"It seems we can't agree," Rothwen mutters. "Let's talk about this … after we finish our mission on Omega Centauri."

Kuzhma-Or opens his curled mouth to respond, but *The Prestige*'s timely broadcast interrupts him.

*Stage Three, T-400, Starting Grand Fleet apex alignment.*

He reluctantly backs down, his searing eyes slitting in a furious scowl as Rothwen calmly announces, "And now, if you'd excuse us, Shaillah and I would like to admire our Invincible Grand Fleet. I'll start the next departure sequence soon after Stage Three."

Kuzhma-Or fumes while rushing towards the flight deck's dashboards and data holograms.

"Well, even though I was expecting it, it went beyond any of my predictions!" Athguer remarks as he follows Kuzhma-Or.

"I must admit, he planned it to the very last detail"—Kuzhma-Or seethes, looking at the sequence data; but he can't help an annoying feeling of admiration for Rothwen—"which angle to enter the hyperspace tunnel, when to deploy the destroyer-crafts in protecting mode, the strength of the magnetic field … every single detail … to win her back!"

"You were right, My Commander. Rothwen would never give Shaillah up. And Shaillah would never give up on the humans," Athguer notes.

"After all, Athguer, I must prioritise our goals. We can see to the humans later—now that we have them under control. What we cannot do now is replace Rothwen. If I had to choose between the largest globular cluster in our galaxy, with its millions of star systems, and a feeble yellow star with its tiny rocky planet, I must surely be inclined to go with the former."

The supreme commander pauses as Shaillah's desperate plea for his mercy keeps ringing into his head. Through his ancient memories, he searches for the face of the woman who once saved his life. His iron heart thumps so violently he has to tighten his chest muscles to make it slow down. Ten thousand years ago, she loved him, risked her life for him. Still, he can't forget her. He swallows his pride as he grudgingly admits, "Besides, maybe Shaillah is right. There's more to these humans than we care to accept."

"Shaillah is a testament to that," Athguer states, his deep assertive gaze fixed on Kuzhma-Or's pondering expression.

At the side gallery's panoramic viewport, Rothwen leans back against the smooth surface separating him from the vacuum of space.

Shaillah wraps her arms around his neck. "I am so grateful, Rothwen, for what you did."

"I know what it means to you. In the end, I couldn't bring myself to destroy your heart, Shaillah."

"What will become of the Earth and the humans?"

"I completely replaced Stage One to make the destroyers-crafts protect the entire solar system against any further Rom-Ghenshar invasions. The humans are protected, not destroyed," Rothwen gloats while exultantly smiling at her. "They'll be able to live with the robots, understand them, even change them … who knows? Humans are so capable, so determined. I learned that from you."

"You risked everything for me, Rothwen. I was so frightened of Kuzhma-Or's reaction," she says, her voice trembling with a mixture of gratitude and worry.

"But, Shaillah, we were never in any danger." He calms her while caressing her cheeks. "He needs me more than you can imagine."

"Does he?" Shaillah looks inquisitively at Rothwen.

"You should know this. I'm not only the Master Navigator of *The Prestige*. I'm the Master Navigator of the entire Invincible Grand Fleet!"

"Oh!" She looks at him, open-mouthed in total awe and admiration. "Why didn't you ever tell me?"

"I wanted to leave all my complications behind when I was with you. But then being with you got complicated," Rothwen admits with a bemused smile.

*Stage Three, T-200, Braking sequence starting.*

The stabilising vacuum waves keep drumming on the fuselage, slowing down the mothership to a braking speed while its synchrotron rings' blue rim lights keep flashing ever faster.

Shaillah's heart is pounding rapidly as she repeats to herself the desperate question lingering on her mind. She holds Rothwen's face with both hands while intensely gazing at him, as she asks him, "Why did you do it? Why did you change the sequence?"

"It took me a long time … but when you tried to leave on the scouting-craft, at that moment, I realised I was fighting for you"—he pulls her up and she wraps her legs around his hips—"Unequivocally, I wanted you. So I made the decision, there and then, that I would never … let you go."

They keep staring at each other as if they have suddenly rediscovered their deep unbreakable bond. Rothwen takes the Quark-Star diamond from inside his uniform's vest and places it around her neck as he keeps intensely gazing at her.

"When I look into your eyes, I see myself in the two brightest stars of this universe," he exclaims, shaking his head, hardly believing what he is feeling, the irresistible passion taking over him.

He presses his lips fiercely against hers as in a final desperate act of futile rebellion.

But Shaillah soothes him with her gentle kisses as she speaks to him, "Say it, Rothwen. Say it. Let it flow out of your head."

Rothwen slowly breathes out as he presses his forehead against hers. "I love you!" He says vibrantly in his deep husky voice.

"I love you so much, Rothwen. I broke down on our departure, went crazy at the thought of losing you," She whispers while tenderly caressing his face.

"I'm getting to know you, Shaillah. I'll be more careful from now on."

They chuckle and kiss under their racing pulses, neither wanting to stop.

*Stage Three, T-60, Taking apex position.*

*The Prestige* majestically glides and comes to a halt at the Grand forefront, hovering at the top of the faultless formation of the millia motherships.

"Falling in love with you was the easy part. Admitting it to myself, t hardest. Everyone, including me, said it was impossible. But here it is … I love you," Rothwen marvels.

"That's what our love is about, Rothwen—doing the impossible!" Her face beams with an ecstatic smile.

"Impossible things are just hard. You only need to find the tool strong enough to break them," he remarks while hugging her tightly until they feel the Quark-Star diamond's edges pressing on their chests.

*Stage Three, Complete.*

"Let's go back to the flight deck and show our gratitude to our great commander for his infinite mercy," Rothwen states while slipping his arm around her shoulders as they start walking side by side.

"He is furious!"

"No. You haven't seen him furious yet. He knew I was going to change the sequence … he didn't know how I would do it, yet he let me do it. But he can't stop himself if something goes slightly out of his way."

"Why did he let you do it?"

"Because he has no other option. It's either you or cancel the mission to Omega Centauri."

"Oh, Rothwen!" She kisses him with her rawest, most intense of passions, the same passion that saved him from his bleak shallow soul.

He draws Shaillah's belt from under his own and hands it to her. She wraps the gem-studded band around her waist, the central buckle sparkling as she fastens it. Under a swirl of emotions, she hugs him while lovingly looking into his pupils. "As long as you're by my side …" he tells her, the flames of his iron-willed spirit glowing through his emerald-green eyes.

"When we finish in Omega Centauri, shall we come back and visit Earth?" she asks him.

Rothwen takes Shaillah's hand. And as they start walking back to the flight deck, he pledges, "Ensheren" (Definitely)!

ller's Lover
of them

leet's
s of

Lightning Source UK Ltd.
Milton Keynes UK
UKHW010720100322
399864UK00001B/8

9 781665 592475